DIRTY SEX

Visit us at www.boldstrokesbooks.com

By the Author

Sex and Skateboards

Dirty Sex

DIRTY SEX

by

Ashley Bartlett

2012

This Trade Paperback Original Is Published By
Bold Strokes Books, Inc.
P.O. Box 249
Valley Falls, NY 12185

First Edition: December 2012

CREDITS
EDITOR: CINDY CRESAP
PRODUCTION DESIGN: SUSAN RAMUNDO
COVER DESIGN BY SHERI (graphicartist2020@hotmail.com)

Acknowledgments

So many queer novels today speak of youth in terms of trauma. The trauma of coming out. The trauma of unsupportive families. The trauma of being alone. I won't say I haven't experienced heartbreak, but I was raised with the luxury of having parents who loved me no matter what I did or who I was. I never came out to my father; he informed me I was gay. My mother's only concern was that she couldn't hold my hand and protect me from those who might not accept me. And the blue hair; she was also concerned about the blue hair.

These books, the Dirties, are cathartic for me. Not to exorcise familial trauma, but as a response to a world that took a brief look at me and wrote me off as queer in so many senses of the word. The story is also a celebration of those who didn't write me off.

To everyone who ignored my loud façade, thank you. To my stepmom who made sure I got into Prom in my suit and tie, thank you. To Mom for buying me the suit and to Dad for teaching me to tie the tie, thank you. To Mare, Jack, Jessica, Jonalyn, and Jean, who have never questioned my place in their lives, thank you.

And to all those who made this book so much better than it was. Metal Dave, your knowledge about guns and drugs makes me question your morality, but in a good way. Thanks for answering my texts, even at two in the morning. Bruce, for showing me your insane collection. And for not making me actually touch any of the guns. My "brothers" for teaching me slang I didn't know existed. Your dedication to smoking weed has clearly paid off.

Everyone at BSB, you guys are all fucking rock stars. Really, all of you. Rad, for signing my books. My bestie, Carsen, without whom these novels might still be sitting quietly on my hard drive. Cindy, for explaining all the stuff I ignored in school. And for making editing painless.

And to the readers. I can't quite believe that you exist, but you do. And that makes me feel all warm and fuzzy inside.

All of you, thank you.

Dedication

For Meg.
If I'm ever an ass like Cooper,
you can totally be a bitch like Reese.

Chapter One

G irls. Booze. Girls. Fighting. Girls. In that order. Because girls are the beginning, middle, and end. They are everything that is terrible and sexy and perfect with the world, but you still need the other two. You need the booze to handle the girls and all that psychological bullshit. You need the fighting 'cause sometimes you just want to hit someone. I'm not talking martial arts. That shit is cool, but I never had that dedication. Same with boxing; too many rules. No matter what, though, you need to have honor, and I thought I had some.

That was why I went to the pub. My almost, but not quite, 'cause I slept with other girls too many times girlfriend had dumped my ass. I deserved it. I also deserved a drink, or six. So Ryan dragged me to Streets of London and lined up shots on the bar. We raced. That was how we did it. Loser bought. He always lost. I let the warmth wash over me, through me. My throat, stomach, hands, eyes burned with each sharp crack of the glasses on the bar. We fell to our pattern of playing darts until it was dangerous for bystanders, drinking more when we started to sober up.

When it got late, we stumbled out to the parking lot. We weren't driving. That would've just been stupid. So we waited for our ride while staring at the dark buildings across the parking lot and trying to stay upright. These guys from inside followed us out. All night they'd stared at us, the type that's too pathetic to say something when they got a problem. They looked young, just out of high school, and looking for a way to prove themselves.

"Dyke," was the first word they could manage. Ryan and I laughed. I could take it. People had called me that before, and I wasn't going to get all worked up over some kid talking shit.

"Good one," Ryan managed to giggle. Neither of us was exactly eloquent when we drank.

"Shut the fuck up, pussy," the shorter one spat at him. He was kind of stocky, like a wrestler.

"Yeah, fuckin' fag," the taller one contributed. Ryan wasn't a fag, though, and he certainly wasn't a pussy.

"You guys should try for some originality." Damn, that was hard to say when I was plastered. Seriously, though, we were in El Dorado Hills, a breeding ground for Republicans in California. Ryan and I were EDH born and raised. We were used to botched gay slurs. He was too pretty to be a boy, and if you couldn't tell I was gay by looking at me then you were blind. EDH wasn't a fan of pretty boys and handsome girls. Last time George W. had been in California for a fundraiser, he did it at our fuckin' country club. That's the best way to explain El Dorado Hills. So dyke or pussy or fag wasn't going to get our heart rates going. We'd heard it all before.

"Yeah, originality," echoed Ryan. "Hey." He turned to me. "Where the fuck is Austin?" I'd been the one to call our ride.

"Fuck if I know." We were dismissing the idiots. If they didn't catch on, it was their issue.

Two hands planted on my back and shoved me forward. "You got a problem, bitch?" It was the wrestler.

I was fine with leaving them to their ignorance, but no one, and I mean fuckin' no one, touched me. Slowly, I turned around. Ryan tugged at my shirt, telling me to leave it alone. Shorty was up in my face, looking pissy.

"Kiddo, you can walk away. If you don't, I'm gonna drop you like a bad habit." Ryan stopped pulling on my shirt. He knew what followed that line.

The kid just laughed. So I placed two hands on his chest and shoved him back a couple steps. When he came at me again, I punched him in the face. That totally pissed him off. He lunged at me and we ended up on the asphalt. That's no good. If someone's a wrestler, don't let him get you on the ground. I was only down for a couple seconds though before I felt hands, four of them, grab and pull me up. The tall kid was holding his buddy back. I struggled a bit before I realized it was Austin and Ryan holding me. They didn't let go when I stopped resisting. Instead, they dragged me and tossed me in the backseat of Austin's car.

"Watch your back, little boy," I screamed before Austin shut the door. From the confines of the backseat, I watched Ryan stumble around the car to climb in the passenger seat. Austin got behind the wheel and peeled out of the parking lot.

"Honey, I've dragged your ass away from more fights than I can count on two hands," Austin said in his singsong voice. "And, sweetness"—he looked at me in the mirror—"one day I won't be there to save you."

"My hero," I managed as I dragged myself upright and found my seat belt.

"What did those guys do?" Austin turned to Ryan.

"They deserved it," Ryan replied. He always sided with me. "One of them pushed her."

"Learn to walk away," Austin said real slowly to me.

"I'll work on that."

"Thanks for picking us up, Aus." Ryan reclined his seat a bit. "What time is it anyway?"

"Just after one. You're lucky you're hot," Austin told Ryan. "I don't leave my warm bed for just anyone."

"You know it, girl." Ryan didn't say girl normally. Just with Austin. The alcohol might have contributed too.

"So what's the occasion?" Austin talked a lot. He didn't like silences. "Your girlfriend dump you again?"

Ryan shook his head. "No, that was two weeks ago. This time it was Cooper's."

Austin gave me another look in the mirror. "That hot little butch number? She finally did it?"

"Yeah. Got a hold of my cell phone."

He grimaced. "Text messages?"

"Yeah. Never let them get the cell phone," I half told him and half told myself.

"You could just stop cheating on them," he offered sagely. Ryan started laughing.

"I don't." They turned in their seats to gawk at me. "They assume we're exclusive. None of them ask me."

"Yeah. They're the ones with issues," Austin said.

"Shut up, Aus," I said like I almost meant it.

A few minutes later, we stopped at the gate of Serrano, the gated community they both lived in. The security booth was empty, but the gate recognized Austin's car and opened automatically. Austin decided to take it easy on the wide, curving roads, which was nice because I really didn't feel like puking.

Ryan clumsily extracted himself from the front seat when we stopped in front of his house, a beige monument to suburban monstrosities. He leaned back into the car. "You coming in, Aus?"

"No. I have work in the morning. I'll see you at Streets though, right?" Ryan nodded and started weaving toward the front door. I followed him until we were upstairs where we collapsed on a couch.

"Are we going back to Streets?"

"Already? We just left." He sort of fell off the couch and started setting up the Super Nintendo. We were old-school like that.

"No. Aus said he'd see you at Streets." I caught the controller he tossed me and righted myself so I could see the screen.

"Yeah, tomorrow night."

Tomorrow night. There was some meaning there. It was hard to think through the drunken haze.

"Shit." It hit me. Reese was coming back, and everyone was going to the pub to welcome her home. "I hate your sister."

"She hates you too." Ryan's shoulder brushed mine as he leaned. The player on his half of the screen did the same thing. Ryan was the type to move with his characters, as if that helped.

"Why doesn't she just stay at Yale for the summer?" Reese went to Yale. Of course, she went to Yale. Me and Ryan, state college all the way. My parents couldn't afford a school like that anyway. Not that I could get in to one. Most days, Ryan and I were proud if we both managed to get out of bed and to class almost on time. Maybe that was pathetic, just like playing video games in the middle of the night while drunk sounds pathetic, but we weren't stupid. We just liked to party. Reese always told me and Ryan that we were like stupid frat boys without the frat.

"You think she should just stay at Yale?" he said like I was being an asshole. "That's nice of you."

"It's not like I'm her favorite either." I paused the game and tossed my controller to the ground.

"I don't care. I'm pumped. I haven't seen her in over a month." He slid to the floor in front of me. His back was propped against the couch, and all I could see was the smooth, dark hair covering the back of his head.

"Do you miss her when she's gone?" I asked even though I already knew the answer. With twins, they're always connected even if they're a million miles away from each other. Or maybe not. But those two were.

"You coming with me tomorrow?"

"To the airport?" I knew someone had to go with him to help Reese carry all her crap to the car. That girl brought so much shit to college and back home it blew my mind.

"Yeah." His head dropped back against the cushions so that I couldn't tell if he was tired or if it was the booze.

"I guess."

A slow grin spread across his face. "I love you." Yep, he was still drunk. His pure cacao eyes, so dark they were almost black, fluttered closed. The long lashes fanned across his creamy, tan skin. Ryan had eyes that were almost sunken in and ringed in shadow, making him look perpetually sleepy. Chicks always said he had bedroom eyes. I just thought he looked stoned.

"You want to get some sleep?"

"Mm hmm. You crashing here?"

I didn't bother answering. We both knew I was staying. Ryan stumbled toward his bedroom and I headed for mine. Technically, it was a guest room, but the drawers had my clean underwear, and I'd picked out the sheets on the bed. They were Transformers. So we just called it my room. It infuriated his sister.

"Good night," I called before he shut his door.

"'Night."

❖

"Get up. Get up. Get up." Ryan fell onto the bed next to me. He took my blanket and wrapped it around himself. Then he tried to take my pillow so I pushed him onto the floor.

"Five more minutes," I said as I curled up with the pillow.

"No, I woke up late," he said from the floor. "We only have an hour."

"That's plenty of time." It wasn't. From El Dorado Hills to Sacramento during rush hour took almost an hour. To get to the airport added another twenty minutes. I rolled off the bed taking care to step on him.

"Oww. I hate you." He pulled the blanket over his head.

"We're gonna be late. If you want a shower, get your ass up." I headed down the hallway and shut the door of the bathroom behind me. When I was done showering, I towel dried my hair as much as possible, found my hair product, and pushed my hair up into a faux hawk. Ryan started pounding on the door.

"Let me in. I want a shower too." So I opened the door.

"Calm down. Does it really matter if we're late?" I didn't see why Reese's plane was coming in so early in the first place.

Ryan just rolled his eyes and said, "You can borrow some of my jeans if you want."

It would have been logical to have more than T-shirts and underwear at Ryan's. Too bad I wasn't logical. At least we pretty much wore the same size.

❖

We were only five minutes late to the airport. Traffic had been kind. As we approached the correct terminal, Ryan handed me his phone.

"See if she's here yet." We couldn't stop and wait at the curb. Obviously. So we just had to circle until Reese showed. That was where I came in. I texted Reese to see if she had landed. She said she was going to baggage claim.

"Let me out. She's here." Ryan stopped, let me out, and immediately pulled away.

I waited on the sidewalk for her. I wasn't going to wander around until I found the right baggage claim. She could come get me. Ryan drove past once, twice before I saw her. If not for the familiar haughty stride she'd maintained since childhood, I wouldn't have recognized her. Her face was different. It was all wrong. The chubby cheeks were slimmer, giving way to the kind of perfect cheekbones and jawline that models were paid serious cash for. For the first time, I saw why women became silent and stared when Ryan looked at them with those eyes. Except hers were more elegant, not quite as shadowed, and contrasted starkly against her light brown skin. My initial urge was to let my jaw drop, my tongue hang out, and start panting like a dog. Instead, I clenched my teeth and summoned the most predatory and bored look I could.

"Buttercup! I've been waiting for you." She turned and glared disdainfully. "Well, come on. Give me a hug." I held out my arms as if she couldn't wait to throw herself into them. The small bag she was carrying hit me hard in the chest. I barely had time to catch it before she spun and walked back toward the building. Her tight little ass twitched in her short skirt with every step.

"My bags are this way. I thought Ryan was smart enough to bring someone who would be able to carry them," she called over her shoulder loud enough for anyone within a fifty-foot radius to hear. "I guess you'll have to make two trips."

"Darlin', you know I can handle anything you've got." There was a slight hitch in her step. "Don't worry. When we get home I'll remind you." I was being a little too obnoxious. It wasn't my fault. I had two semesters of annoying her to make up for.

"I haven't even been in California five minutes and I already feel nauseous," was all she said to me until I'd pulled all the bags she silently pointed out. I should have gotten a cart to carry them. I didn't because I wasn't going to let her win. I stacked and slung them until my T-shirt wasn't visible through the straps and I couldn't really feel my arms.

"Is that everything, princess?" I pretended that my extremities were not tingling and my lungs were perfectly capable of filling with air.

"Why? Can't you carry any more?" She wasn't even watching the bags going past us.

"I'll carry you if you don't get your ass moving." I nodded in the direction of the doors.

"Oh, Cooper, I'm so impressed," Reese responded flatly. At least she also started walking.

When Ryan pulled to the curb, he jumped out, opened the back of his 4Runner for me, and tackled Reese in a massive hug. She squealed and let him spin her around. I was going to hurl from the sibling love. I channeled my disgust into throwing her luggage in the back. They were like that the whole way back to El Dorado Hills. She would reach over and play with his hair, tell him she liked the new cut. He acted affronted when he saw the little glint from a new piercing at the top of her ear. Apparently, it's uncool to get a piercing without your twin present. Reese pulled her hair back to give him the full effect. Her hair was way longer than when I'd last seen her. It hung halfway down her back in thick, deep brown waves. When was the last time I'd seen her? Not Christmas. My parents had forced me to visit my grandparents in Oregon, my own potpourri-filled hell. It must have been when she left last summer. Almost a year.

As soon as we got to their house, I took off. As much as I loved Ryan, I hated Reese. I didn't care if it was just because I was jealous.

CHAPTER TWO

S treets of London was packed when I showed up. Everyone was in the backyard, a little fenced in place with dilapidated picnic tables and foliage to hide the road. After giving hugs and high fives to everyone and a single dramatic kiss to Austin, I sat on the tabletop with my feet on the bench. Ryan and Reese were on the bench next to me, Austin on my other side. Carson and Derek sprawled in wooden chairs across from us.

"You want me to get you a beer?" Carson offered. My twenty-first birthday was coming up. Sadly, the bartender frowned on being almost twenty-one so I couldn't order my own drinks.

"Yeah. Here." I pulled a couple bucks out of my pocket and gave them to him. "Thanks." He nodded and sauntered off.

"Hey, Coop," Reese said.

"What's up, buttercup?" I asked in the most sickly sweet voice possible.

Reese looked like she swallowed something disgusting. It took a second for her to compose her face. "Why don't you kiss the boys?" she asked like she was actually interested. It had to be a trick.

"'Cause they have scratchy faces. Why don't you kiss boys?" Cynicism should always be met with sarcasm.

"That's not what I mean." Reese leaned back against the table to see me better. "I mean you kiss Austin, but you give the rest of the guys high fives."

"I don't follow." I looked at Derek and Ryan to see if they got it. They looked lost too.

ASHLEY BARTLETT

"Don't follow what?" Carson returned with my beer.

"Reese wants to know why I don't kiss boys," I explained.

"Eww." He looked appropriately disgusted. "Why would you kiss a dude?"

"Not a dude," Reese cut in again. "You guys."

At that, Carson's eyes got big and his mouth turned down. "That would be wrong. Like queer, but…" He thought real hard for a second. "What's the opposite of queer?"

"Straight," everyone responded.

"No," Carson said. "If Coop kissed a guy, it would be like me kissing a guy." It was fun to watch him try to explain why I kissed girls. "Like, I was born to like girls." The guys and I nodded in encouragement. "So was Coop, so it would be sick if she kissed a dude, just like it would be sick if I did."

"That was kind of poetic." Austin sounded appropriately reverent.

"Okay, but you still didn't answer my question." Reese hated when we all agreed. "Because I kiss all of you guys on the cheek when I see you, but—"

"Oh, but you like chicks too," Carson cut in. "So you're wondering, if you're both gay, why doesn't Coop kiss"—he grimaced again—"us if you do."

"Yeah."

"'Cause she's one of us," Derek offered. "You're not." He was never one to think before speaking.

Reese looked pissed. "I'm not one of you?"

"He didn't mean it like that." Ryan put a comforting hand on Reese's shoulder.

"Coop chases girls. I think that's what he means," Austin jumped in, always the peacemaker. So helpful.

"Okay, so she is a womanizer and I'm not?" Leave it to Reese to make me sound like an asshole.

"Exactly. If only you abused more women you could be part of the club." I gave her my sad, serious face. This was why I hated Reese. She could turn the most innocent conversation into a discussion of how evil I was. She only did it to make me feel shitty. She knew that when I went home I would obsess for days about whether or not I was a womanizing asshole. So I just did what I always did, played it cool.

"I'm confused," Carson said. He looked it too. His beer was clutched tightly between his hands and he was staring into it. "I think I should ask my dads." Carson was kind of a daddy's boy, so if he got in any kind of trouble he just called home. Trouble included confusion, a common occurrence. He would probably get out his cell any minute.

"I wasn't trying to be a jerk." Reese tried to backpedal. "I was just making an observation."

Derek started laughing. "You were trying to be a jerk. It's cool. We love to watch you guys argue."

"Fuck off, Derek," she said.

"Why doesn't everybody just chill?" Ryan was the only one who hated it when I argued with his sister.

A chorus of "fine," rippled through the group finished by Reese and me.

I just wanted to take a piss. When I went inside the pub, I started weaving through the masses of people toward the bathroom. Halfway across the room, I saw something that made me stop dead. Reese was at the bar and some guy was all up on her. She was holding her ground, but I could tell she wasn't having fun. Her shoulders were squared and her eyes narrow so that even in the dim light I could see them killing the guy a foot away from her. Ryan and the guys were all outside. Fuck it. I pushed my way to where they were.

"How's it going?" I positioned myself just barely in between them. The guy looked me up and down and decided I wasn't a threat.

"Fine. We're trying to, ya know, talk." He angled his back against the bar so his body was brushing against Reese. I almost decked him.

"It's fine, babe." Reese touched my arm. "I was just coming back outside." She smiled so that it seemed like she couldn't see anyone or anything, only me. It was all a lie, but he didn't need to know that. I slid an arm around her waist protectively. Suddenly, I remembered that I was taller than her. It was a fairly recent improvement. Go me.

"You sure?" I said in her ear like it was meant for only her, but I made sure I was loud enough for the prick watching us to hear. He looked like he might throw up on his K-Swiss. Who still wore those?

"Sorry." Reese looked at him like she cared. "I've really got to go back outside." She threaded her fingers into the hair at the base of my neck and started playing with it. My spine slowly started melting at her soft touch.

"Fuck that shit," he muttered as he turned away and sauntered back to his friends.

Reese leaned against me so she wasn't facing the guy anymore. "Is he still looking?" Her lips brushed my ear slightly.

"Oh, yeah." He was scowling from across the room. Reese moved her mouth down my neck kissing and licking my skin. "He doesn't look happy." We were putting on a show. I had to keep her updated.

"I think he's had enough." Her lips were on my ear again. "Come on." She slid her hand into mine and pulled me to the back door. The guy was still scowling. Right before we rejoined our friends, she dropped my hand and said, "Thanks, Coop."

I nodded in response. We'd run the same scam a thousand times when people didn't understand the meaning of no. I tried to act like this time was the same. But it was the first time her warm breath and lips against my skin had made my entire body feel seared.

❖

Someone was pounding on my door. It had been going on for a while.

"Go away," I shouted.

"Come on, V. It's noon," my little sister shouted back.

"Go away." She ignored me. There was a scrape against the door that I knew was her stretching to reach the top. After a second, I heard a key slide into the lock and jiggle around. On top of a doorframe is a terrible place to hide a key. The door pushed open.

"Wake up." She sat on my bed and started bouncing.

"Fuck off, Adriana." I pulled the sheet over my head even though my room was already like eighty degrees.

"No, I need a ride." She was fifteen and without transportation. Life was tough.

"Learn to walk." It's what I did at fifteen.

"It's almost ninety out." She stopped her bouncing and started to tug at the sheets. I gripped as hard as I could in my just-woke-up haze.

The sheets were immediately yanked out of my hands. Ade put her head on my pillow inches from my face. I turned and stared into eyes so like mine it was freaky. They were a bright lime green, just like Dad's. Most people thought we all wore contacts.

"Bring water," I suggested as a remedy to the heat.

"I need to go to the Galleria." I doubted she really needed to go to the mall. It didn't matter anyway. We both knew I was going to drive her there.

"Ask Mom to take you."

"She's at work." Coyly, she grinned at me. "I've got a Jamba card. If you want to stop, I'll get yours." Bribery always worked.

"Fine. Fine. Let me shower," I said like I was doing her the biggest favor. Actually, I kind of was. "I'll be ready soon."

"Thanks. You're awesome."

"I'm just doing it for the smoothie." I headed for the shower, leaving her on my bed.

❖

"Did you tell Mom I was taking you to the mall?" I asked once we were in the car with our liquid breakfast.

"I texted her." Adriana started playing with my stereo.

"You're not supposed to text your mother. It's disrespectful." Someone had to teach her these important life lessons.

"I'll remember that."

"You know you're getting to be a smartass." I swatted her hand away from the stereo and plugged in my iPod.

"Can't imagine where I learned that." Pointedly, she stared at me.

"Gee, it will be so sad when you have to drive yourself."

"What kind of car do you think Mom and Dad will buy me when I turn sixteen?" she asked, all spoiled innocence. "An Acura like yours?"

I almost pulled the car over. "You have got to be fuckin' kidding."

"What?"

I turned down the stereo so she could hear me. "I paid for half of this car." Lovingly, I petted the dashboard. "And I paid for that stereo and this bass." I turned it up again until her seat vibrated, then turned it back down. "I paid for the custom headlights and all the engine mods.

I worked my ass off for this car, little sis. Our parents are not going to just give you one."

"They still paid for most of it. I'm sure they'll get me one." For the first time, she looked a little worried. "Anyway, I'm the baby. You're paving the way for me." She was the most obnoxiously petulant brat I'd ever seen.

"Get over yourself."

"Oh, whatever. You love me." She was right.

"Let me put it this way. When I was fifteen and a half, I already had my permit and Dad left out the ads for me every morning. He would circle promising cars."

"So?"

"How long until you turn sixteen?"

Slowly, she counted. "Two months." For such a smart kid she was a little slow. "I haven't finished driver's ed yet. That's why I don't have my permit." More like she couldn't pass driver's ed. "And Dad probably just doesn't leave out the ads because he knows I wouldn't know what to do with them. I'd look online. I want to see pictures."

"You want advice? Get a job. Your chances of having a magical car drop into your lap are better that way."

She looked horrified.

❖

Austin was awesome. Not the best for picking up girls though. That's why I loved Ryan. He knew what was up. But we were at the gay club, which meant Austin was my wingman and Ryan was at home getting stoned and watching James Bond movies. Ryan didn't like to watch pretty girls all night if one of them wasn't going to fuck him.

"What about that one?" Aus used his drink to indicate a very pretty boy.

"You are the worst wingman ever." He was unconcerned.

"Okay, okay. There."

"The one with the mullet?" It was a scene kid mullet, not a circa 1980s mullet.

"Mullets are soooo back."

"Doesn't make it okay," I clarified. He shrugged. "There. By the bar." I pointed subtly with my bottle.

Aus gave me a weird look. "Dark hair, dark eyes, short skirt? Looks kinda haughty? Not hottie, but haughty." He giggled.

"That's the one."

"I can see her nipples from here." He said it like it was a bad thing. "You notice anything about her?" I shook my head. I didn't know what that meant. "She doesn't remind you of anyone?"

"No, what do you mean?" She was super hot. Other than that, I didn't know what the hell he was talking about.

"Nothing. Go get 'em, tiger." It was an awkward sort of encouragement, kind of skeptical.

❖

Her name was Andi. She seemed cool. And she didn't want to dance. Big plus for me. She was fully content to lean against my Abercrombie shirt and tuck a hand into my belt. The warm breath on my neck was making me horny. It had been too long. Okay, my girlfriend had dumped me less than a week before, but I was young and I had needs.

Up close, her dimples were too deep for normalcy. Upon more careful inspection, I could see the piercing scars at the center of each.

"Those hurt?" I lightly touched one. She leaned in even closer.

"Not really." The words poured from her thick, like honey. "I like getting new piercings."

"I've never gotten one."

Her eyes widened in shock. "Never?" There was a quick inspection of my ears, which were without adornment. "Ever think about it?"

"I guess." I shrugged. It never seemed to be a priority to shove a metal bar through my skin. "Seems painful."

"It's not bad. Addicting though." As we talked, her face seemed to get closer and closer to mine. Fine by me. Her breath smelled of mint and cloves. When she spoke, she whispered against my lips.

"I have plenty of vices. Promise." Andi laughed in response. The laugh was what bothered me I decided. It was too infectious, too bubbly, giving the impression that she found everything funny. Maybe it wasn't the laugh. Maybe I just didn't feel like it. No, that couldn't be it. I was twenty fucking years old. Anything that stood still long enough should have been potential humping material. And I was definitely horny. It was probably the laugh. I was contemplating the meaning behind that when I looked up. Reese was on the edge of the dance floor locked in a slow, sensuous grind with a gorgeous girl. Their heads were bent forward so their hair mingled together shielding their faces. The chick's hand was delicately resting on Reese's ass. I was instantly wet and disgusted at my body's response.

I did the sensible thing and kissed the girl in front of me. I couldn't take it anymore. At the velvet glide of her tongue, I braced my back against the wall, pulling her into me. She was holding on to my shirt like it might suddenly fall off. It was excruciating to keep my hands from sliding up that short skirt into the waiting heat. Instead, I dug my nails into the soft flesh of her thigh. Andi moaned into my mouth. She circled her fingers around my bicep and slid them down until they intertwined with mine against her leg. I thought she was going to push me away, but instead she directed my hand up. My fingertips brushed damp cotton. Just as I eased a finger underneath to push the underwear aside, she pulled away. Her eyes looked over bright and she was breathing damn hard.

"Let's go."

"Yeah," I responded brilliantly. As she grabbed my hand and started dragging me toward the door, I looked up. Reese was still dancing, but her eyes were following my progress. To anyone else looking she would have appeared totally nonchalant and unconcerned with anything happening around her. If I didn't know her brother so well, I would have seen the same thing as everyone else. Instead, I saw a sort of cold fury that she thought I was oblivious to. She was glaring with distaste at the girl dragging me. For a second, I deluded myself into reading jealousy in her expression. Then I realized it was what I always got from her, unbridled hatred. Reese saw me with a chick and assumed I was somehow manipulating the girl. Fuck Reese. The girls I hooked up with wanted me for what I could offer them, a couple hours of fun.

We had to go through the mass of people dancing to get outside, which brought us continually closer to Reese. With every step, Reese's eyes got darker and narrower. I couldn't see in the dim light, but I knew that as she got angrier her brown eyes would be invaded with flecks of charcoal. Ryan's did that same thing when he got mad or high. I wondered if hers went gray when she was high too. Probably never tested the theory. I pulled my keys from my pocket and let go of Andi's hand.

"I'll meet you outside. I need to give these to a friend." She nodded and left.

"You might want to check her ID," Reese suggested wisely. She stopped dancing, but her partner continued her fondling.

I leaned forward so Reese could feel me everywhere. I wanted to make her forget the foreign hands roaming her body. A vein in her neck jumped and her jaw clenched. "Thanks, buttercup. I'll keep that in mind," I whispered in her ear. "I won't need these tonight. Will you give them to Aus for me?" I slowly pushed the keys into the pocket of her super tight jeans. She gasped in response and looked ready to deck me all at the same time. "Thanks."

When I joined Andi outside, I was primed and ready to go. She looked sexier under the streetlight. We made it down two streets to 19th before we started groping like teenagers again. The blood in my head was quickly draining and pounding through my hands, my clit; even my mouth tasted metallic. Maybe that was from her teeth. She smelled like girl. I love the smell of girl. Slightly perfumed, like an afterthought and the way skin tastes. I wanted to fuck her right there.

It was another two streets before I stopped at the window of a store. Done with waiting, I pushed Andi back against it, yanked her skirt up around her waist, and pushed her panties aside. Her mouth was in the open collar of my shirt sucking, biting, so I'd remember in the morning. Each wet connection to my skin made my clit twitch with need. When I buried two fingers in her pussy, she bit down hard. My thumb found her distended clit and started the smooth beat of pressure and release making her slump forward against my chest. With my other hand, I tilted her chin up and took her mouth. I like to kiss when I fuck. Hopefully, we'd get to finish before someone found us. One of her legs wrapped around my thigh, opening her wider. I slid a third finger in.

"Fuck. Yeah, like that." She encouraged me so I went deeper. "More." And deeper. I ground my thumb into her clit, guided by the forward jerk of her hips. The skirt was almost up to her tits and she'd gotten my shirt unbuttoned somehow. With every thrust into her cunt, my hand got wetter. The moisture spread down my arm slowly, the strands of wetness stretching between my naked stomach and her thighs.

With a final grind, her body electrified and shuddered before collapsing with a whispered, "Fuck."

Carefully, I withdrew my fingers, flexing my hand. My boxer briefs were soaked and the material was pressed insolently against my aching clit.

"How close are we to your place?" I closed my shirt with trembling fingers. She pulled her skirt down and straightened her top.

"Close." Andi smiled and started strutting down the street again, forcing me to stare at her scantily clad ass.

I stayed a step behind to admire the view.

CHAPTER THREE

Before dawn, I slid from the bed, leaving the sleeping woman without looking back. On the way to the door, I picked up the remnants of my clothing. Everything was sore. My nipples hurt, my thighs, even my face, and I wasn't sure how that was possible. I remembered drinking a lot after we fucked and then I remembered fucking some more until the alcohol wore off. I didn't remember sleeping.

I let myself out onto the street. It wasn't quite cold, the way summer mornings are where the lack of heat is refreshing. I started walking toward the Capitol after figuring out where the hell I was. There was no way Reese and Austin were still in Sacramento. And without my car, I was fucked. I thumbed through my cell until I found Austin. After it went to voice mail, I hung up. Carpooling to the bar suddenly seemed like a terrible idea. There was a light rail station near Naked Lounge. Maybe I would grab some coffee at Naked and then catch the light rail. It would at least get me within fifteen miles of home. Great. I could call home, "Hi, Mom. Got stranded after hooking up at a bar. Want to pick me up?" My phone rang.

"'Lo."

"Coop." It was Austin. "I'm so glad you called." A sentiment I shared. "You woke me up in time to get out without morning awkwardness."

"Please tell me that means you're still in Sac." I was guessing Reese still had my car and was home in her warm little bed. If Austin was still downtown, I would at least have a buddy to catch a ride with.

"You know it. I'm on, umm, Nineteenth and P."

"I'm Seventeenth and N. Meet me at Naked?"

"Yeah, I figured. Do you have your car?"

"I gave the keys to Reese." Something I would never do again. She probably crashed it just to spite me. I had no idea what I was thinking.

"Damn, we're kind of fucked, huh?"

"Yeah, I guess we'll figure it out. Maybe we should call Ryan."

"Maybe. I'll see you at Naked, 'kay?"

"Yeah."

Five blocks later, I stood in front of the coffee shop. The sky was just turning the blue gray of morning. Despite the chilly walk and the intoxicated all-nighter, I was pretty awake. Austin wasn't inside yet so I leaned against the lamppost outside to wait. Naked was a converted Victorian like most of the buildings in midtown. With the exception of two bored employees, the place was dead. I heard pounding footsteps behind me and turned in time to have Austin half jump, half crash into me.

"Morning, sunshine," he said all excited and sarcastic.

"Darlin'."

"Sweetness, what did you do last night? You smell like lesbian sex and scotch." Aus backed away like I offended him.

"Whatever you did to smell like boy sex, but more." I held the door for him.

"Uh-huh." He grinned at me just a little too knowingly.

We got coffee and went out to the little yard on the side of the building. It was shielded from the sidewalk by a high fence and a couple overly huge trees. There was a chick in the corner smoking a slim cigar and drinking coffee. Reese.

"Jesus fuckin' Christ," Aus said. "What the hell are you doing here?"

"Drinking coffee." Rather than sounding sarcastic, Reese made the words sound sexy and aloof, like some exotic drink I'd never try and would always want to.

"Reese, honey, tell me you went home with that beautiful thing last night," Austin probed.

"Maybe." Ambiguous. Thanks for that, Reese.

"You did not," Austin said breathily as he sat down.

"I did." She merely raised an eyebrow at Austin's incredulous expression.

"I always took you for the type to stick around for breakfast." I yanked out the chair holding Reese's feet and collapsed into it. "Careful. You don't want to pick up my womanizing habits." If I said it before her, it was better for everyone.

"Not everyone fucks the women they go home with."

"Actually, they do," I responded after a microsecond of contemplation.

"Come on, Reese," Aus crooned, "details."

Reese looked him dead in the eye. "I told her I wasn't going to sleep with her. We spent the night drinking wine and discussing philosophy."

"Bullshit," I said immediately.

"Fine." She smiled at me coldly. "It wasn't philosophy, but we did stay up all night talking."

"Fucking," Austin whispered to me.

"Fucking," I whispered back.

"I suppose whatever you did for the last six hours allows you to criticize my behavior?" She made it sound like she was asking both of us. She wasn't. Just me.

"Don't act so high and mighty, princess."

"Sweetheart," she said like the bitch she was, "how does your face feel?"

What the hell did that mean? It was especially weird because my face hurt like a bitch. Like I'd been punched in the eye. Did I get in a fight or something the night before?

"Oh. My. God." Austin jumped out of his chair. He grabbed my head and turned it so I was looking directly at him.

"What the fuck?" I tried to push him away. Reese was laughing her ass off. "What the hell are you doing?"

"Come with me." Austin dragged me back inside the coffee shop. He opened the door of the bathroom and shoved me inside.

"Seriously, what the fuck?"

"That." He squared my shoulders in front of the mirror. And then I remembered.

"I got my eyebrow pierced." I told his reflection in the mirror. Apparently, I will do just about anything to impress a girl. That was a whole new side of myself I wasn't aware of. Not a pleasant realization.

"And you had no idea." He was absolutely gleeful.

I leaned in close to the scarred mirror to inspect my eye. The piercing was red and a little crusty. Gross.

"I'm never drinking again."

"Of course not, sweetness." Austin patted my back reassuringly, then steered me out of the bathroom and back to our table. Reese was still sitting there snickering.

"You guys ready to go?" I allowed my frustration with myself to bleed into my tone. They nodded. "Where's my car?"

"The street." Reese nodded in the general direction, which made her hair flutter provocatively around her face. We definitely needed to leave.

❖

Bed was good. That was my only thought as I fell into mine. I didn't take off my jeans or shower. I just crashed. My wonderful sleep was interrupted throughout the morning by my phone vibrating. The noise became increasingly insistent until I shut it off. My mom was downstairs making the normal morning kitchen noises. There were voices too. I blocked it all out in favor of sleep. I needed to get my own apartment.

I was asleep again when my door flung open, and before I could open my eyes, a body landed on me, followed by one, two more. Ryan, Carson, and Derek, the bastards. It was Saturday morning. How could I forget? My mother liked to make breakfast, and she liked to make enough to feed a small army. So every Saturday morning, about twenty of our closest friends descended on the blue house on the corner.

"I hate all of you," I told them without opening my eyes. "And your mothers, and your future children, and the mothers of your future children. And I hope they all die painful deaths." They responded to my tirade by bouncing up and down on me like six-year-olds.

"Come on, Cooper." Derek.

"Yeah, Coop." Ryan.

"Miss Vivian Cooper." Carson. I hated my name.

"None of you guys will live to see twenty-two." I curled up in a ball. "And don't call me that."

"The way I see it is this," Ryan put it down for me. "Your mother is making breakfast. You need to wake up and shower."

"Definitely shower," confirmed Derek.

"So you can do all of that on your own," Ryan went on.

"Or we can help you out," Carson finished.

"If you guys don't get the hell out, I will kill you." I opened one eye. "Slowly."

"Sounds like she needs help." I wasn't sure how Ryan drew that conclusion.

"Don't even think—" But they were already going. The three of them wrapped me in my sheet, despite my kicking and yelling and empty threats, and carried me into the bathroom. Unceremoniously, I was dropped into the tub. It didn't feel good.

"Get her shoes off, Derek," Ryan directed. I didn't even know I was still wearing my shoes. Derek yanked them off my feet and tossed them over his shoulder while Carson and Ryan held me down. I began screaming creative obscenities at them. They turned on the cold water full blast and ran out of the bathroom, slamming the door behind them. By the time I freed myself from the cold, wet sheet, it was pointless to chase them.

I made future plans to make their lives hell as I turned the water to hot and stripped off my soaked clothes. I'd start with stealing Ryan's stash and his little pot plant called "Peggy Sue." For a moment, I considered letting Derek's dog out of his backyard. No, that was too mean. The dog wasn't that smart. It would be better to take Austin's gay porn and poorly hide it in Derek's room where the housekeeper could find it. Yeah, that sounded like a good idea. For Carson, I would siphon the gas out of his car while he was at work. By the time I went downstairs, I was almost calm.

The kitchen table was crowded with plates of hot food and twenty-year-olds. As I rounded the corner into the kitchen, Derek and Carson both looked me straight in the eye. They quickly turned the opposite direction when I put my finger to my lips. Both were probably hoping I would punch Ryan instead of them. I did. Right in the kidney.

"Ohh, you bitch," he yelled at my feet. They were all he could see from his bent over position.

"Language, Ryan." My mom didn't even turn from the stove to admonish him.

"Sorry, Mrs. C." He straightened up with what I imagined to be a little tear in one eye.

"You had it coming, asshole," I whispered.

"I know." He at least tried to smother the grin. "But, damn, bro. In the kidney?"

"Both of you. Language." This time she did turn around.

"Sorry," we said simultaneously while giving each other the how-the-hell-did-she-hear-us look.

"Breakfast is going to get cold. Sit down." My mom set another platter on the table. Pancakes.

Ryan and I sat down with everyone else and started filling our plates. Ryan sandwiched himself between my sister and Austin. I joined my dad and Carson, who looked like he might wet himself.

"I'm sorry." Carson leaned over and started whimpering. "It seemed like a good idea at the time."

I didn't even look at him. "You'll get yours."

"Come on. Are you really mad? We were just playing." He actually looked sincere.

"Don't worry, Carson." I looked up at Reese to see what she could possibly contribute to my empty threats. "She's all talk."

"Anyway," my dad pointedly cut in. "How was your semester, Reese?"

"I'm not sure. Grades aren't in yet." She grinned to accentuate what I could only interpret as an attempt to be charming. Dad laughed accordingly. My parents loved Reese.

"I'm sure you did just fine, honey," my mom reassured her from where she was still screwing around in the kitchen.

"Mom, sit down," I said. "We like it better when you eat with us."

Mom shot me a look then leaned over me to set a pitcher of juice on the table.

"Honey, you need a haircut." She ran her fingers through the back of my hair.

"I think I can handle it." I tried to brush her hand away. It didn't work.

"Your dad needs one too." She started playing with his hair at the same time. "Mitch, take V with you next week when you go to the barber."

"Mom."

"Vivian."

"Mom."

"I know you hate it when it gets long in the back," she offered in explanation.

"Sit down and eat." This time everyone at the table loudly agreed with me.

It was rather hard to follow any sort of conversation in my house on Saturday mornings. My mother had started the tradition of weekend breakfasts when I was really little, and during the summer when everyone was home from college, she still insisted on them. I didn't even invite people anymore. They just showed up. I was actually surprised none of Adriana's friends were there. Half of them were in love with Austin, and the other half were in love with Ryan. They were all afraid of my dad though. He looked like a fifty-year-old version of me. He had the same slightly muscular build and pale blond hair that people said made him look like a handsome all-American guy, and just made people say I looked like a boy.

"Did everyone see the, umm, what shall we call it, Aus? The fruits of Cooper's labor last night." I hated Reese. She was such a bitch.

"Huh?" Ryan brilliantly looked up from his pancakes and sausage. "What's that mean?" He looked back and forth between Reese and me, as did everyone else at the table. Austin started laughing.

"Nothing." I shot Reese an I-hate-you look. "I just, never mind, it's nothing." That got their attention. Good job me.

"None of you noticed her eyebrow?" Reese acted totally affronted on my behalf. As if I wanted the goddamn piercing.

"The eyebrow ring? I thought she always had that," Carson spoke up after they all stared at me.

"No way. You got your eyebrow pierced?" I could always count on my little sister to encourage me.

"Get this." Austin stopped giggling long enough to explain my stupidity. "She picked up this chick at Twenty-One and…" He had to pause to gulp air and laugh some more. "They go and somehow the girl convinces Coop that she should get a piercing."

"How?" Ryan asked.

"I'm guessing the very short skirt the chick was wearing and a lot of booze."

"Enough. Stop. You're done," I told him. "My mother is at the goddamn table. Just a little respect, please."

"Language, Vivian," was all she said.

ASHLEY BARTLETT

"Well, it looks good," Derek told me.

"Yeah, it's kind of sexy," Reese said. Every person at the table stopped staring at me to look at her. A piece of bacon fell out of Derek's mouth.

Ryan recovered first. "Did you just say Coop looked"—he swallowed loudly—"sexy?"

"What?" She sipped some orange juice then slowly licked her lip. "I was just making an observation."

My pulse skyrocketed and my hands started shaking.

"So are you guys going camping soon?" My mom thankfully changed the subject.

"I hope so." Ryan sounded a little surprised. "I made reservations already. For next, next weekend." He interpreted the blank looks properly and explained further. "Two weeks from now."

"You kids might want to straighten out who is bringing what," my dad suggested. "That is, if you've only got two weeks to plan. If you want to discuss everything in the living room, I'll clean up in here."

That seemed like a good idea, mostly because cleaning the kitchen sucked. So we all gradually moved into the living room. Carson and Ryan helped my dad clear the table. I went upstairs to get The Camping List. It was the same list we'd been using since the year we all turned sixteen and could drive ourselves to the campsite. Every year, something new got added or crossed out or changed until it was as close to perfect as possible. I knew it was in my room somewhere.

"So, V." My sister followed me upstairs and into my room. She shut the door behind her. "You want to talk about it?"

"Talk about what?" I started digging around in my closet.

"Reese."

"What about her?" The folder with The List was dark red. I was pretty sure I could see it on the top shelf. I grabbed for the corner.

"How you're in love with her."

"What?" As I yanked the folder, a couple of shoeboxes came with it and poured out half my childhood on my head: photographs, essays, third grade drawings, and letters from my grandma. "What did you say?" I asked again once everything hit the ground. I must have heard her wrong.

"Maybe love is a strong word." She was way too observant. "You think she's hot, gorgeous, sexy. You want to get into her pants. You're having impure thoughts. Does that cover it?" Damn, my sister was annoying.

"Adriana." I stepped out of the pile of papers and detritus so I could walk closer and place my hands on her shoulders and stare into her eyes. "You're out of your mind."

"Are you being cool or are you in that much denial?" She tilted her head to one side like she was actually curious.

"Neither. I hate Reese. I have hated her since—"

"Second grade. I know." Ade pushed my hands off her shoulders. "But this…" She walked over to the pile of crap from my closet and started digging through it. After about a minute, she straightened with a photo in her hand. "This girl is easy to hate." She gave me a photo from high school. It was the twins and me sitting by their pool. There she was, the chubby girl who broke my Gameboy in second grade, the one who buzzed half my head when I was asleep on our sixth grade overnight trip. That bitch who outed me in our freshman English class because I stole her girlfriend. "Now, not so easy."

"She was a vindictive bitch then and, believe me, she hasn't changed." I tossed the picture back onto the floor.

"Vivian." Her tone got my attention more than the use of my name. "That is debatable. Anyway, you've dated tons of girls who were half as attractive and twice as evil."

"It doesn't matter. I don't see her that way." She opened her mouth to protest. "No, we're done."

CHAPTER FOUR

R yan and Reese's place was fucking huge. They practically had
their own wing. It was a whole new, sad level of McMansion.
No joke. Their stepdad hated them and it was way mutual, so everyone
kept to their sides. I let myself in and walked through the house trying to
find them. A sort of common room was on the second floor of the twins'
side that housed every video game system known to man, a functional
couch, and a TV that was bigger than me. Bedrooms branched off that.
Mine and one other guest room faced the street. Ryan and Reese's
rooms faced west affording a crazy view of the Sacramento Valley. Not
sexy, really, but at night with all the lights, it was kinda cool. I looked
out the window when I couldn't find them upstairs. They were out back.
The backyard was in darkness except for the light coming from the pool
that bathed everything in a sick blue-green glow. I changed into a pair
of jeans that didn't smell like a restaurant and went to join them.

"How was work?" Ryan called from his lounge chair. Reese was
sitting in another one facing him. She was wearing little more than a
couple scraps of material that, I supposed, doubled as a bathing suit.

"Same shit. Scoot," I told Ryan. He moved forward so I could slide
behind him. I stretched my legs out on either side. He reclined back
against me so his head was planted in my stomach. That would have
been fine if his long locks hadn't been wet from the pool. But they were.

"Christopher's out of town again." The evil stepfather. Ryan
stretched out a hand to the small table next to us. He grabbed his silver
cigarette case and matching lighter. The case was lined with perfectly
rolled joints. Carefully, he selected one and placed it between his lips.

"Where does he go on all those trips?" Christopher was only home about half the time. None of us knew what he did. The CIA wouldn't have surprised us. Neither would the mob. They both shrugged.

"Who gives a fuck?" Ryan repeatedly flicked the lighter to no avail.

"Give me that." I took the lighter and joint from him and lit it. After taking a slow hit, I held it to his mouth. His bottom lip brushed my thumb and the light scruff on his faced rubbed against my hand. When he was done puffing on the jay, I pulled it away.

"You guys are kind of creepy. You know that?" Reese broke her silence.

I took another hit and held it in as long as I could. Then I put the joint to Ryan's lips again.

"We're non-sexual soul mates," Ryan informed her. He must have already smoked before I got there. Otherwise, he wouldn't have told her that.

"What the hell does that mean?" She seemed disgusted.

"It means if Ryan were a woman, we would be destined for each other," I said.

"It's true." Ryan tilted his head back to look at me. I could barely see the shine of his eyes through the dark curtain of his hair. He let out a big sigh. "Too bad I don't have like a sister or something."

"Yeah, like a super hot twin sister." We started giggling. Reese did not look amused. The joint went out so I lit it again.

"Pretty much any woman as smitten with you as my brother is would do the job." She mustered as much sympathy as possible. "But as soon as you start talking, your looks don't really cut it."

"Did you just say I was hot?" I pulled on the joint again, leaving a thin ash. Aiming for the ashtray on the table, I tapped it off.

"Yeah, sis. I think that was a compliment," Ryan deadpanned. He leaned his head back again so I would let him take another hit. Obligingly, I placed it in his mouth upside down so my fingers were splayed across his chin. He held the smoke in his lungs before exhaling in a long stream of dark, dank vapor. "I'm gonna get some food." He braced a hand on my thigh and pushed up, then sauntered into the house.

"Let me get some of that." Reese sat up and stretched out her hand.

"No." The joint was almost gone. "Get your own."

"Come on. I don't want a whole one, just a little."

"There's nothing left." I held it up so she could see. "Probably only one more hit."

"So give it to me." She stood and towered over me. Her bikini bottoms were at my eye level.

"No." I sucked on the jay until it was almost to my fingertips. The smoke burned my lungs, but I held it in.

"Shotgun it then." I shook my head. Reese swung a leg over my lap and planted a knee on either side of me. She knew I'd have to exhale soon. I turned my head away. "Please." When she knew I wasn't giving in, she took my face in her hands and turned it toward hers. I tried to jerk my head away, but she twisted her fingers into my hair and held me still. Our lips were inches apart.

I wanted to ghost it. Hold it till there wasn't anything left to shotgun. But it was the end of the joint and I was about half a second away from coughing. Totally not sexy. Or cool. So I exhaled. I couldn't hold it in anymore.

"Fuck you." The smoke poured out as I spoke. I'd already lost. I blew the rest of the thick smoke into her mouth. She inhaled slowly, pressed her lips closed, and held her breath.

"Thank you." Reese blew the smoke out into my face. It was pungent and distinct, the way only good pot smells.

"You're a bitch."

"I know." Her face was still next to mine.

"Now go away." I tried to push her off one-handed. The joint was still in my other hand.

"No. You're going to kill that"—she pointed at the roach—"and I want more."

"No."

"Fuck, Coop, just do it."

I knew what she meant. That didn't mean I had to interpret it that way. I tilted my hips up so they rubbed against her inner thighs.

"I'll do it. Just tell me how you want it, babe." I lifted the joint to my lips and inhaled from it again. This time it did burn my fingers. I tossed the roach into the ashtray.

"You know how I want it." She dropped low and ground against my crotch. Automatically, I pressed into her. Her breasts brushed mine when she took a deep breath. The charm on her necklace rested against the skin exposed by my open shirt. The metal was warm.

I wanted to kiss her. I tried to think of my poor, broken, second grade Gameboy. I tried to think of freshman English class. No luck. I still wanted to kiss her. Before blowing out the smoke, I cupped a hand around her neck and pulled her closer. Our lips just barely brushed together, not exactly kissing, but on the verge. Then I exhaled. She took it in stride, staring straight into my eyes as she drank in the smoke.

Buddy Holly started playing over the outdoor speakers. My hand fell and Reese leaned back. She didn't stop staring at me. Calmly, she dropped back onto her chaise lounge and just watched me.

"Pizza's on the way," Ryan announced as he shut the door and walked back over to us. He drew a lazy finger back and forth on the thin chain around his neck. Reese started doing the same thing. I don't think either realized how often they did that simultaneously.

Their necklaces were really cool, a present from their mom when they were little. The matching St. Christopher charms that hung from them were just bigger than a nickel, but more oblong. Carissa had worn one too. Hers was slightly larger and less elaborate. I wanted one and I wasn't even Catholic. Actually, the twins weren't very Catholic either.

"Hey, man. I think your sister wants me," I told Ryan without looking away from Reese. I wasn't sure what had just happened, and I didn't want to think too hard about it. All I knew was that I was so turned on it was painful. My underwear were wet, and I was sweating in weird places.

"Yep. I'm into teenage boys. All that charm and sex appeal." Reese was still staring at me too.

"Great." Ryan wasn't even paying attention. "Does that mean you'll stop fighting?"

"I doubt it," I said.

"Oh, well. Wanna go swimming?" He was already stripping his shirt off.

"Sure. Let me go change into my suit." I started to walk inside then turned back. "Sorry, buttercup, I didn't even think. You okay with me swimming? I mean, if I'm half naked and all wet it might send you into a frenzy."

"Don't worry. I think I have the gag reflex under control this time." Damn, why did she always have a response?

"Why don't you guys just shut the fuck up and swim with me?" Ryan asked before diving in.

❖

"Oh, did Reese tell you?"

"Tell me what?" It was nearly three in the morning, but we were still out by the pool. It had finally cooled down to seventy so Reese and I were wearing jeans and sweatshirts. Ryan, however, was oblivious to the temperature. He was still wearing damp board shorts and an equally damp towel.

"That we need an extra tent for next week," he told me. Derek and I were in charge of most of the camping equipment. Ryan was handling the reservations and getting a keg, as usual. Carson and Reese were in charge of food, and Austin was getting the Jet Skis and a truck. Everyone had a job.

"Why do we need another tent?" I asked, all sleepy. "I thought we were doing the usual." Gay and straight tents, or sometimes we called them the boy and girl tents. Ryan, Derek, and Carson had one; Reese, Austin, and I had one. There were many reasons for the sleeping arrangements, but it was mostly about cleanliness. The boys were dirty; we weren't.

"I'm bringing a friend," Reese said.

"A what?"

"A friend. I already asked everyone and they said it was cool."

"You didn't ask me."

"Uh-oh." Ryan stood. "I'm going inside. Let me know when you clean up the blood." He let himself into the house.

"Sorry." She didn't look sorry. "But she is only coming here for a little while and I want to see her and I don't want to miss camping. Plus, I want her to meet my friends."

"Why doesn't she just come the week after?"

"Why does it matter?"

"It doesn't. I was just wondering." I tried to sound cool. I wasn't even sure why I was irritated. "Who is she anyway?"

"I know her from school. Her name is Kerry." The way Reese slightly smiled when she said the girl's name tipped me off.

"So why can't you and Kerry just share a tent with me and Aus?" If she wasn't going to volunteer the information, I'd make her give it up. Mature.

"I don't know. You figure it out." Reese closed her eyes and leaned her head back like she was bored.

"She snores? Maybe she should have her own tent."

"Stop acting like a child."

"I'm not acting like a child." I was. "You are. Just tell me why you need a separate tent." She opened her eyes to glare at me. "Come on, tell me."

"Because she's my girlfriend. Happy?"

"Yes." No. "Do you really think our camping trip is the best place for you to get laid?"

"Please spare me the lecture. I really don't think you qualify as an authority on the most appropriate places to hook up." Reese wasn't even looking at me anymore. Instead, she began to peel the label off the water bottle she was holding.

"What the fuck does that mean?"

"It means you're a fucking whore." Her lips seemed to embrace each word like she was kissing them.

"Fuck you."

"I'd rather not." She made actual eye contact when she said it, then looked back at her water bottle.

"No, really. Where do you get off calling me a whore?" I knew she was just trying to piss me off. She knew it was working.

"I was just making an observation." Reese flicked some moist paper onto the ground. "You fuck any girl who stands still long enough." She shrugged. "That means you're a fucking whore."

"Babe, that means I'm a fuckin' playa." I stood and braced an arm on either side of her. "I'm a motherfuckin' pimp."

"Please, please, please, Cooper," she grabbed my hands and begged. "Get over yourself."

"Oh, fuck you."

"Fuck you."

Yep, that was a constructive conversation.

❖

"Cooper," Ryan whined through the phone like a three-year-old. "I'm going crazy."

"Why?" I asked even though I knew the answer.

"It's been three days. Three days. You know how many times I've seen them?"

"I don't know, six?"

"Twice. I mean, I met this Kerry girl and then they disappeared. For three days. Three days." I was starting to get the point, three days.

"So what?" For all we knew, Reese and her girlfriend were playing board games. So I told him, "Maybe they're in Reese's room playing Scrabble. Or Monopoly. Reese loved that game when she was little." We both knew that wasn't what they were doing. Reese was known for marathon fucks. She could disappear with a girl for weeks at a time. I didn't have that attention span.

"Don't give me that bullshit. I'm bored out of my mind."

"So leave. You really don't need to bring them food every day." I knew that was exactly what he was doing. The twins were completely warped. Three times a day, Ryan would bring up food and put it outside Reese's door. Maybe bring them a bottle of wine at night for good measure. It was so twisted.

"You're right. I should leave. Plus, it's super gross to know what they're doing. I mean that's my sister. Ewww." The fact that he put any thought into the specifics of what was happening behind Reese's door was also sick and wrong.

"All right. Enough. My dad is making dinner right now. Come over, eat, and we'll go see the new James Bond movie. You can crash here."

"Yeah. Okay. I'll be there in ten."

Five minutes later, Ryan let himself in the front door. From my room, I could hear him wander into the kitchen, eat something, and get reprimanded by my dad. Then he meandered down the hall to the office and said hi to my mom. A few minutes after that, he started up the stairs, but only made it halfway down the hall before sticking his head into my sister's room. He must have been really starved for human contact.

"Ryan," I shouted from my room. "Stop annoying my family."

"He's not that annoying," Ade called back. I heard the rumble of his voice and they both started laughing. A couple seconds later, Ryan finally walked into my room and shut the door behind him.

"Sorry, but I'm dying."

"We should get an apartment. Down by school maybe," I let him know. It was time. I was twenty years old and living at home. How sad.

"Yeah, just a couple little, tiny, insignificant problems." Ryan collapsed on my bed and stared at the ceiling. "One…" He held up a finger so I could see. "You can barely make tuition even with your parents' help."

"So I'll get another job."

"Two…" A second finger joined the first. "That annoying legally binding agreement from my dear mother."

"Yeah, I don't know how to fix that."

"You ever wonder if she knew what she was doing?" He propped himself up on his elbows to look at me. "I mean she wrote her will or whatever, right? But that document is so simple and so…" He snapped his fingers repeatedly.

"Complex?" I offered.

"Cruel." The will his mom left was all of those things. To get their inheritance, the twins had to finish college and live at home until they were done. If the college they chose was too far for a commute, like Yale, they had to return home for all breaks. They couldn't even go on vacations longer than two weeks unless their stepfather was with them.

"Please tell me you're not complaining. Sure, it must be hard to have everything paid for." Like cars, tuition, and each had a credit card with, count it, a ten thousand dollar limit. Yes, all of those things were stipulations of her final document. And in no way did I pity him.

"You're forgetting something, Vivian."

I was. "Don't call me that."

"Christopher." The man who wouldn't get his share of the money unless he maintained a home for the twins until they graduated from college. Sucked for him.

"Okay, he's a douche bag," I conceded. Christopher was an asshole who managed to skirt physical abuse, but still made their lives a living hell.

"Douche bag? That's all? Dude, he comes home tomorrow." Ryan seemed a little nauseous at the prospect. He even went slightly pale.

"We're going camping. You won't even have to see him."

"Oh, fuck." He definitely went pale.

"What?"

"What if he comes home early? With Reese and Kerry upstairs. I can't leave them alone with him." Ryan was right. Christopher maintained a no overnight friends rule. That was why I slept in the guest room and not on Ryan's floor like when we were little.

"That's true."

"Remember last time?" When Christopher literally threw a half-naked, very pretty girl in the front yard. A girl he happened to find in Ryan's bed.

"Yes, I remember." I remembered Ryan calling me because Christopher wouldn't let him give the girl her clothes or a ride. I remembered going to pick up the girl, giving her something to wear, and driving her home. "So call the front gate and ask the security guard to call you if Christopher comes home early."

"Do you think that would work?"

"Why not? We'll drive up before the movie and you can bribe the guy or something."

"Okay, yeah." We both looked at the door when my dad yelled that dinner was ready. As we meandered downstairs, Ryan said, "I always feel like James Bond when I bribe someone." I wasn't sure why he was proud of that. Fuckin' rich kid. Still, I couldn't help but love him.

CHAPTER FIVE

Packing was hell. There was yelling and cussing and sometimes a good fistfight. Austin and I had thought that breaking into the beer at six thirty a.m. was a good idea. It wasn't.

"All you had to do was get a truck. What the fuck is this supposed to be?" I threw a hand up at the truck parked on the street that was big enough to carry a small house. "I can't fit shit in there." Maybe I was being a little overdramatic. Only a little.

"I'm sorry. I didn't realize we were going to war. Otherwise, I would have brought the Hummer," he screamed back. "Anyway, I was a little worried your fuckin' ego wouldn't fit in the cab." He cocked his head to one side and considered. "You're right; the Hummer would be a better idea." He snatched the truck key out of my hand.

"Shut the fuck up." I grabbed the keys back. "We don't have time for that."

"Why don't both of you shut the fuck up?" Carson yelled at us. He and Derek were up by the house making sure the ice chests were all properly sorted.

"Fuck off," Austin and I screamed back at him.

"You guys are annoying the shit out of us," Derek returned in Carson's defense.

"Stop crying, you little bitch," Austin said. Carson's neighbors were probably loving our little display.

Derek and Carson looked at each other. Carson shook his head. Derek nodded his. Then they both ran straight at us. Austin and I started running, but we didn't get far. We ended up with our faces pressed to the window of the truck, which our heads barely even reached. Derek trapped my arms behind my back and pulled up until I was on my tiptoes and in serious pain. Carson held Austin in the same position.

"Help," Austin cried out in a rather high-pitched voice. "Rape, molest, assault."

"Shut up and take it." Carson pushed him harder against the truck. I started laughing at Austin.

"You think that's funny?" Derek rewarded me by raising my arms even higher until I whimpered.

"Now say you love each other," Carson demanded.

"No." I refused to give in.

"I give up." The pain on Austin's face was replaced with a sneer. "I love Vivian."

"Hate you," I spat at him.

A car door slammed, followed quickly by another. Two seconds later, Ryan was pulling off my captor and Reese was doing the same to Austin's.

"What is wrong with you guys?" Ryan tossed Derek back against the truck. His head narrowly missed the side mirror. Carson landed on my other side.

"It's seven thirty in the morning," Reese stated the obvious. "Have all of you been drinking?" The four of us looked at one another sheepishly.

"Can you even drive? We're leaving in less than an hour," Ryan said. Damn, we didn't think of that.

A chorus of, "Sorry," sounded down the line.

"Great impression, by the way." Reese turned and held out her hand to a chick standing behind her. "This is Kerry." Kerry was pierced and tatted everywhere. She had a dark faux hawk like mine, but mine was better. I guess she was kind of hot, if you're into pretty eyes and toned arms.

"Hi, Kerry," we responded like school kids.

"The twink is Austin." He looked outraged. "Blond hair and blue eyes is Carson. Blond hair and green eyes is Cooper. I know they look the same, but the one with green eyes is a girl."

"Thanks for clarifying, buttercup. That's a toughie," I said like I was thankful when I just wanted to knock her out.

Reese smirked in response. "And finally, the tall, dark, and handsome, self-appointed God's gift to women is Derek."

"Lovely to meet you, Kerry." I shook her hand. "Sorry to make such a poor impression."

"It's all right. You guys lived up to every one of Reese's descriptions." She smiled in a way that made it sound funny instead of rude.

"Fabulous." Austin pushed off the truck and shook her hand as well. "Let's get this shit packed up now. Hey, Kerry, do you want a beer?"

"Or a Bloody Mary?" Derek asked. "It's like breakfast. But with vodka."

"You know? A beer sounds great." Reese shot Kerry a look. "I'm still on East Coast time." She shrugged like that explained it.

"Follow me," I told her. We walked toward the house past a Reese who looked like she might kill.

❖

"Seriously, guys." Austin stood surveying the pile of gear in the driveway with Derek and me. "Do we need all of this?"

"We could leave your sleeping bag," Derek offered.

"Can I share with you?" Austin asked innocently.

"Sorry. I'm already sharing with Carson. Too bad." Derek pursed his lips like it was a real tough call. "You know how we love to spoon."

"You know straight guys aren't supposed to say things like that, right?" I said.

"I'm enlightened," Derek said.

Austin and I rolled our eyes. "We went over The List extensively," I told Austin.

"This really is the bare minimum," Derek assured him.

"Okay." Austin shrugged, resigned to the task. "You and Ryan and Carson load up the coolers and the keg in the 4Runner. I'll get the lesbians to load the truck."

"What are you going to do?" I asked him.

"Look pretty and direct." He walked back toward the house. "Hey, lesbians," he called to Reese and Kerry. He was so annoying.

We started loading. Kerry and I stood in the bed with Reese and Austin handing shit up to us. I had to help Aus lift some of the heavier items, but we made good time.

"What the hell is this?" Austin asked when we got to the bedding. A rolled up sleeping pad was tossed over his shoulder. Next to him, Reese held a pile of blankets.

"Bedding," I told him. "Kerry, you want another beer?"

"Yeah, it's only eight. We should probably drink throughout the day," she said. I was starting to like this chick.

"That's the plan."

"I'll go grab 'em," Kerry said. "Austin, you want one?" He shook his head. "Baby, do you?" Reese just glared at her some more. "I think I'm in trouble," she whispered to me before jumping down.

"Cooper." Austin was still standing there waiting.

"What?"

"What happened to air mattresses? And sleeping bags?"

"We're still using them," I said. They looked skeptical.

"Then what's the deal with this?" He hefted the bulky sleeping pad onto the truck bed.

I considered answering, but decided against it. "You know what? None of your damn business. There's room up here. It's going with us."

"Fine, whatever." Austin strutted off.

"Really." Reese set the blankets next to the sleeping pad. "What's with this stuff?"

"You ever share an air mattress with someone else?" I sat on the tailgate.

"Yeah."

"Was it comfy?" I asked even though I knew the answer.

"Not really."

Kerry walked up and handed me a beer. "Can you guys handle this? I'm going to help Austin with the rope." She pointed to where Austin was standing surrounded by a tangle of rope. He was staring at it like it was algebra.

"That's probably a good idea," I said. "Thanks for the beer."

"No problem." Kerry went to help Austin.

"Coop?"

"Yeah?" I said like I forgot what we were talking about. Reese set a hand on the blankets. "Oh, yeah. You, uh, ever had sex on an air mattress?"

"Can't say I have." Reese raised an eyebrow.

"It's really, really not fun." Her mouth opened a little in surprise. "You can't get any rhythm, you know?" I rocked my hips back and forth a little and grinned. "Anyway, guess you'll never know." I set my hand next to hers on the blankets. Not touching, but almost. Then I jumped down to join Austin and Kerry.

"Wait," Reese called.

"What?" I turned back to look into those shadowed eyes.

"Thanks. That's sweet, in sort of a Cooper way."

I was pretty sure she meant that as a good thing. I mustered all of my strength for a sort of apology. "I was an asshole before. You didn't deserve that."

"I kind of did. I called you a whore."

"You did." I contemplated. "But I guess I am. If you think about it."

"No, Coop. You're a playa." For once, she wasn't mocking me. She was still lying, but in a nice way.

Reese drove Ryan's SUV. Ryan and I took the truck. He drove. They were the only people who hadn't been drinking all morning. After the two-hour drive up winding mountain roads, I was pretty sober. We rolled down the windows as soon as the heat tapered off. At home, it was supposed to be pushing one hundred, but up in the mountains, we were loving the high seventies. I thought they would beat us up there since we were towing four Jet Skis and they only had one, but we only got there fifteen minutes behind them. With seven people, it didn't take long to unload everything. Set up was another story.

"So you guys ready?" I asked everyone. We were all relaxing in chairs around the empty fire pit.

"Ready for what?" Kerry asked. We all smiled back at her.

"The Race," Ryan said.

"You guys are kind of into competition aren't you?" she asked.

"What gave you that idea?" I smirked.

"The brawl I witnessed," Kerry stated unnecessarily. "And 'The Race' sounds a little competitive as well."

"They want to race putting up tents," Reese told her. "You guys can count me out. I'll be the ref."

"What about the third tent?" Carson asked. "We'll need to change the rules."

I looked at Aus for his approval. He smiled and nodded. "Me and Aus will do both the small ones."

"But we get Kerry," he added. "Three on three."

Ryan, Carson, and Derek had a very intense conversation with their eyes. Their tent was more complicated to put up. We were getting one more player than usual, but also an extra tent. The conversation must have gone well.

"Done," said Ryan. "Stakes in the ground. Tops on. Losers blow up air mattresses."

"You guys are all losers," Reese informed us. "I'll go place the tents."

"Your girlfriend's a bitch," I said to Kerry.

"Cooper, I kind of like you." Was that supposed to be nice? "Don't make me hurt you."

We watched in silence as Reese looked around our massive campsite and chose three promising places. In each one, she placed a bag with a tent. Then she sashayed back to the truck, found the two mallets, and handed one to me and one to Ryan.

Calmly, she looked at her phone and waited. "Ready?" We nodded even though she wasn't looking. "Go."

We jumped up and ran. Chairs hit the ground. Derek pushed Austin. I pushed Ryan. And then we were in the clear. I shoved the mallet into my belt at the small of my back.

"Kerry, build the poles." Austin yanked the tent out of the bag. I gripped the nylon so he could pull. A bag of stakes fell out followed by a bundle of poles, and we tossed them to Kerry. Austin unrolled the tent in my direction and we unfolded it.

"Where's the door?" I asked him. "Where's the fucking door?"

"Over there." Kerry pointed. Austin and I each grabbed two corners and half walked, half ran in a circle until she shouted, "Stop."

"Here's the first pole." She nudged a fully assembled pole on the ground with her toe. The second was already half done in her hands.

As we fed the first pole through Aus slowly chanted, "Careful, careful, fucking careful, dude." Kerry assembled the last pole for the rain cover. Then she spread the nylon cover out for easy access.

"Is it in?" she asked.

"Almost," Austin told her.

"Done," I shouted a second later. "Hold the center so we can put the poles up."

Kerry did as she was told, carefully stepping in the open door of the flat tent and lifting with us.

"Are you in, Aus?"

"Yeah."

I bent the pole in my hands until I could slide the pin into it. "Done."

"Three minutes," Reese called out. Behind us, the guys were feeding their first pole through. They had three times as many poles to work with. We got our second pole in. All three of us started tying the tent to the pole. Three corners done.

"I got the last one and the stakes. You guys get the cover." I finished tying the final corner and Kerry threw me the bag of stakes.

"Go, go, go," Austin helpfully suggested.

I pounded the last stake in as they secured the cover. We only had the stakes for the cover left.

"You get those, Cooper. We'll start the next one," Kerry shouted back as she and Austin sprinted to the next tent.

I glanced over at the guys. They had the poles all in and were struggling to stand the tent up. Carson, the tallest, was standing in the flaccid tent holding the ceiling above his head. Ryan and Derek were spinning in circles trying to fit pins into the poles.

"Cooper," Austin screamed. "Stop staring, build poles."

"Five minutes," Reese shouted.

I ran to the pile of poles, tore off the rubber bands, stuffed them in my pockets, and started fitting the first pole together.

"First one," I yelled to Kerry and Austin. They grabbed it and started feeding it through. When I finished the third pole, I opened the rain cover like Kerry had done.

"Hold the middle, Coop," Austin instructed me. They pushed both poles in the air and we started tying again.

When I began pounding in the stakes Reese called out, "Seven minutes." We were getting close. The guys were putting on their rain cover. Austin ran back to the first tent and shoved all the nylon bags and such into the tent bag. I fished around in my pocket and pushed the rubber bands into Kerry's waiting hand. I hit the remaining stake into the soft ground.

Austin ran back to the fire pit. I grabbed Kerry's arm and dragged her with me.

"Done," Austin shrieked the second we joined him. Triumphantly, Austin handed Reese our tent bags.

Reese took the bags calmly and said, "I'll check."

Behind us, the guys finished with their stakes and clean up. They sprinted to the fire pit and started wishing one of our tents would fall over.

Reese circled our first tent. She shook it, nothing happened. Lightly, she tugged on each pole. They stayed in the ground. The guys looked pissed. After the same inspection of the second tent, we waited for the verdict.

"Ryan, Carson, Derek." Reese somberly touched each of them on the shoulder. "Have fun with the air mattresses."

For hours, we had to hear about how unfair the competition was.

The first day was uneventful. We spent most of it setting up camp and walking around aimlessly. In the afternoon, Ryan managed to convince Reese to join in an impromptu game of football down by the lake. We put her and Derek on the same team because they pretty much amounted to one player. Derek was a disgrace. And Reese didn't give a fuck.

The next morning, I woke up first, as usual. I started the fire and the first pot of coffee. Sleeping while camping isn't fun. It's too cold and uncomfortable so I always went to bed last and woke up first.

Reese was the next one up. We didn't talk. I listened to my iPod. She read a book.

"Is that one good?" I asked.

"Yeah." Reese turned the book and glanced at the cover. "I'll let you borrow it when I'm done."

I nodded. "I left a stack for you with Ryan."

"He gave them to me," she said.

We went back to our own shit.

"Do you want to help me with breakfast?" I asked once the sun was actually visible. "I'm sure they'll wake up soon."

"Sure." Her eyes never left the page. "Let me finish this chapter."

I left her to it. The food was all in Ryan's car so I started hauling out the stuff we would need. We had learned during our second year of camping that the rangers weren't joking about bears. After that, we put the food away and covered the ice chests every time.

"Let me help you." Reese joined me when I got to the big ice chests. We each grabbed a handle and lugged the coolers out. "You want a Bloody Mary?" she asked as we set the last one down.

I looked up to see if she was serious. Reese wasn't a big drinker anyway, let alone this early. She looked serious.

"We're camping," she said by way of an explanation. "Plus, Carson did a homemade mix."

Carson did make one hell of a Bloody Mary. "Sure, why not? We are camping."

Reese smiled and dug around in the cooler until she found an unlabeled bottle with a ruddy brown liquid. She was more liberal with the mix than the vodka.

"Here." She handed me a camping mug, one of those blue tin ones with white flecks.

"Thanks." I didn't really want to think too hard about the truce we seemed to have. It was better to just go with it. The bed I'd packed for Reese and her girlfriend probably helped. I was pretty sure it was the first time I'd been overtly nice to Reese in fourteen years. At least she was receiving it well.

Silently, we went about making breakfast. Reese mixed pancake batter. I started cooking turkey bacon and making more coffee. The turkey bacon was a concession to Ryan and me. Everyone else ate real bacon. But they'd given up on trying to convert us. Mostly 'cause one year Ryan and I packed turkey and chicken substitutes instead of the real shit. We made it through hot dogs and sausage before they noticed. They caught on at the bacon. That was when they gave up. So our camping meals were beef and pork free.

The smell of bacon lured Derek and Ryan out of their tent. They were easy to please.

"Can I have a piece?" Ryan tried to take the tongs out of my hand.

"It's not cooked yet, but sure." I pulled out a half-cooked slice of bacon.

"Gross." He scowled and walked away.

"Why don't you guys wake everyone up?" Reese asked. "Breakfast will be ready soon."

"They can starve." Ryan collapsed in front of the fire. It wasn't warm enough for him though so he went back into his tent and remerged with a blanket in his hands and a joint in his mouth. Then he checked back on the bacon to see if it was done.

"Not yet," I said. He leaned down and lit his joint off the camp stove. "Go away. That's dangerous." His sleepy eyes held no remorse. I took the joint from him and inhaled deeply. When I blew out the smoke, I directed it toward the cherry to make it burn hotter. The end flared.

"Give it back," Ryan whined. So I did.

"You ready for pancakes?" Reese set a bowl of batter next to the stove.

I checked the coffee brewing on my second burner. It looked done. "Sure. You want to take the coffee for me?" She did and I set a big pan next to the bacon.

"Brother, darling, dearest," Reese addressed Ryan.

"Huh?" His eyes were all red, the pupils dilated so they filled his irises.

"Don't smoke pot this early. You will get even dumber." He was unconcerned. "And go wake Austin and Carson."

"Fine."

"And don't bring the joint with you. You'll burn down the tents."

Ryan handed the joint to her and strolled to the closest tent. Reese handed it to me and went back to her tent to get Kerry.

CHAPTER SIX

"Took you guys long enough," I called back to shore where Reese and Kerry were wading into the water. Ryan pulled up on his Jet Ski next to me.

"Yeah. Where you been?" he called to them.

They both blushed then Reese yelled back, "Changing into our suits." At least someone was getting laid.

"Put on your life jackets and come on." Ryan waved them closer to us.

They clipped the jackets shut and swam out closer.

"Jesus, it's cold." Reese reached us first.

"Who is going with who?" I asked.

"Are you going to let us drive?" Kerry wanted to know.

Ryan and I looked at each other. "Hell no."

"Then I guess I'm with you." Reese tried to pull herself up. I grabbed her hand and hauled her out of the water.

"Why me?"

"'Cause I'm not riding with my brother. Is that cool, Kerry?" she asked.

"Sure." Kerry clasped the hand Ryan held out to her and let him help her up.

Once they were both secure, I looked over to Ryan. "Race you out to the guys?" I barely waited for a response before I gunned it. Reese screamed and held tight to me. Ryan was right next to us so I turned just enough to spray him and Kerry with water. At the movement, Reese threaded her fingers into the side of my life jacket. They were warm and soft against my skin.

Reese and I made it to the center of the lake first where the guys were riding in circles and screwing around. That was how the day went. We raced around the lake, we drenched each other with waves, we attempted to do tricks and failed. After lunch, I rode with Austin so Reese and Kerry had their own Jet Ski. They surprised Aus and me by killing us in a race to the center of the lake. Bitches.

❖

The third night we made s'mores. None of us really liked them, but we were camping so we made them anyway. Actually, Carson liked them, but he always ended up covered in melted marshmallow. Kerry and Reese went to bed first. Carson drank so much we had to carry him into his tent. Austin and Derek crashed soon after, leaving Ryan and me alone by the fire.

"I think I'm going to bed too." Ryan stood and stretched.

"I'm gonna stay out here for a while."

"You want me to get you some more beer before I go?"

"I think I'm good." Even with the massive amount of food I'd eaten for dinner, I was tipsy. Drunk seemed like a bad idea. "You want to turn off the lantern for me?"

"Sure." Ryan turned it off and my eyes were temporarily stunned from the darkness. "Hey." He turned back. "What's with you and Reese?"

"What do you mean?" I fought to stay cool. If Ryan knew I suddenly thought his sister was hot, he would kill me.

"I don't know. You guys are being…" He stopped like he wasn't sure how to describe it. "…nice."

"I don't know. I guess we have a truce," I said all casual.

"Cool." He nodded his head. "Well, good night."

"Yeah, good night." I watched him unzip his tent and crawl inside.

I almost fell asleep sitting by the fire. My jacket was super warm and the fire was putting off a lot of heat even though it was dying down. I felt good.

A noise broke through the night. At first, I thought it might be a bear, but then I heard it again. It was the sound of a tent moving. I looked hard at all of ours. There was no movement. Then I heard giggling. Someone was awake. A girl. No guy laughed like that. Voices started to carry to me, also girls. I couldn't tell what they were saying. I stopped trying to figure it out. It was kind of messed up to listen in on someone else's conversation.

A car drove by, some latecomer looking for their campsite. The headlights washed over our campsite briefly. The voices stopped. I should have gone to bed. I just knew my sleeping bag would be cold and my chair was warm, so I stayed. Reese and her girlfriend would probably go back to sleep.

The next noise was different. Distinct. Un-fucking-deniable. The wet sucking sound of fingers buried in a cunt. Low moans emanated from the tent, and it definitely started moving, rocking back and forth. I was either in my worst nightmare or a seriously fucking wet dream. Both, because I was getting really turned on and I couldn't believe my misfortune. A wet lapping joined the gentle cacophony. A fresh flood of moisture soaked my boxer briefs. My clit was pounding. Demanding. Something had to be done. I pressed my hand against my stomach, edged up the elastic on my boxer briefs, and slid my hand in. I was so fucking wet. I dipped down, drew moisture over my engorged tissues, and started slow circles at the base of my clit.

The moaning got louder, interspersed with "baby" and "honey." Damn, I was so almost there. I circled faster, listening to the sound of Reese's voice. The beginnings of an orgasm curled around my spine, through my stomach, my throbbing clit. My hips jerked of their own accord. The car got close to our campsite again. I froze. Headlights washed over everything, burning me, shining through the girls' tent. For a split second, I could see Reese's perfect silhouette. She was kneeling with her head hanging forward and strands of her hair covering her face. The flash of light lasted long enough for me to see the slow roll of her hips as she fucked Kerry. I jerked my hand away. I was infinitely more aroused and equally disgusted with myself.

My heart raced and my clit pounded with every beat. I wasn't entirely sure if I wanted to throw up or come. I couldn't listen to them anymore; that much was obvious. I couldn't go in my tent without them hearing the loud rasp of the zipper. My iPod was in one of the cars, so that was out. No walking because I didn't have a flashlight. It seemed my only option was to sit there and listen. How long could they last, really?

Reese was crying Kerry's name now with serious fucking conviction. I couldn't take it. I pulled up my hood and covered my ears.

It didn't work. Kerry was moaning now. Reese was nearly screaming. When she came with a flood of groans that sounded like incantations, I could see her. In my head, she was slumping over, Kerry was gathering her in her arms, whispering to her, kissing her cheeks and lips and forehead. Around me though, it was just dark and cold and I was alone.

❖

Morning was killer. I woke up late to the sound of people moving around, talking to each other, laughing. I despised all of them. It took a seriously flat air mattress to force me out of the tent. Ryan gave me one look as I slumped into a chair in front of the fire and grimaced. Kindly, he poured a cup of coffee and pushed it into my hand.

"You look like shit."

"Thanks."

He took the chair next to me. If I felt like shit for normal reasons I would have told him then. My reasons were far from normal so I didn't say anything. Reese and Kerry were sitting across from us looking happy. Reese was all sleep tousled, her eyes looked deeper than usual, and she hadn't brushed her hair. I was still horny.

"You want some breakfast?" Ryan asked.

"No, I'll get it." I didn't want to stare at Reese anymore. "Hold my coffee." I shoved it at him.

Austin was manning the stove and he looked up as I approached. "Eggs will be done soon." He had a concoction of sausage and eggs and cheese in the pan. "Grab a plate."

"I'll get it." Reese came up behind me. "I'm getting one anyway."

"I got it." Damned if I was going to let her be nice to me.

"Don't worry about it." She nudged me out of the way and pulled out a stack of plates.

"Thanks." I tried to grab one.

"You're pushy this morning. Go sit down. I'll bring you some food." Clearly, Reese was determined to make me feel guilty.

"I got it." She was still in the way so I reached around her to take a plate. Bad idea. Instead of moving like I thought she would, she just turned around to face me.

"What is wrong with you? I'm just trying to be nice." The length of her body pressed against mine. Her hip pressed between my legs applying just short of lethal pressure. I looked down into her eyes and almost came. Instead, I gulped hard and loud and blinked my eyes until my head felt clearer. It didn't help.

"Sorry. I'm kinda blue ballin' this morning and you're really not helping." My solitary vow to never speak about the night before crumbled.

"What's that supposed to mean?" She wasn't ignorant, just confused how she was contributing to my condition. Also a little irritated.

"It means that last night you and Kerry were loud enough to get me going, but I just couldn't finish jacking off after you said her name." I played it all nonchalant like I always jacked off while listening to my friends getting laid. "You killed my mood. But Kerry seems satisfied." I took Reese's hand and pressed it against my crotch. "Maybe you could ease my pain."

Reese moved so fast I didn't have time to stop her. I didn't even have time to turn my head to absorb the blow. The slap reverberated across our campsite, silencing every other sound. Reese and I stared at each other hard. Her hand still hung in the air and my cheek stung like a bitch. I could feel all of our friends watching us, but I didn't dare turn away. Suddenly, Reese pushed past me. She stopped in front of Ryan, demanded his keys, and jumped in his car. I thought she was going to sit in there forever with her arms braced on the steering wheel and her face hidden in them. After about five minutes, during which everyone glanced secretively between me and the 4Runner, she started it up and gunned it out of there.

I had no clue what the hell to do. Kerry looked like she might kill me. Ryan was resigned. As usual, he would listen to both sides of the story and decide which of us to be mad at. The rest of the guys were just shocked. Reese and I fought all the time, but neither of us had ever hit the other. I stayed motionless, just looking at the spot where the SUV had been parked, willing her to come back. No luck.

I went back into my tent and changed out of the clothes I'd slept in. When I emerged from the tent again, everyone was trying really hard to act normal. Ryan was studying his breakfast so hard I thought it might ignite. I reached into the breast pocket of his shirt and pulled out his cigarette case. He let me. One joint went behind my ear, the other between my lips. I put the case back in his pocket. Then I walked away.

As I strolled, I lit the joint, sucking on it hard. I didn't get far before I heard footsteps. Ryan.

"Hey, wait up."

"Leave it alone," I warned him.

"I'm not really sure what to do." He took the joint I held out. "I'm mad at her for slapping you. But damn, dude. She looked mad. You must have done something."

"Honestly, Ryan." He looked at me, all ears. "I deserved worse."

I'm not sure if he was more shocked by my admission of guilt or the fact that I'd clearly done something messed up.

"Well, what was it?"

"I really, really can't tell you." A mirthless laugh pushed its way out of my chest.

"Oh, come on, nothing is that bad."

"It is. I'm not sure if it's worse for me or her. Probably her." I thought about that for a while. Was it worse being totally violated or realizing you really are a twisted asshole? "I don't know. Just let me walk, okay?"

Ryan let me go.

❖

Summer continued in the usual vein. Reese and I conducted a silent war. Most of our skirmishes revolved around pizza toppings. Reese would order pizzas and accidentally request stuff I hated on each one. There would be one with anchovies, one with ham, another with bell peppers. My attacks were equally subtle, drinking her favorite juice in the fridge, leaving the bathroom counter covered in hair product, taking naps in her bed with my shoes on. The games hadn't changed a whole lot since we were kids. By the middle of June, we hadn't spoken directly to each other in weeks.

I was almost living at their house. When Christopher would come home, Ryan would stay at my place, but when he was gone, we partied it up. When I let myself in one afternoon, I couldn't find Ryan. Instead, I found Reese sprawled on the couch watching soap operas in Spanish. A glass of wine dangled from her limp hand. The bottle on the table next to her was empty.

"What is this?"

"A telenovela."

"Can you understand it?" I dropped over the back of the couch so I was upside down.

"Most of it."

"I can't." Sure, we both took four years of Spanish in high school. That didn't mean I remembered it.

"I took Spanish in college too. Not just high school," Reese told me. I wondered if she could read my mind or something.

"They're talking really fast."

"You're just slow at listening." There wasn't any malice in her voice. It seemed like we were actually having a conversation. Big step.

"So why are you watching a telenovela?"

"It's more educational than the soap operas in English?" Reese offered in place of an actual reason. "You want some wine?" Her tone was really flat. Actually, everything she was saying was kind of lacking emotion. "We can open another bottle."

Was this some sort of an olive branch?

"Are you okay? You seem a little out of it."

"I'm fine." She drained the remaining wine in her glass and set it on the table.

I studied her from my upside down position. Her eyes were a little red and puffy and she was frowning at the TV. She didn't seem stoned, but it was that or crying.

"Are you stoned?"

"No."

"Then why were you crying?"

A self-deprecating smirk grew across those full lips. "I hate how you know me." I waited for an answer. "Kerry broke up with me."

"What?" I pushed myself upright. "Why? What's wrong with her? She doesn't like sexy, smart chicks?" Reese and I might have hated each other, but that didn't mean other people could be mean to her.

"Thanks."

"You know what? We need a real drink. I'm breaking into Christopher's liquor cabinet. And then, peanut butter, you can tell me all the disgusting, invasive, embarrassing details."

Reese flashed a real smile, only for a second. "I'll have—"

"Scotch. Neat. Give me a little credit." I went downstairs and returned five minutes later with an unopened bottle and two heavy crystal glasses.

"He's going to kill you if you open that," Reese said.

"I know." I studied the bottle. "Damn, it's like older than me." With that, I opened it. I wasn't a complete idiot. I knew that Christopher was going to be livid and I also knew he would get over it. Most importantly though, I knew I was a bit of a snob. It was the result of only drinking Christopher's liquor growing up. He shouldn't have kept such a nice supply if he didn't want us to consume it.

"I'm blaming that on you."

"Blame it on Kerry." I poured the deep gold liquid and handed Reese hers.

"Fuck Kerry."

"Charming, darlin'. You want to tell me what happened?" I settled across from her on the arm of the couch.

"No, I want to get drunk and watch telenovelas."

"Good. Constructive."

"Don't start. It's your fault anyway." Reese took a healthy swig. The glare she shot across the glass had just the right amount of authenticity.

"That's a damn good single malt. Please don't chug it." More glaring. "How could Kerry dumping your ass be my fault?"

"She thought we were hooking up." Distractedly, she pointed back and forth between us.

I nearly spit a mouthful of booze. "Huh?"

"I wouldn't tell her why I smacked you. Somehow that equated to…" Reese waved her hand in the air vaguely.

"I'm sorry."

"It's her problem. If she trusted me, it wouldn't have mattered. No, if I trusted her enough to tell her, it wouldn't have mattered. Anyway, it's over."

"I'm sorry about what I said. And did." It took balls for me to say that, so when it came out, my voice was barely a whisper.

"How much of what you said was true?" There was an attempt at her previous nonchalance that just came off harsh and cold.

We both should have had a lot more booze. I tried to answer, but I blushed instead. That was a first.

"I thought you were screwing with me." There was something resigned in her eyes that made my clit shrink and my stomach turn.

"Oh come on, Reese. You're fucking beautiful." As if hormones could explain my behavior.

"It was dark. You couldn't see shit." Damn, she had a point. Still, I was surprised when she set down her glass and went for the stairs.

"Whoa, hey." I ditched my scotch and rushed to block her way. "Where you going?"

"Somewhere else."

"How long are you going to be mad at me?"

"It's you, so I'll probably hold the grudge for life," she said like she wasn't kidding.

"Fine. I can't change that." I couldn't very well argue with her. So I decided to move on. "Will you watch crappy TV with me now?"

Reese glared at me as she considered. "Okay, but stay on your side of the couch."

CHAPTER SEVEN

The next morning, I woke up to screaming. There was one voice that didn't fit. Fuckin' Christopher. As quickly as possible, I pulled on some clothes and brushed my teeth. The hair could wait. On my way downstairs, I distinctly heard the word scotch. For the last few steps, I slowed. Feigning ignorance, I strolled into the kitchen yawning and rubbing my eyes.

"Hey, Christopher. Good to see you back," I said like I meant it. He was in the middle of the kitchen with his back to me. The twins were on the other side looking scornful.

"Hello, Vivian," he turned and greeted me cordially. Christopher Lagorio, douche bag extraordinaire.

"How was the trip?" I sauntered to the fridge, which brought me even closer to him. A position I didn't exactly relish. I would rather swim in sewage than touch Christopher. He gave off bad fucking vibes.

"It went well," Christopher replied noncommittally. He was decked out in the usual weekday splendor. Perfectly cut suit, shirt, and tie that cost more than my tuition, shoes shined until they were mirrors. Every hair was combed into place, and he was cultivating a close cut beard. His eyes were particularly bright and clear that morning. Glittering like sapphires. If he were anyone else, he would have been unbelievably handsome. Since he was Christopher, my hands were shaking and my stomach hurt.

"Great, great." I gave up on the fridge.

"How is your summer going?" He clapped a hand on my shoulder and squeezed. It brought me just a little closer to him. Why did he have to be so much taller than me? "Do you have anything exciting planned?"

"Not really." I blew him off. "So I was just wondering if we were still going to get breakfast. Sorry, if I interrupted you guys." I looked at the twins like it was our plan all along.

"No, no. Not at all. The kids and I were just talking." Christopher seemed to think I would buy that. He didn't like to expose family matters. As if Ryan didn't tell me everything. Christopher also had grudging respect for me. None of us were sure why, but I sure as hell didn't question it.

"Yeah," Ryan piped up. "Are we going to Old Folsom?" That was our breakfast place. The mugs were all mismatched and the gravy was made with chicken sausage so Ryan and I could get biscuits and gravy. Reese called it Grandma's Kitchen, but no one knew the actual name of the restaurant.

"I figured." The three of us started to leave the kitchen.

"We need to finish our discussion when you two return," Christopher ordered like he was talking to twelve-year-olds.

"Oh, hey." I turned back. The twins were headed for the nearest exit. "I opened that bottle of scotch you had. Hope it's no big."

The muscles under his stubble clenched. "That was you." It wasn't a question. "That was a thirty-year-old bottle."

"Oh, shit. Sorry, I didn't realize." Yeah, yeah I did. Take that, asshole. "You want me to hit you back?" I asked all innocent, as if I had cash to throw down for booze like that.

"No." More jaw clenching. "Just ask next time."

"Yeah, sure, no problem. I forgot to even tell these guys." I waved toward the twins then I grinned. "Okay, see you later."

We didn't start breathing again until we were in Ryan's car with the doors closed.

"My life flashed before my eyes for a second there," I declared melodramatically.

"Your life flashed before my eyes too." Ryan started the car and backed out of the driveway. "I don't even know how that bottle got opened. It wasn't us."

Reese met my eyes in the side mirror.

"It was me," I said from the backseat.

"What?" Ryan looked a little pissed.

"No, it was me." Reese gave me a look in the mirror that said shut the hell up. "And I'm not talking to you." She glared to make sure I knew she was still pissed. "But if I were talking to you, I would kiss you for taking the heat."

"First of all, I opened the goddamn bottle, so don't start," I told her. Ryan began studying the road to hide his confusion. "And second of all, you seem to be talking to me, so I would like my kiss now. Oh, and please take off your shirt beforehand," I said like I was ordering a beer, not a woman.

Reese turned to Ryan. "That's why I'm never talking to her again. She's a fucking pig."

"Could you guys at least try to get along?" He was on the verge of begging.

"Ryan, could you please tell your sister that I'm sorry?"

"Ryan, could you please tell your friend that sorry won't cut it this time? She's disgusting and womanizing and I don't appreciate being treated like a whore or a piece of ass."

Ryan looked ready to kill himself.

"Ryan, please tell your sister that if she didn't act like a whore or a piece of ass, I wouldn't treat her like one; however, that shirt she is wearing implies otherwise." The top really was skimpy. I'd already seen far too much of her pristine tits that morning, and if I looked down her shirt once more I'd have to do something about it. Like touch them.

Wordlessly, Ryan pulled to the side of the road. He turned off the car and slowly turned in his seat so he could see both of us.

"Neither of you is a whore or a piece of ass or a womanizer or a pig or any of the other bullshit names you come up with. But you guys are both acting like complete bitches. I have no idea why you hate each other or why this summer you are being unbelievably cruel, but I can't fucking take it. So stop. Both of you." With that, he turned away and gripped the steering wheel hard. His hands twisted on the leather until his knuckles were white. "Now, can we go enjoy a civil breakfast?"

"Yes," Reese and I quickly promised. Ryan looked like he might cry. He nodded curtly and started the car again. He was right about everything.

❖

"I know what's gonna happen, but my heart still gets going and shit. I think it's the music," Ryan said.

We were halfway through *Scream*. It wasn't scary and we'd seen it a thousand times. He was still squeezing my hand like that would stop the killing spree unfolding before us.

"Definitely the music," I agreed and squeezed back. "You want some food or something?"

"Yeah." His eyes were still glued to the screen. I paused it and we wandered into the kitchen. My parents had work in the morning so they were already asleep, and my sister was at a friend's place so we had the house to ourselves. I left him quietly foraging in the fridge so I could grab some Mountain Dew out of the garage. My dad refused to keep it in the house. He hated junk food. My mom was a little nicer, but not much. When I got back, Ryan was carting ice cream bars, frozen chicken taquitos, pita chips, and hummus into the living room. The taquitos were for him. Who the hell ate frozen taquitos? That was just disgusting. Other than that, it was a good mix.

"We're gonna get sick," I said. He shrugged.

After ice cream and hummus, we moved on to the second *Scream* movie and pizza. I swear Ryan thought pizza was a food group. Down on the bottom of that food triangle, the largest section was occupied by pizza.

Sarah Michelle Gellar was getting slaughtered in a sorority house when Ryan's phone vibrated on the table. He ignored it until it vibrated onto the floor.

"Damn." He picked it up and read the screen. "It's Reese." His thumbs flew over the screen. "Wants to know where I am." The phone was tossed back on the table. Five minutes later, someone knocked on the door.

"Who the hell is that?" I asked Ryan.

"Probably Reese." He shrugged. "Dunno why."

"You get it. I'll get more soda." I was halfway through the kitchen when Ryan screamed my name. Not just called, fucking shouted. "What?" I sprinted back to the front door.

Reese was standing there clinging to Ryan. Her chin tucked against his shoulder. When Ryan slowly turned to shut the door behind her, I saw her face. The whole left side was swollen and discolored. A nice gash across her cheek oozed blood. It didn't look like she could open her eye.

"Oh my God," I whispered. I was going to throw up. After a deep breath or two, I was able to direct them to the kitchen. The light was best in there. We sat her down at the table.

"Stop staring. It's bad enough," Reese said. She might have been trying to be funny.

"What happened?" Ryan finally asked.

At first, it didn't look like she was going to answer. Finally, she muttered, "Christopher."

"He fucking hit you!" I shouted.

"Be quiet. Your parents are probably sleeping," Reese said.

Every muscle in my body tensed. I stood and slammed my fist into the wall. Then I pretended I hadn't. Without looking at Reese, I got an ice pack, wrapped it in a towel, and handed it to her.

"He hit you." Ryan found his voice finally. "I can't believe he hit you. I mean he's been bad before, but never, never..." He wasn't even talking to us. The only connection he seemed to have to the room was the hand he was clutching Reese's with.

"Well, believe it," Reese said. She was the only calm one.

"Why? When? What the fuck?" I struggled to keep from screaming. I still couldn't look at her. Instead, I gripped the sink with a hand that hurt like a bitch and stared into the darkness outside the window. All I could see was my own reflection.

"I told him I was applying to grad school. He hit me. That's it."

"Come on, there's got to be more," I said, turning to make eye contact with her. It hurt to see.

"Really, that's it. I wish there was more." Reese shook her head then immediately stopped as if she might puke. She probably had a concussion.

"You need to go to the hospital." I forced myself to sit at the table next to her, her needs suddenly winning out over mine.

"No, I'm fine."

"Really, babe, I think you do." I placed two fingers on the right side of her face and made her turn toward me. "You might have a concussion and your eye looks pretty bad."

Ryan's head snapped up at my suggestion. "She's right, Reese."

"No, guys. I don't want to." She was adamant. "I just need to ice it and sleep."

"I'm going to get my mom." I stood and dropped her hand. "I'll be right back."

"Cooper, stop. I said no." Great. Now she was going to stick up for herself.

"I'm sorry. Someone needs to look at it." I looked at Ryan. "Keep her here." He nodded.

I took the stairs two at a time trying needlessly to be quiet. Lightly, I tapped on my parents' door. After a second, I pushed it open. Disadvantage of having kids; even when they're twenty, they'll walk in uninvited.

"Mommy," I whispered as I got closer to her side of the bed.

"What's going on?" she whispered back.

"Are you okay?" my dad asked. "I thought I heard shouting."

"You did." I had no idea why we were still whispering. The entire household was awake. "Mom, I need you to come downstairs."

My dad flicked on the light. "What's going on?"

"It's Reese. She just showed up and the whole side of her face… Christopher hit her. Looks like he punched her." I'd never seen my dad move so fast. He jumped out of bed and started pulling a pair of sweats over his boxer shorts. "Dad, no. Stay here. She's really freaked. Come down in a couple. I don't want her overwhelmed."

"I'm not going down there. I'm driving up to Serrano to give that piece of shit what's coming." Wow, my dad was cooler than I thought.

"Mitch." My mom could probably kill someone with that voice. "Reese is probably scared, so stay in bed. I'll send Vivian up to tell you what's going on."

He did as he was told, but he didn't look happy about it. My mom followed me downstairs. In the kitchen, both twins were vacantly staring at points on the wall. Reese had the ice pack on her face.

"Hi, sweetie," my mom greeted Reese.

"Hey." I wanted to kill Christopher for making Reese sound like that.

"Let me take a look." Slowly, my mom pulled the ice away. The towel had blood on it. Ryan and I stared dumbfounded as my mom did a little inspection. It didn't take longer than a couple minutes. I'd never felt so useless.

"Is she going to be okay?" Ryan sounded like an old man, all raspy.

"Yes, of course. But we do need to go to the hospital." She pushed Reese's hair back and kissed her forehead. "I want to find out if your head's okay and I think you might need your cheek stitched up."

"Okay. Fine," Reese conceded. It's good to know when to give up.

"Good." My mom flashed one of those mom smiles. "I'm going to get dressed. You two"—she pointed at Ryan and me—"we need another ice pack and an extra towel." We nodded, happy to be told what to do.

"My car's in the driveway," Reese announced after my mom left the kitchen. "I should move it."

"Nope, I got it." Ryan held out his hand for the keys. She handed them over somewhat reluctantly. "Be right back."

I fixed the ice pack my mom requested and set it on the table. "You want to go get in the car?" I asked.

"Sure. Can I drive it off a cliff?"

"Nope."

"Oh, well." Reese braced a hand on the table and pushed up.

"I got you." I slid an arm around her waist and pulled her close even though she could walk just fine. "Want me to carry you?" I tried for a charming smile.

"I'm all right, thanks." She set her head on my shoulder and let me walk her out to the garage. "You feel good."

When we got home from the ER, my dad had already left for work. He left a note telling us that my bed had clean sheets on it. Reese resisted the whole way, but we finally got her in my room for some sleep.

"I can get dressed myself," she said irritably as I chose some clothes for her.

"I realize that, peanut butter, but my mom told me to help you and I'm more afraid of her than you." That was a lie.

Reese scowled at me and sat on the bed. The swelling had gone down, but not much. A perfect line of stitches marred her face. The doctor said it wouldn't scar too bad. I would have given my life right then for the mark to disappear.

"I'm not even tired," Reese said.

"I know. Put your arms up." I slowly pulled her shirt up over her head and dropped it behind me on the floor. It was spattered with blood. It only took me a second to take off her bra and drop that too. I tried really, really hard not to look at her. I didn't do so good. She was smokin'.

"You're fast at that," Reese teased me. For a second, I wondered if she caught me peeking. She didn't.

"Lots of practice," I countered. I hadn't given much thought to my bra removal technique since I'd started dating girls.

"I thought you didn't wear bras." She let me slip a baggy shirt over her head.

"I don't."

"You're such a pimp." Her eyes were closed now. I let her fall back on the bed. Taking off her jeans was even more of a challenge. Not because they were tight, because I was a perv. "Stop staring," Reese whispered.

"Get over yourself." I made her stand up to put on a pair of my shorts. "Now, try to get some sleep, okay?" I guided her back to the bed. Her eyes fluttered closed again and she leaned her forehead on my stomach. Automatically, I threaded my fingers into her hair at the base of her neck. I could feel the tension drain out of her in the droop of her shoulders and the soft sigh that lingered between our bodies.

"Mm hmm." Her breathing was getting deeper. "Hey. You should stay. I hate you, but you should stay." Any second now, she would fall asleep.

"You want me to get my mom? Or your brother?" There was no way I was sitting there and waiting for her to fall asleep.

"Nope, they can't snuggle. You're a girl. You can snuggle." Maybe she was talking in her sleep. It kind of sounded like it.

"I'll just go get Ryan." I stepped away. Immediately, her eyes snapped open and the set returned to her shoulders.

"No. I will really hate you then." Her eyes started to close. "I'm not snuggling with my brother."

I told myself she would fall asleep soon so it was okay. Quickly, I shed my jeans and tugged on a pair of gym shorts. Then I climbed in bed next to her. She turned to her side and pressed back against me. I curled my arm around her stomach and pulled her close.

"Cooper, I only kind of hate you," Reese whispered as she wove her fingers through mine. Moments later, she was asleep. I couldn't bring myself to move.

❖

"How is she?" my mom asked an hour later. I'd finally forced myself to leave Reese and go downstairs.

"All right." I fell into a kitchen chair across from her.

"Ryan is asleep on the couch. You can sleep in Ade's room." She leaned closer and brushed a hand down my face.

"I'm not tired," I lied. "Don't you have work?"

"Not today. I called in." That was cool of her. "Do you want some coffee?"

"Sure." I nodded. "What are we going to do?"

"Nothing, sweetie." My mom flashed a sympathetic smile as if that would make it better. Actually, from her it did. I still needed my mommy. "If Reese doesn't want to press charges, we can't make her." She placed a cup of coffee in front of me.

"Why not?" I asked even though I knew the answer. All I got was a look.

"They are both staying here. They can stay as long as they want." My mother was adamant. "Maybe we can move the office around." She wasn't even talking to me anymore. "Get some bunk beds so they don't have to share. No, we should give Reese that room." Once she got started, she'd never stop. "You and Ryan can share."

"Mom," I cut her off. "You might want to ask them first."

"I didn't say it was optional. You kids will always be my babies. So If I need to lock you up here to keep you safe…" She shrugged like it was out of her hands. Mothers.

"They might not be able to. They have to go home sometime."

"According to whom?"

"The law. Okay not the law, but their mother. Close enough. That stupid two-week rule thing."

"I wish Carissa had spoken to us. Before she was killed that is." No shit, Mom. A lot of people wish that. The whole dying in a car accident thing kind of made that more difficult. "Don't look at me like that. I was talking about the twins. We would have taken them in a heartbeat instead of leaving them with Christopher. We had no idea he had gotten so bad."

"That's nice of you," I replied sarcastically. "Really, but since they're twenty-one, it might be a little late in the game."

"When did you get so obnoxious? You must have gotten that from your father. I didn't teach you that." Actually, it was a mutual effort. Thanks, guys.

❖

"Ryan, we need to talk." Reese stomped into the kitchen. The twins had been at my house for two weeks. They went home to sleep and get stuff once so Christopher couldn't kick them out.

"What's up, sis?" Ryan asked through a mouthful of macaroni and cheese. We were at the table with one of those party-sized ones between us. We were only a third of the way through and already feeling sick.

"This." She tossed a thick file onto the table.

"What's this?" He pointed at it with his fork.

"How much do you think Mom left us?" Reese sat at the table and grimaced at our choice of food. Her face looked much better and she could fully open her eye now, which really added to her ability to glare. Neither of us had mentioned me holding her while she fell asleep, and I sure as hell wasn't planning on it.

"How much what?"

"Money."

"I dunno. Couple million." I loved how nonchalant he was about that.

"Wrong." Reese was on some sort of mission.

"What? Please don't tell me we put up with that douche bag for ten years for a lousy couple hundred thousand." Ryan was really distressed. "How am I supposed to buy a house in Hawaii, smoke pot, and live off the interest if it's only half a million? I can't even buy a house for that."

"Wow, great plan for the future," I interjected.

"It may be simple, but it will make me happy." Ryan shouldn't have smoked so much pot that morning. Or in the last six years.

"I think it's time to cut back on the weed," I said.

"I agree, but could we focus?" Reese said.

"Okay, how much money?" he asked.

"She left a total of almost forty million." Ryan dropped his fork into the mac and cheese. "We each get about twelve million. The remainder goes to Christopher."

I inhaled the food in my mouth and had to rush to the sink to cough it up. "You should have pressed charges against the bastard."

"It wouldn't matter. That's what I want to talk about. The money's gone." Reese delivered her information like an executioner, with precision and entirely lacking remorse.

"What do you mean the money's gone?" I sat back at the table. It looked like Ryan was still in shock. His fork was still in the mac and cheese.

"I mean the accounts have all been closed and there's no trace of the money."

"But what does that mean?" Yes, I was dense.

"My best guess would be that Christopher somehow bribed the lawyer in charge of the trust to close it out and transfer the money."

"How did you figure this shit out?" Ryan found his voice.

"When he hit me, I knew there had to be a reason, but I couldn't figure anything out. And then I thought maybe he was stressed or something. So I hired a lawyer and a private detective. The kind who look at paper trails. I wanted them to figure out what he does for a living. Because we still don't know and that's weird."

"Wait. He hit you so you decided to figure out what his job is?" I asked.

"Yeah. Why?"

"That doesn't make sense."

Reese looked annoyed. "Sure it does. I had to figure out why he didn't want me to apply to grad school."

"I don't get it," I said.

"Don't worry about it. Just keep up for a sec, 'kay?"

I was confused. But with Reese, I was usually confused. "Whatever."

"So what's he do?" Ryan wanted to know.

"Nothing. Oh, and those business trips he takes? There's no record of it. Or at least no flight records. He apparently drives wherever he's going."

"But I thought he had a job," I said.

"No need. The trust and interest pay for everything. The way it's set up, Christopher has access to it with the permission of the lawyer so he can pay our expenses. You know, tuition, health insurance, food, things like that."

"So where's our fuckin' money?" Ryan was starting to comprehend what she was saying.

"I don't know. The people I hired couldn't find it."

"Isn't that totally illegal?" I was there to ask the obvious questions.

"Of course." Reese looked at me like I was stupid. "Get this. The lawyer is gone. My private detective couldn't find him."

"So call the cops," I said.

"What good would it do?" Reese asked.

"Um, dude did something illegal. So you call the cops on his ass." It seemed like a logical move to me.

"They can't bring the money back."

I was missing something here. Or Reese was hiding something.

"Uh, I think Coop's right. We need to call the cops," Ryan said.

"And what? They'll find what I found. The money is gone. So is Christopher. So is the lawyer. They'll just dig into the paper trail." Reese stared hard at Ryan. He shrugged.

"Good call." Ryan.

"Yeah." Reese.

"Cops suck." Ryan.

Something had just happened. That look. I decided to roll with it. For now.

"So what are you going to do?" I asked.

"Not a damn clue. Mooch until he kicks us out."

"You guys are fucked."

"Thanks, asshole." They both glared.

"Okay, no, maybe not." I figured it couldn't hurt to throw out some dumb ideas. "Your credit cards are paid by his account, right?" They nodded.

"So what?" Ryan didn't follow.

"So buy your house in Hawaii, he'll have to pay it off. Buy cars in your names and sell them off later. Run your credit cards up to the limit until he stops paying them off. He'll probably catch on pretty quick, but until he does buy everything you can."

"It's better than nothing." Reese was resigned. "I wonder if we can use our credit cards for mutual funds."

"Fuck, Reese. You're so boring." It was actually a good idea. "Anyway, you can probably get cash advances."

"I can't believe I'm saying this, but you're a genius."

"Why? You guys would have thought about cash advances."

"No, the whole buy everything thing," Reese said.

"You guys are taking this really well." They shrugged. Maybe they were in shock. "When Christopher gets back into town again you should probably confront him." I knew they weren't going to like that idea.

"I guess," Ryan told his mac and cheese.

"If he gets back in town, that is. The dude is probably long gone." If I stole a bunch of money, I would take the fuck off.

"We'll deal with that when we need to." Reese was all business. "In the meantime, let's spend some money." She grinned.

"So are you guys going to throw me a kick ass party for my birthday?"

"Fuck, yeah." Ryan and I slapped our palms together.

Whatever had just happened was weird. But Ryan would fill me in later. I was sure of it.

CHAPTER EIGHT

The newest slasher flick was playing at midnight so we were totally going. There's nothing better than thirty-year-olds playing teenagers bleeding all over the screen.

The theater was insane. Not in a good way. After graduation, you really don't want to see most of the people you went to high school with, but it was unavoidable at the theaters in the middle of summer. Midnight releases of big movies increased the chances. By the time I got to the ticket window, I'd seen at least twenty people from my graduating class, three girls gave me their new numbers, and two guys gave me the evil eye. It wasn't my fault about the guys. Their girlfriends had wanted me and were hot. What was I supposed to do? Anyway, that was for days ago.

"Coop, did you see Melanie Hendricks?" Derek asked as Ryan and I approached.

"Who?" I tried to remember a Melanie.

"You know." Carson smacked my arm. "Hendricks. We went to middle school with her. And she had government with us senior year." This was why I went to theaters in Sacramento.

"No idea. Should I remember her?"

"Sweetness," Austin said. "You made out with her at homecoming when we were juniors. Remember?" he said like there was a reason for me to remember.

"Did I go to homecoming?" Dances weren't my thing. Neither were games.

"Yes. I was playing so I made you go. Instead of watching the game, you got drunk with Melanie under the bleachers." Carson seemed to know more than I did. But the story did seem familiar.

"Coop? Cooper, I knew you'd show up." I turned and should have looked at her eyes, except my gaze strayed a bit south. "Oh, yeah, definitely you."

"Shit, Mel?" Out of the corner of my eye, I could see the guys rolling their eyes and fighting laughter. "How are you?" Now I remembered her. Mel Tricks. I thought Tricks was actually her last name. Guess it was just a not-so-flattering nickname. Last names would be a good idea in the future. I promised myself that I would know the last name of the next woman I kissed.

"Great. I'm going to school in LA now. You?"

"Still at Sac State with these losers." Ryan was standing close enough for me to yank him next to me. I hated talking to people. No way I was talking to her alone.

"I'm not a loser," he replied indignantly. "How's it going, Mel?"

"Not bad. I was kind of hoping I'd run into you." One of her hands landed on my arm. Interesting. No, not interesting. I managed to smile when I really just wanted to watch a psycho massacring teenagers on a very large screen. Over Mel's shoulder, I caught sight of Reese. Maybe she'd help me since the guys were no help. She still owed me from the bar that night she got home.

"Hey, peanut butter," I called to see if she would bite. Then I remembered why Mel and I were under the bleachers. So her girlfriend wouldn't find us. Her girlfriend Reese. Shit.

"Hey, babe," Reese called back.

Mel turned to see who I was talking to. Simultaneously, they straightened their shoulders and narrowed their eyes. Mel started looking back and forth between Reese and me. We weren't known for nice pet names.

"Hi, Reese." Mel attempted to be cordial. Their breakup had been one of the most fucked up I'd seen. They did it in true high school fashion, screaming matches in the quad, vandalizing cars, sabotaging grades.

"Mel." Reese nodded at her then committed to the scene. She marched past her ex and draped an arm over my shoulders. I slung mine around her waist.

Hoping I wouldn't be heard over the noise outside the theaters, I whispered to Reese, "I'm sorry."

"You'll pay," she returned just as quietly.

"Jesus, Reese, what happened to your face?" Mel started staring.

"You should have seen the other guy," I said. No one other than my family knew what happened. We planned to keep it that way. "No, for real. We were coming out of Twenty-One a couple weeks ago and these assholes were ragging on a kid who just came out of the club, right?" This lie was inspired. "Reese was fuckin' brilliant." As if I were proud, I pulled her closer.

"It wasn't me. Obviously." Reese indicated her face. "I just got hit. You should have seen Coop."

"I'd show you the bruises, but Reese said I need to keep my shirt on in public." Then I started laughing like I was hilarious. Reese joined in.

"They're crazy." Ryan couldn't let us just tell lies to Mel Tricks, especially when it was so obvious. "You should have seen them when I picked them up. My car is still being cleaned."

"Oh my God." Melanie finally added two and two. "Are you guys together?" It was better than what I remember of her performance in high school math. "Weird."

"It seems like we've been this way forever." Reese started doing that play with my hair thing. I gave her a look to stop it. She opted for brushing a kiss across my cheek. This movie was going to suck now. It's way too hard to be scared and grossed out by blood at the same time as being horny.

"Gotcha." Mel dug around in her purse. "Sorry, just a sec. Just wondering where my girlfriend is." She turned away and started texting like mad. Reese and I watched her like we had all the time in the world, as long as we had each other. When another high school reject emerged from the crowd and sidled up to Mel, it took every ounce of my energy to not laugh out loud.

"Brittany, how are you?" Reese greeted my ex to save me the trouble.

"Awesome." A big, dumb smile took over her face. Reese was right. My standards were low.

I took a stab at making conversation. "I didn't know you were still around here. I thought you were moving to Australia or something."

"Yeah, I totally was gonna 'cause you know, I thought it would be warm. Like it was on *The Real World*. So I went to check it out last summer and it was hella cold." Brittany made it sound like a personal attack, as if Australia decided it didn't want her. "So Daddy bought me a ticket home. I'm never leaving California again."

"Wow. Sounds tough." I shrugged like it was news to me that the rest of the world had seasons. "Who knew it would be cold in summer?" Reese was still pressed against me. I could feel her body vibrating. She was really trying not to laugh out loud.

"I know. Isn't that crazy?" As an afterthought, Brittany threaded her arm through Mel's.

"Yeah, good season of *The Real World* though, huh?" I'd never seen an episode.

"Totally. God, it's so good to see you." She reached out and ran her hand down my arm. Reese's eyes narrowed and Brittany snatched her hand back.

"Okay. So I think we better go in," Reese announced. The hand that wasn't entwined in my hair tugged lightly on my shirt. "You ready, babe?"

"Did the guys already go in?" I asked her.

"They're in line."

"No way." Brittany joined Mel in her brilliant deduction. "Are you too, like?" She pointed at us and waggled her fingers.

"I don't know, peanut butter. Are we, like?" The smirk I'd been holding back finally surfaced.

"Come on." Reese slid a couple fingers down the front of my jeans and started pulling me. "It was nice to see you guys." She smiled back at Mel and Brittany as if it was normal to lead me around by my crotch. Actually, it was.

"Did they really just pretend they were together to show us up?" I asked once we were inside.

"Does it matter?" Reese was back to hating me. "That's what we were doing."

"No. I just didn't want to talk to Mel and it got out of hand." My excuse was lame, but they really did seem more pathetic than us for some reason.

"Right. Whatever." Reese began to stride away from me.

"You should be thanking me."

She stopped dead. "Why?"

"Because right now Mel is the loser and you got the one thing she never could." That sounded conceited and arrogant. It was.

"Please tell me you're not referring to yourself." She waited for me to deny it. "Oh, God. You're serious." The guys walked up in time to hear the last part.

"Nice show, you guys," Derek commented. "Mel must be dying right now."

"Why?" Reese demanded.

"'Cause she always wanted Coop," Derek said like it was common knowledge. "But after you and Mel broke up, Coop never spoke to her again."

"Well, they spoke plenty under the bleachers."

"Shut up, you guys." I said. "And, by the way, someone could have told me that Melanie Hendricks was Mel Tricks."

"You didn't know?" Ryan was looking at me like I was crazy.

"Cooper doesn't pay attention to names," Reese shot at me.

"Would you two please shut up?" Derek asked. "Let's just go in the theater and watch the movie." They took our silence for affirmation.

Below us, the revelers covered the backyard in a swaying mass of eveningwear. It felt like we were adults instead of just playing at it. Even so, the scotch in our heavy glasses and the suits couldn't change us. We were children drinking and dancing, filled with that feeling like life is real and heavy and amazing when in reality we were horny and stupid and enjoying every second of it.

Music reverberated up so that it seemed like the house was shaking, not just the bone and muscle housed in my chest. Ryan turned to me, lifted his glass to his lips, and smiled.

"Pretty happy with yourself aren't you?" I said.

"Fuck yeah." Ryan lowered his glass to the railing of the balcony. "Why does booze always taste better when it's stolen from Christopher?"

I sipped mine and thought a second. "The sweet taste of revenge?" I mustered every bit of cheesiness I could.

"Yeah, that's probably it." He laughed. "You seen Reese yet?"

"No, why?"

"I almost locked her in her room when I saw the dress she was going to wear."

"Slutty?" A girl could dream. "Skimpy? Sexy?"

"All of the above. Well, maybe not slutty." Ryan appeared mildly concerned. "I hate when people check her out. She is my sister, you know?"

"I'm pretty sure she can take care of herself."

"So I can't be protective?"

"Yeah, I guess," I said. Seeing my sister talk to teenage boys drove me up the wall, probably because I knew what they were thinking.

My attention turned back to the crowd beneath us. The makeshift dance floor took up most of the space not occupied by the pool.

"I think I'm going to join the masses," Ryan said.

"Have fun." We saluted each other with our glasses and he let himself inside. It was rather boring on the balcony alone so I trailed after him. Austin found me on the stairs and immediately dragged me outside to dance with him.

"You're looking very dashing." He had to shout to be heard over the music.

"Thanks." I glanced down at the pale gray suit and dark blue shirt I was wearing. I was looking pretty dashing. "You ain't so bad either." Austin was his usual immaculate, gorgeous self in a very fashionable, but not overly trendy suit.

I didn't mind dancing with Austin even though I hated dancing with girls. It was too distracting with chicks. After five minutes tops, I would want to fuck the girl, and that lacked certain decorum.

"Have you checked out Reese?" Austin unknowingly mimicked Ryan.

"No. Is she totally smokin'?" Reese had to be.

"Even you won't be able to resist her." He grinned like he knew too much. I cupped his elbow and led him into the house.

"Why are you smiling?" I asked once we were out of the fray.

"I'm not."

"Oh, yes, you are."

"Very sensitive tonight, sweetness," he said.

"Austin." I had to focus. "What are you thinking in that twisted mind of yours?"

"You need to get laid." That smile was back. Instead of explaining further, he sauntered off.

❖

"Down here." I led the girl down a hallway on the forbidden side of the house.

"I thought we couldn't go down here." She didn't seem too concerned. What was her name? Kristy? Katie? Something like that.

"Don't worry about it." I opened the door to Christopher's office. It fit him perfectly. It was dark wood and leather and totally lacking imagination, a designer's idea of masculinity that fell short. The desk was perpendicular to expansive windows, and behind it stood the now virtually empty liquor cabinet. Surprise, surprise, there were no bookcases. Christopher wasn't the type to read.

I tossed my jacket in the direction of the desk. She started kissing me. All tongue. No lips. Not great. So I backed her up until we landed on a previously unused and perpetually uncomfortable couch. I already had her dress up around her waist and her almost sexy panties hanging off one ankle. The leather of the couch creaked as I slid to the floor. My ears were filled with the deafening rustle of her skirt as it was dropped over my head. It allowed me to forget the unlocked door and the hardwood beneath my knees because there was only that sound and the feel of soft thighs encasing my head, the smell of teasing girl, and smooth anticipation.

With the first touch of my tongue, she shifted forward. Her hand settled on my head urging me further with light pressure. I circled, teased, brought her to the edge and away again without thought. This was what I did and I did it well. In my cocoon of fabric, I couldn't hear her so I was guided by the twitch of her muscles as she neared release. Juice dripped down my chin slowly, exquisitely.

Suddenly, I was yanked back and to my feet. The rush was gone, replaced by a second of fear, then anger. A boy, or maybe a man, stood before me. The jacket he was wearing was slightly loose on his frame, like it was made for someone else. His tie was terrible. It was tied too short making the knot fat and exposing the lower buttons of his shirt. His breathing was laborious to match mine, but without the benefits.

With the back of my hand, I wiped off my face. My lips and chin were drying already. Experimentally, I opened my mouth, moved my jaw a bit. He watched this display with revulsion.

"What the fuck are you doing?" he asked.

"You want me to give you some pointers?" My manufactured confusion was lost on him.

"Baby, leave her alone," the girl on the couch protested. Her dress was pushed back down, but one of her heels, a small purse, and her used underwear were still scattered across the floor.

"Don't fuckin' talk to me." The boy didn't even look at her. "I asked you a question, bitch." He punctuated this with a shot to my shoulder.

I stepped back to absorb the blow and remained silent. I didn't have to answer to this punk.

"What? You can fuck my girlfriend but you can't talk?" Uh-oh.

"I didn't hear her complaining." It was the truth. I wasn't responsible for their issues.

"You assaulted her." His shouting sounded crazy in comparison to my even tone.

"Don't give me that shit. I didn't assault anyone." There was serious effort involved in ignoring his bait. I'd still throw down though if that was what he was looking for.

"She's not a dyke." He didn't need to add the "like you are."

"That's not really for me to judge."

"I said she's not a fuckin' dyke." He stepped up so our chests were almost, but not quite touching. As if proximity would change my opinion of his girlfriend.

"Back up, kiddo, or I'm gonna drop you like a bad habit." To facilitate him, I planted my hands on his chest and pushed back. The desk stopped him from falling.

The door next to us opened and I made a mistake. Instead of watching the guy in front of me, I stared at the most beautiful woman I'd ever seen. Ryan and Austin were right about the dress. There was a splash of deep blue over golden brown skin and then there was a fist connecting with my stomach.

I indulged myself with enough time to fill my lungs before I punched the fucker back. In an instant, Carson was hauling him backward and Reese was in front of me. She was pretending to stop me, but she didn't have to try hard.

"Hey, stop it," Carson said. "Everybody cool down, all right?"

"Yeah, fine." I wasn't even that heated up. Just annoyed.

"Whatever. Let me go." The boyfriend shrugged Carson off.

"All right. I think it's time for you to go," Reese told the guy. She kept a cursory hand on my shoulder as she turned to look at him.

"That bitch attacked my girlfriend," he protested loudly.

"No, she didn't, baby," the girl finally spoke up.

"Listen to your girlfriend," I advised him a little unnecessarily.

He moved too fast for anyone to stop him. He tackled me and we slammed into the wall. Actually, I slammed into the wall. Behind me, I felt the drywall give way. The girlfriend screamed. Carson picked the kid up unceremoniously and dragged him out of the office. The girlfriend watched them go looking all distraught and shit.

"Fuck, Coop. Are you okay?" Reese rushed over and pulled me up.

"Yeah, yeah. I'm fine." But she wasn't even looking at me, just staring at the wall. It was going to be a bitch to fix that. I turned to check out the hole. It was six inches wide at least, but instead of the dark hole with wood beams that I was expecting, I saw the glint of gold.

CHAPTER NINE

"Get her out of here, Reese." I stepped in front of the hole so the girl couldn't see.

"Yeah, okay." Reese's face was a mixture of confusion and slow comprehension. The girl looked even more baffled as Reese led her out of the office and hopefully out of the house. I locked the door behind them and started pacing, looking everywhere except that hole. There was no way. I just imagined it. When there was a subtle knock at the door, I jumped.

"Who, uh…" What followed who? "Who is it?" I asked.

"It's me." Reese.

"Are you alone?"

"Yeah, of course." I could feel her glaring though the heavy wood.

It took me a minute to unlock the door and open it. The second Reese was in, I locked it again. We stared at each other, both waiting for the other to look at the wall.

"Are you okay?" Reese cautiously turned me around and brushed off my shirt. Anything for a distraction.

"My shoulder is kind of sore."

"Unbutton your shirt." Her heels clicked on the floor as she walked to the windows and pulled the curtains closed. Without the bright lights set up outside, the room was nearly dark. Only a small lamp on the desk afforded any light. Clumsily, I started unbuttoning. Reese pulled the shirt from my pants and finished opening it. Meticulously, she pulled it off my shoulders and pushed aside the ribbed tank top I was wearing to examine my back.

"I'm sure it's fine, Reese."

"You're going to bruise." Her fingertips traced over my skin. I could feel goose bumps raise on my back and arms. "Why did you let him hit you?"

"I didn't expect the tackle."

Reese pulled my tank top back into place. "Maybe, but you should have expected the first hit. The one we walked in on."

"What were you doing here anyway?" I took the shirt she handed me and slowly put it on.

"We were getting more alcohol." With a twitch of her wrist, she pointed at the liquor cabinet. "Why did you let him hit you?" She was relentless.

"I didn't let him." I unbuttoned my pants to tuck my shirt back in. Reese wasn't looking at my face anymore. Her gaze was lower. Much lower. "I just got…distracted."

"Oh," was all she said.

"Should we?" I waited for her to say it.

"Look at the wall?"

"Yeah. There's no way."

"Right, yeah. It's probably some electrical unit or something." Reese could always be counted on for logic.

"Or something. Yeah." My stunning intellect shone through.

We slowly turned and looked. It was so not an electrical unit. I pulled away some of the drywall. Reese reached in and, with a loud clunk, extracted a gold bar.

❖

Ryan was sprawled in an armchair. Reese and I were on the couch. We all had big mugs of coffee to compensate for the fact that it was six in the morning and we hadn't slept.

"Did you guys have a good time?" Ryan pulled his St. Christopher necklace out of his shirt and slid it back and forth on the chain.

"Uh huh." I blinked through gritty eyes. Sleep wasn't in my near future.

"Yeah." Reese's long eyelashes drooped.

"You both seem kind of out of it." He was way too observant. Reese shot me a look and I nodded toward the stairs. We couldn't talk there. At least five other people were asleep in the rooms surrounding us.

"Come here, Ryan. We want to show you something." I stood and started for the stairs. It didn't take the twins long to follow me.

"What's up? Where are you taking me?"

"Just wait," Reese said. At the door of Christopher's office, she handed me the key. Where she'd been keeping it in that dress, I'd never know.

"Guys, this is a little weird. Is this about the fight last night?" Ryan slouched against the doorframe while I unlocked and pushed open the door. We filed in and Reese locked the door again.

"Whoa. Hole in the wall," Ryan remarked casually. "Guess we'll have to patch—" He walked closer, examined it, then turned back to us. "You're fucking with me."

"I found your money." It was supposed to be funny. It wasn't, just weak.

"We wanted to tell you last night, but we thought it was best to keep it on the down low," Reese offered in explanation.

Ryan slumped to the couch. "How much is in there?"

"We don't know." Reese perched on the arm of the couch next to him.

"What are we going to do?" Ryan knew we didn't have any answers.

"No idea." I was just along for the ride.

"Who else knows?" He was straight up shocked, but at least he was thinking.

"The girl I was with might."

"Kristin," Reese supplied. At least someone caught her name.

"Let me guess." Ryan looked at me half proud and half annoyed. "Her boyfriend isn't too happy."

"She didn't tell me she had a boyfriend." That sounded pathetic.

"Any chance she'll tell him and he'll want to teach us an expensive lesson?" He really tried to not sound like an asshole.

"I think you're giving the girls Cooper hooks up with way too much credit," Reese said.

"Fuck, Ryan." I ignored Reese. "I don't think she even saw, but I don't know, okay? How about being happy I found your money?" They just glared. "Right. What's the plan?"

They made some meaningful eye contact with each other. "How do you feel about Mexico?" I wasn't sure if Ryan was kidding.

"Let's see how much is in there," I said. "Make sure it's worth it."

They seemed to think that was a good idea. Ryan went to get a couple hammers from the garage. Then we started to pull the drywall down. Reese said it made her hands hurt. I didn't see how that was possible. All you had to do was put the hammer in the wall and pull. It was messy as hell.

"There better be a lot in there. 'Cause I am so not cleaning this up." I wasn't too worried. We'd already removed quite a few feet from the wall and more gold was still visible.

"We're doing all the work. If it needs to be put back, Princess Reese can do it."

Reese looked up at the sound of her name. The midnight blue dress she was wearing was pristine. Ryan and I were head to toe white powder.

"Maybe you should have changed clothes," she said.

"Fuck you." Maybe I was a little cranky.

"Okay, I think we can start pulling the bars out," Ryan said to shut us up.

"All right." I set my hammer down. Ryan started handing me bars one at a time so I could stack them on the desk. "These are fuckin' heavy."

"Don't you watch movies? Of course they're fuckin' heavy." Reese picked one up off the desk. "Oh my God. How much do they weigh?"

"Why don't you do some research, princess?" I leaned over and turned the computer in front of her on.

After all of the bars were out of the wall, Ryan and I started counting them. Reese was super helpful. She kept updating us while we counted.

"What's a troy ounce? How do you convert that to pounds? I think this website has today's gold prices. Why is it listed for New York and London? I don't see how the price in Singapore is going to help me."

"Reese, would you please just shut up?" I asked after I lost count at twenty again.

"Ryan, she's being mean."

"Reese, I love you," Ryan said. "But if you don't shut up I might kill you."

"Fine."

Ryan and I each counted in absolute silence. "You done?" I asked after my second count.

"Yeah, I counted three times." Ryan said. "You?"

"Got the same both times."

"So how many?" Reese asked. We told her.

"How much is it worth?" Ryan asked.

Reese typed, deleted, and typed again, shaking her head. With a low whistle, she leaned back. "Thirty-four million."

❖

"What else do we need?" The front hall of the twins' place was piled with duffle bags of clothes, pillows, blankets, a small bag with Ryan's handguns, grocery bags of junk food, and water. Off to the side there was a neat pyramid of gold bars.

It was scorching in the foyer. Actually, it was scorching everywhere. At two o'clock in the afternoon, the temperature outside was approaching its triple digit height. I wondered why the air-conditioner wasn't on.

Reese ignored me. She ran her hands through her hair and pulled it up off her skin. Beads of sweat stood out on her neck.

"You look good, Reese." She let go of her hair.

"Are you sure we need to take two cars?" Reese pretended not to hear my comment.

"I don't think either car will hold that much weight." I thought she went to Yale. Didn't they teach common sense there? "We don't want them riding suspiciously low."

"I just think we should try it."

"It won't work," I said. "Do you want your precious Mercedes scraping the pavement?"

"What about Ryan's?"

"His is lifted."

"Whatever." She walked out and returned a couple minutes later with a bottle of cold water.

"Thanks for bringing one for me." Sometimes I thought Reese just couldn't hear me.

"We need to pick up your stuff. Ready to face your mother?" She knew I was putting off saying good-bye to my mom. At my grimace, Reese laughed. "You are such a mama's boy."

"So?" I sauntered closer and made a show of leaning down to look in her eyes. If she thought I wasn't going to play up the whole being taller than her thing, she was crazy.

A delicate fist gripped my polo shirt and yanked me closer. "It's kind of pathetic, you know?"

"And?" I could smell the sweet tang of her sweat. "You're sexy when you're all sweaty."

"We need to talk."

"About my mother?" I wasn't pretending to be confused. It was all real. Maybe the heat was making me stupid.

"You know, we don't have to bring you with us." She wasn't asking, just telling me. I nodded. "And you know we don't have to give you a cut."

"I didn't think you were."

Reese looked at me like I was an idiot. "We are." That was a surprise. It was probably going to be out of Ryan's half. "So if you want your cut, you play by our rules." She pulled me even closer.

"What rules?"

"Stop hitting on me. Stop looking at me like I'm a piece of meat. Don't act like you're calling the shots because you're not."

I pretended to consider her rules. After a second, I brushed her hair away from her ear so I could lean close and whisper, "If I give up my cut, can I still hit on you?"

The grip on my shirt eased up and Reese snaked a hand behind my neck. Her cheek pressed against mine. "No," she murmured. I was breathing hard, but I think she was too. With every breath, I could feel her tits brush against me.

I backed away like it was no big deal. "All right, buttercup, but it goes both ways." Indolently, I tugged my sweat-dampened polo over my head to reveal an equally damp tank top.

"Believe me, it won't be a struggle."

It would for me. Not that I was going to tell her that.

Thankfully, Ryan walked in two minutes later. I didn't think I could glare disdainfully much longer.

"Cell phones for everybody." He tossed each of us a pre-paid cell phone.

"Gosh, we're just like spies now," Reese mocked Ryan.

"Why do you have to kill my buzz?" Ryan threw up his arms and turned away. "You ready to go to your parents'?" he tossed over his shoulder. We followed him out the door.

My parents and sister were all home when we got there. It was impossible to act normal. I didn't want to leave my mommy and daddy. Okay, I was a child. Reese and Ryan waited downstairs while I ran up. Ryan explained that we'd decided to go on a road trip, but we'd be back soon. No, we didn't know where we were going. Ryan was a way better liar than me.

I tossed a bunch of clothes into a duffle bag. What did people bring when they ran away? I grabbed another bag and added a couple books, my laptop, my iPod. Toothbrush, that was important. Where was my passport? I definitely needed it for Mexico. And whatever the hell country Reese would pick after that. I found the file folder in my desk with my important documents and riffled through until I got to the passport. With everything packed, I grabbed my bags and headed out. I lingered on the stairs debating.

It wasn't like I was moving out. I couldn't go back to visit my parents. Not for a while at least. I could let Reese and Ryan go on their own. They would be fine. Except I couldn't do that. The twins won over my parents. It still felt shitty though.

I told my parents I loved them. I might have hugged my mom longer than necessary, but so did Reese. After my parents' house, Ryan drove to my bank.

"This shouldn't take too long," I said before getting out.

"We'll be here," Ryan said.

It was surprisingly easy to pull the majority of the cash in my account out. All I had to do was ask for it. Ten minutes later, I was climbing into the back of the SUV.

"How much was in there?" Ryan drummed his fingers on the steering wheel and leaned back to look at me.

I tossed a bank envelope onto his lap. "Three thousand. It won't get us far."

"Far enough." He handed the envelope back. "Until we can sell a bar at least." He assumed we'd be able to sell them. If not, we were fucked. We didn't know how to move gold bars. You didn't just walk into your bank and ask to have your gold bar turned into cash. Or maybe you did. How the hell would I know?

"So I was thinking. If we want to cover our tracks we should get some fake IDs."

"Totally," Ryan said.

"God, you two are hopeless," Reese said. "Too many movies."

"Whatever. Ideas?" Ryan was practically vibrating at the mention of falsified documents. What a loser.

"Remember Paulie Montrose?" Paulie'd had a monopoly on fake IDs in El Dorado County until he moved away. The kid had some serious skill.

"Oh, yeah. He's in San Francisco now, right?" Ryan asked.

"I seriously doubt Paulie is still making fake IDs," Reese said.

"No, he totally is. And I heard he's gotten better. I bet he'd hook us up," I said.

"So we'll detour to San Francisco before we leave?" Ryan asked.

"Can't hurt. You can head straight down to Vegas," I told Reese. "We'll hit up Paulie."

"What's your name going to be?" Ryan wanted to know.

"Anything you want, babe." All that earned me was a loud sigh from Reese and rolling eyes from Ryan.

"We didn't buy cigarettes." Ryan started whining after ten minutes on the freeway.

"You don't smoke," I reminded him.

"You wouldn't let me bring any weed. I need something to smoke."

"Too bad. We just started driving. You'll just have to deal." I leaned back in the seat and studied cars opposite us on the freeway. I wondered where all of them were going. Home, probably, to their normal lives with a failed marriage and two point five brats. How unappealing.

"I'll probably get withdrawal or something. I could die." Ryan was such a drama queen. That was probably why Reese had been okay with driving alone. She didn't want to deal with his shit.

"Fuckin' come on, bro. We're supposed to be under the radar now. We can't just keep going into gas stations and liquor stores."

"We aren't that far from home. Who cares if we go into a gas station?" He was so annoying.

"Fine." I said. "Pull off here. I'll go in."

"You rock." Thanks, Ryan, I was aware of that.

Ryan pulled into a gas station. "Wait," he said before I could get out. He climbed into the backseat. "Wear this." A baseball cap was thrown over the seat. "You'll be incognito."

"Yes, I'm sure the hat will totally disguise my identity." I pushed my hair back and put the hat on anyway. "Too bad it's dark or I could wear sunglasses too." A pair of aviators landed in my lap. I tossed them back. "What kind do you want?"

"Camel Wides."

"All right." I hopped out of the 4Runner and went into the gas station. "Can I get a pack of the Camel Wides?" I asked the kid behind the counter.

"Wides?" He stood on his tiptoes to pull the pack down. "Anything else?"

"Nope."

I handed him some cash. When he gave me the change and handed the packs over a, "Thank you, sir. Have a good night," accompanied it.

I debated correcting him, but I didn't care. Even though it wasn't a common occurrence, it still happened often enough. When I climbed back into the SUV, I tossed Ryan his Wides.

"Did anybody recognize you?" Ryan played it up as if that were even a possibility.

"Nope. The hat worked. Actually, he thought I was a guy." He started laughing. "Oh my God. I got it." I realized how to fly under the radar.

"Got what?" Ryan opened his pack and lit a cigarette.

"I know how to stay incognito."

"Baseball hats?"

"Drag," I answered.

CHAPTER TEN

Paulie's loft in San Francisco was in the heart of what he called SoMa. We just called it South of Market, but Paulie liked to pretend he was in New York.

"Damn, Paulie, this place is amazing." I hugged the guy I'd known since childhood and stared openmouthed around his apartment.

"I know, right?" He grinned. "Come on. I'll show you around." Showing around mostly entailed looking out from the balcony off the twenty-third floor. The sun was beginning to set and it glinted off the glass buildings surrounding us.

"I thought your mom cut you off." Delicacy in speech wasn't one of my attributes. It was better to just ask.

"Yeah. Fags don't get college money." Paulie managed to say it without crying. I would have cried.

"So how the fuck did you get this place?" Ryan prescribed to the same social functions I did.

"I upgraded."

"In boyfriends?" I picked up a framed black-and-white photo from the counter. It was Paulie in his scruffy, muscled glory with a gorgeous model type who had softly curling hair. They had matching shirts on. I was going to puke from the domesticity of it.

"Isn't he beautiful?" Paulie took the photo and gazed lovingly at it. "He's Canadian. And so fucking smart. I think I'll have to marry him to keep him here."

"Good luck with that."

"Don't worry; you guys will get to meet him. He should be home soon. Anyway." He sighed and put the photo down. "I mean, I upgraded in illicit forms of identification." What a geek. "You guys are going to die. You said on the phone you wanted licenses, which are no problem. We just need to take photos." He waved a hand like it was nothing. "But wait until you see what I've been working on. It's an art form. I swear, I wish I could put them in a gallery."

"Paulie?" He looked up at Ryan. "What the hell are you talking about?"

"Driver's licenses, military IDs." He ticked them off on his fingers. "Those are easy. Birth certificates, passports, not so much."

"Fuck, dude. You're awesome," I said.

"You guys want? I could cut you a deal." He always was a salesman.

"Are they any good?" Ryan should have known better. Paulie wouldn't sell them if they weren't perfect.

"Good? Sweetie, no. Amazing, brilliant. Art, I'm telling you. I do the birth certificates and my wonderful, sexy Marc—he works at the embassy—he pushes the paperwork through for a passport. So it's fucking real."

"You really are brilliant." I congratulated him with only a hint of surprise.

"I know." He gloated. "I about had a heart attack when they announced that they were going to do biometric passports." Ryan and I must have looked appropriately blank. "You know RFID?" Still nothing. "Electronic ones." That we could understand. "But as long as we can fabricate the documentation, it's no problem. That's when I started doing the birth certificates."

"We didn't really follow that, but it sounds cool." I figured we should give him some encouragement.

"How long does it take?" Why did Ryan have to kill the excitement?

"Depends on how much cash you have. I can get it done in two weeks, but normally it takes about a month."

"How much?" Ryan asked.

"For the two weeks," I added.

He named an amount. We didn't argue. "I'll include any manufactured documentation like the birth certificate. And that's fucking cheap so don't tell anyone." As if we would know who to tell.

"Done." Ryan didn't even ask me. "We need one for Reese too."

"Great. You still want IDs?"

"Yep," I said.

"So three Canadian passports and three California driver's licenses? Or you want Canadian licenses too?"

Ryan and I looked at each other. He raised an eyebrow.

"You want the British Columbia license," Paulie said. "The holograms are beautiful."

"Paulie, are you as good as you say you are?" He always was a cocky bastard. I just wanted to make sure.

He just laughed. "Come on. We need to take pictures. Do you have the pictures of Reese?"

"Right here." I gave him a flash drive with the pictures we took before leaving.

"Did you use a plain background?"

"We did everything you said on the phone."

"Perfect." Paulie ran a finger down Ryan's chest. "Just like you." He turned away smiling. "Follow me, boys and girls."

Five hours later, Ryan woke me up. It was just past midnight. The pillow I had propped against the window fell between the seat and the door.

"You want me to take over?" I asked all groggy.

"Yeah, I'm dead tired."

We switched and Ryan was out in five minutes. We were somewhere on I-5 between San Francisco and LA. The sporadic headlights on the other side of the freeway lulled me into a half awake, half asleep state. Periodically, I sipped from the Mountain Dew I'd pulled from the cooler to keep myself alert.

When you've got a shitload of gold bars in the backseat, it tends to slow you down so we were barely at the speed limit. I wondered how long it took Reese to drive. We knew she was already there because she'd called to tell us she checked into a hotel, but it was going to be hours before we arrived.

After I'd been on Highway 15 for a while, Ryan's GPS said we were about an hour outside the city. I pulled onto the shoulder.

"Ryan." I shook him. "Hey, it's time."

"Shit." He rubbed his face and shook his head. "All right. Let's do it."

I took the 4Runner off the asphalt and drove straight out into the desert for about ten minutes. Periodically, Ryan would consult the GPS and tell me to go a little to the right or the left.

"How's this?" I put on the emergency brake.

"Works for me." Ryan hopped out and opened the back. I chugged the rest of my Mountain Dew and joined him. Both shovels were already on the ground. Ryan was strapping on his shoulder holster.

"What are you doing?"

He opened the side compartment and pulled out his Glock 21.

"Seventeen million," he said as if that answered my question.

"You can't dig a hole when you're strapped."

"Watch me." He grinned his pretty boy grin and grabbed a shovel.

My arms were going to fall off. Followed by my shoulders and legs and neck, and then I was just going to die.

"I can't dig anymore." Both holes were about three feet deep and four wide. They were separated by about six feet. "It's three a.m. Why is it so hot?"

Ryan tossed his shovel to the ground and sat with his feet in the second hole. "It's too hot to think."

"Too hot to breathe." I sat next to him

"To move."

I dragged myself back to the 4Runner and pulled out two bottles of water. "We haven't been digging that long."

"Thanks." Ryan caught the bottle I tossed to him. "It's the heat, I'm telling you." Or the fact that neither of us had slept more than a couple hours since before the party.

"Should we get this shit over with?"

Feebly, Ryan stood and joined me. He found a bandana in his duffle bag and tied it around his forehead to keep his hair back.

"Come on, gorgeous. Give me a hand." I palmed a bar and handed it to him.

"You're brutal."

"I want a shower and some sleep and a drink." Dreams of cool water and soft sheets were already filling my head. A naked girl would complete the picture, but I didn't want to get carried away. "I can't have those things until we finish."

"Bro." That meant he agreed.

We began the laborious process of stacking the gold in one of the holes. Each bar was wrapped in a piece of cloth, duct taped shut, and numbered. Ryan crouched by the hole and I carefully lobbed the bars into the dirt next to him. I tried really hard not to hit him.

"Shit, Cooper." He jumped out of the way for the third time. "I swear if you hit me I'll kill you."

"If you kill me, you'll have to bury my body." I tossed another bar at him. "Do you really want to dig another hole?"

"Just be careful, all right?"

"Okay." Another bar landed with a spray of dirt. "Stack faster."

Ryan's cell phone rang. "Shit." He dug it out of his pocket. "You here?" It had to be Reese. "Yeah, cool. Fifteen minutes."

"Reese?" I asked after he hung up.

"Yeah. Let's unload and you can go pick up her half. I'll stack this while you're gone." Worked for me. Five minutes later, the remaining half of the bars were scattered on the ground around the hole. Ten minutes after that, I got back to the highway. Reese was parked on the shoulder looking the part of lost girl. I parked behind her.

"You look like hell," Reese kindly informed me. Sure, I was sweaty and dirty, and I smelled like dirty sweat, but I thought it was a little unnecessary to point it out.

"Thanks. Open the trunk." I was all business. Shower, drink, sleep, shower, drink, sleep. I just had to keep my goals in mind.

"Here are your room keys." Reese handed me two red plastic key cards. "We're at the Wynn. In the Tower Suites. It's on the Strip." All of which meant nothing to me.

"Just help me move the gold." I pocketed the cards.

"You're a little uptight." Dutifully, Reese started moving gold from the trunk of her Mercedes into the 4Runner. Hers were wrapped like Ryan's except the numbers were written in green instead of black.

"I'm tired and hot and sore. I just want to get this shit finished." I turned around to grab more gold and she was right behind me.

"Maybe you should get a massage at the hotel." Somehow, her hands ended up pressed against my lower back. "You're tense."

Damn, that felt good. I had to bite my lip to keep from moaning. Hopefully, she couldn't see that in the dark. "Of course I'm tense. Stop that. We need to get this finished." I stepped around her and continued loading.

"You are such an ass."

"Took you long enough to catch on." We finished working in silence after that. Reese didn't seem too talkative.

"So I guess I'll see you guys in a couple hours."

"Yep." I immediately got back in the SUV and retraced my steps. When I pulled up, Ryan was just starting to bury the gold.

It took us the better part of an hour to unload the second set of bricks, stack them in the second hole, and fill it with dirt.

"We should clean up." I dug around in the mound of gear in the 4Runner until I found the larger containers of water.

"Clean up what?" Ryan looked at me like I was crazy.

"Us. If we walk into a hotel looking like this we'll draw too much attention to ourselves."

"Oh, okay." Ryan took the shoulder holster off and stashed the gun properly. Then he uncapped a gallon bottle of water and poured it over his head. The water ran down his face collecting dirt and leaving streaks behind. With a shake, he flung the damp hair out of his eyes. "Your turn." Before I could move, he dumped the remaining half gallon of water over my head.

I screamed like a girl. "Asshole." The water ran down my hair into my ears and eyes. It went down the back of my grubby shirt and collected in the waistband of my underwear. Ryan was already dying of laughter. I felt surprisingly good.

"Was that what you had in mind?" He stripped off his shirt and used it like a towel on his hair and face.

"Not entirely." I followed suit with my shirt. "I'll get you back though."

"Sure you will." He was totally mocking me. "You ready to go?"

"Yep. I want first shower." I called dibs.

"I don't care."

Ryan drove the rest of the way. He seemed to know where he was going so I just watched in a semi-comatose state until we pulled up to the private entrance.

❖

Eighteen hours later, I woke up. It was already dark again. Wearing only my boxer briefs, I padded out to the main room of the suite. Below me, the Las Vegas Strip flashed and blinked and screamed. I pressed against the cool glass to see it all. Our room was dark and quiet. I wondered for a second where the twins were until I heard movement behind me.

"Isn't it beautiful?" Reese asked softly.

"In sort of a corporate America kind of way, yeah."

She chuckled at my response. "You want some champagne?"

"Yeah, that sounds good." I spun around and leaned back against the window.

"I'll pour it if you put on a shirt."

I glanced down at the expanse of skin that was showing. "If you insist." I let out a big sigh and went to find a shirt. A minute later, I reemerged wearing tight jeans and an oxford shirt with a single button done. Reese was still in front of the expansive windows. A flute of champagne dangled from her long fingers and another stood behind her on a low table. Mine, I assumed.

"Where's your brother?" I joined her.

"He's still crashed. Did you guys sleep at all on the drive?"

"For a couple hours. Before that, the last time we slept was before the party."

"No wonder you were so tired." Reese turned to look at me. The gaudy lights from outside reflected in weak imitations of color across her face and chest. She pushed her hair back and took a slow drink of champagne. Girl was sexy. She knew it. I searched for something, anything that would distract me.

"So, uh…you think he'll come after us?" I gathered the courage to ask. I knew the answer, but I wanted someone else to say it.

"Christopher?" she asked. I nodded. "If you took the time to put thirty-four million in gold bars in a wall and someone stole it, would you go after them?"

"Fuck, yeah. But, technically, it is your money," I pointed out.

"He thinks he's entitled to it or something."

"Why?"

"I'm not sure really. I think he helped my mom get it in the first place."

"So? It's from some business she ran, right?"

"I guess." Reese stared out the window. "You want to go walk around?"

"Sure."

"You'll need to button up your shirt." She dragged two fingers down my bare stomach. My boxer briefs got suddenly wet. I'd need to change those.

"You ask me to put on clothes and now you want them buttoned? You're so demanding." I went to find shoes.

"Where are we going to go?" Reese asked me in the elevator.

"You tell me." She looked at me like I was crazy. "I've never been to Vegas, but you have, right?"

"Oh, yeah. I guess."

Either she had or she hadn't. Maybe she'd gotten really trashed or something and didn't remember.

"So you can show me around then?" I slung a casual arm around her shoulders as we cruised down the street. Surprisingly, she didn't punch me. She didn't even move it.

"Sure. Whatever."

A mile later, we stood in front of what was supposed to be a spectacular water show. I leaned against the wide railing next to Reese "So these are the Bellagio fountains?"

"In all their glory." Her sarcasm was duly noted.

"They seem so exciting in movies."

"I think they improve with alcohol consumption." Reese was so smart.

"Want to find out?" I couldn't think of anything better to do. "We could get trashed and walk around. That fake Eiffel Tower will be way cooler."

"You make it sound like Disneyland."

"I think Vegas is supposed to be like Disneyland, but for big kids."

Reese looked around, but I guess she didn't see much because she shrugged and said, "Why not?" Then she took off through the crowd. So I did the logical thing. I followed her.

I probably should have asked what she was looking for.

Drunk Reese was awesome. She couldn't walk a straight line to save her life, and she couldn't focus on a single subject longer than thirty seconds, yet her speech was impeccable.

"I am not entirely sure if that is a good idea." Reese clung to my arm to stay upright as we stumbled back to our hotel. Navigating through people, around trees, and past the sidewalk vendors peddling beer merchandise was apparently far more than she could handle.

"Nope, it is."

"Cooper, I believe we are intoxicated and should not engage in certain pursuits."

"Are you trying to sound like a pompous ass?" I genuinely wanted to know. "I love it. Really. It's like you're compensating for not being able to function at all."

"I am perfectly capable of functioning."

"Really?" She nodded emphatically. "Then let's do it."

"Oh, fine. Now will you open the door?"

Belatedly, I realized that we were in front of our door and that Reese couldn't unlock it. I took the key card and slid it through the reader.

"No, wait for the red light."

"That's why it's not working. You wait for the green light." I pushed the door open.

"Oh. Well." She grasped about for something to say. "Thank you." Then she sashayed into the room.

"Where the hell have you guys been?" Ryan was perched on the small desk with a handgun tucked into his waistband.

"Where the hell have you been?" Reese countered.

"Put that away." I pointed to the gun. "Why the fuck do you need that?"

"What? This makes you nervous?" He pulled it out, waved it around, and tucked it back into his pants. "Well, I've been fuckin' nervous. So deal. You guys have been gone forever and neither of you were answering your phones."

"Damn, Ryan. Calm down." I put up my hands in surrender. "And put the gun away, please."

"I don't know why they freak you out so much. You're a better shot than I am." He was right, but just because I could shoot like a cowboy didn't mean I liked guns. I didn't see why he had to bring that shit in the first place. Ryan took the gun and put it back into the small safe on top of five gold bars.

"It's a machine made to kill people." Exasperated, I fell back onto the designer sofa. We'd had this conversation before.

"Hey, Ryan?" Reese collapsed next to me. "Guess what we're doing?"

"How drunk are you?" he asked in response.

"Suitably," she said.

"What does that mean?" I'd never been suitably drunk in my life.

Reese ignored me. "Ryan, I said, guess what we're doing?"

"Getting married?"

"No. We tried. It's illegal here." She wasn't exactly telling the truth. We'd been walking down the strip, and I asked where all the chapels were and Reese said she didn't know. That wasn't exactly trying. "We are going swimming."

"No, you're not." Ryan sounded the voice of reason.

"Sure we are." I backed Reese up. It was my idea after all.

"No, you're not."

"Ryan, we are." I used my serious tone.

"Not happening." His serious tone was better. Maybe the deep voice helped.

"Yeah, huh," Reese brilliantly contributed.

"Come on, Ryan," I whined. "Why not?"

"You're both drunk," he said.

"If we keep annoying you, will you give in?" I didn't think he'd actually go for that.

"Not even a little bit."

"Come on." Reese jumped up and immediately fell down.

"Definitely not now."

"Is it weird that I'm totally attracted to her right now?" I asked Ryan.

"Yes."

"Let's go swimming," I said again like it was a new idea.

"No. The pool is probably closed and my sister is about to pass out." And then she did.

"Damn."

CHAPTER ELEVEN

Your sister sure knows how to pick accommodations." After two days, we'd taken full advantage of the disgustingly opulent hotel Reese had chosen. Mostly, that meant Reese and I had gone shopping for Ryan. Weird, but we liked to dress him. Ryan knew his marijuana, he knew computers, he knew wine, and he even knew a little Spanish, but he didn't know shit about clothes. After the age of fifteen, Reese and I didn't let him pick out his own clothes. Even weirder, Reese had picked out some clothes for me. I think the girl just liked men's suits, but she didn't like to wear them so she dressed Ryan and me up like Ken dolls.

"That she does." We were at the virtually empty private pool watching the heat rise in waves from the ground. It was sort of hypnotic. "Hey, happy birthday." Ryan held out his mimosa and I tapped mine against it.

"Thanks."

He hooked a finger in his oversized aviators to look at me. "You feel old?"

"Yep."

"Me too." The sunglasses went back into place.

"So what's with the bathing suit?" I'd been holding back all morning. It was time to ask.

"What's wrong with my bathing suit?" We both looked down at the very slim mid-thigh length trunks. They were cream and deep blue, which looked damn good against his dark skin, but I wasn't going to tell him that.

"Just a little shorter than usual." Actually, they weren't bad. Ryan had the muscle in his legs to pull them off. "Way shorter. And super tight. You see James Bond wearing them and thought you'd try it out?"

Ryan's jaw dropped. "Daniel Craig. How'd you know?"

"You're so transparent, darlin'. At least you kept your chest hair." We both looked down at all four of his chest hairs. His St. Christopher hung on its long silver chain just below them. It was bigger than the patch of hair.

"Sometimes I hate you," he said unconvincingly. "Should I put on my shirt?"

"No, you're hot." He was. "Just lacking hair."

"You know I was going to give you your birthday present, but now there's no way in hell."

"I thought the party was my birthday present." News to me. I wasn't going to complain about more presents though.

"Sort of. Reese and I talked about something else though. I couldn't convince her last year, but…" He waved his hand through the air, which made him look exactly like his sister. "Never mind, you'll see."

"That really didn't tell me much."

"Doesn't matter. Be patient."

"Why'd you mention it in the first place? Now I'm all curious."

"It builds the anticipation." He smirked.

One of the cell phones on the table between us vibrated. It was mine. "Damn." I fumbled the phone open. "What's up?" Only two people had the number and one was sitting next to me.

"Happy birthday," said Reese. "Are you as hung over as I am?"

"Totally. The cure is to drink more." A mantra we'd been living by for most of the summer.

"I'll keep that in mind." Not much of a drinker, that girl.

"We're having mimosas."

"Well, I just ordered brunch. You guys want to come back to the room? I can order more mimosas if you want."

"You rock."

"I know." She hung up.

"What did she want?" Ryan asked when I set the phone down.

"She ordered brunch for us. You want to go?"

"Yeah." We stood and Ryan's phone went off. "Why's she calling me now? Hello?" Ryan reached out and grabbed my arm. "No way.

All right, cool. Yeah, I'll call." He hung it up and looked at me with feverish eyes. "Our first shipment is ready."

We weren't so good at codes. I was pretty sure that meant the fake IDs. "No way. Are we driving up?"

"One of us will have to. Paulie said he'd overnight them, but it's probably not a great idea."

"Considering what they are, no shit." Sometimes I had to help him with the most obvious things.

"Let's go eat breakfast and then we'll figure it out."

"Works for me."

❖

I'd never had such good French toast. Reese ordered all my favorites right down to the coffee. Italian roast. The girl knew what was up. After we ate, we collapsed facing the windows and watching the Strip. It was way less sexy in the daylight.

"So I figured I'd drive back up to San Francisco," Ryan said. "I mean, it's your birthday and Reese drives so slow it would take days."

I considered arguing. Driving sixteen hours there and back sounded really unappealing though. "I'll go with you if you want."

"No, it's cool."

"Okay," I folded.

"Hey, wait. Don't I get a say?" Reese didn't look happy at the evaluation of her driving.

"Not really," Ryan said.

"Do I get my present before you go?" I really couldn't follow too many trains of thought at once.

"You told her?"

"Only that there was a present." Ryan moved out of hitting range. Reese swatted at him anyway. "I didn't tell her what it was."

"I guess we have to give it to her now." Reese disappeared into her bedroom and came back out with a velvet box the size of my fist. She tossed it into my lap.

"You guys got me jewelry?" Boxes like that are pretty distinctive.

"Just open it." Ryan was literally on the edge of his seat.

"Okay." So I did. Inside was a St. Christopher like theirs. It was a little bigger and wasn't quite as ornate. It was also very familiar. "Oh my God. No way." I glanced up and Ryan nodded. Reese was smiling but trying to hide it. "No, you didn't. You can't give me this."

"Sure we can." Ryan reached out and took the box from me. He pulled out the long silver chain and put it over my head. "She would be proud to give it to you."

"This was your mom's. You can't give me it."

"Cooper," Reese cut in. "You've always wanted one."

"Not this one." My fingers automatically started playing up and down the chain.

"We want you to have this one." She placed her hand on top of mine. "It looks good on you."

It was kind of hard to argue with both of them. "You guys are sure?"

"Yes," they both nearly shouted.

"Thank you. I love it."

"We know." Ryan leaned over and kissed my cheek. I kissed him back. "If you lose it there will be hell to pay."

"Hell." Reese kissed my other cheek. It felt entirely different kissing her back.

"Thanks."

"Okay, now that that's over with, I'm going to go." Ryan stood. "I'll be back tomorrow probably."

"What? Right now? No, you're not." I abandoned the couch to follow him into his room as he picked up stuff to bring with him.

"It's one o'clock. If I go now I can be back by tomorrow morning."

"Hell no. We're partying tonight."

"We should really pick up the IDs."

"Why rush? It's my twenty-first birthday and we're in fucking Las Vegas." It seemed logical to me. "We have to live it up."

"Fuck." Ryan dropped the backpack he was holding. "We're in fucking Vegas for your fucking twenty-first birthday," he screamed. "How the fuck did that happen? Reese." He sprinted back out to the main room. "Reese. Vegas. Twenty-one."

"Ryan." I followed him out. "Hey, Ryan." He finally looked at me. "We already knew that."

"Yeah, but I didn't, like, catch on, you know?"

Reese and I stared at each other, a little worried about him. I decided to step up. "Darlin', remember how we always tell you to smoke less weed?" He nodded. We'd only told him a million times. "I think you just proved why."

"You guys are mean." He pouted.

Reese and I nodded. We were mean. "So are you going to stay so we can go out?"

"Duh." My best friend was such a genius.

We lost Reese five minutes after stepping onto the casino floor. It was probably good that she had suggested that we stay in one casino all night. Didn't want to get lost or anything. Not that it mattered. We were there to have a good time. The hotel casino was a step up from the usual. Just like our hotel suite, it was all trendy and art deco and subtle class, but underneath that, it was still a casino. Slot machines covered the elaborate carpet, and there were still unshaven, unclean men wandering around looking decimated. Ryan and I were just playing the part of gamblers. Mostly because we had no clue how to gamble. Slots were fun because they required no thought. Blackjack was cool because we could add to twenty-one. Craps looked cool, but we couldn't follow it so we stayed away. After all those James Bond movies, we probably should have understood it, but, oh well. A couple hours in, we were pretty much breaking even. I was up ten bucks. Ryan was down about fifteen. Not too bad.

"Where do you think Reese is?"

"Dunno." Ryan handed me another beer from one of the beautiful, though slightly vapid waitresses.

"Should we find her? I want to go hit up that club."

"Yeah, I don't want to lose any more money. Makes me feel like a loser." He pouted his beautiful lips and tried to summon some tears to his eyes. They were shot through with sensuous gray. He was definitely drunk.

"Darlin', when you lose money, you are a loser. That's where the name comes from."

"You always know how to make a boy feel good." He gave me a sloppy smile. We slung our arms around each other and started wandering through the casino looking for Reese. Our efforts didn't get us far. Thirty minutes later, we were drunker and no closer to finding Ryan's sexier half.

"Excuse me." I got the attention of a waitress. "Have you seen a really hot girl who looks like him?" I pointed to Ryan. "But like super hotter than him." That was kind of what I was trying to say.

"You mean Ms. DiGiovanni?" she asked. Whoa.

"That's her." Ryan didn't seem to notice that some waitress knew his sister by name. Or if he did, he didn't care.

"She's in the back playing poker. If you'd like I can show you where." The woman offered with a smile. Helpful.

"That'dbegreat." No more beer for Ryan.

The waitress took off weaving through people, smiling at some, ignoring others. At the back of the casino, she escorted us into the poker room and pointed us toward Reese.

"Thanks," I attempted, but she was already gone.

Ryan and I leaned against the wall and watched Reese. She didn't look nearly as lost as she should have. Actually, she looked totally sexy. Her soft, pale pink shirt was unbuttoned about halfway down her sternum giving an appropriately tormenting view of tanned cleavage. Wide cuffs were turned up to just below her elbow, which made her look like a swindler and a poker player all at the same time. I couldn't see her eyes; they were hidden by Ryan's oversized aviators. She was smoking a slim cigar. I wasn't close enough, but I knew that, under the reek of cigar smoke, it smelled faintly of honey.

In a practiced motion, she pushed her hair back and deliberately placed her cards on the fabric-covered table. Around her, the other players and few spectators leaned back with resigned faces.

"Ryan." He stopped playing with his tie long enough to look at me. "She looks like she knows what she's doing."

"So?" He leaned over and tried to play with my tie. His must have gotten boring.

"Stop it." I smacked his hand away.

"Come on. Let's go." Great, he'd entered his drunk and whining phase.

"Fine. I'll go get her." I left him leaning against the wall and made for Reese.

I leaned down to whisper in her ear. "You look like a real poker player."

Her shoulders stiffened, only for a second and then she relaxed. "Gentlemen." She turned to the only other woman at the table, a striking blonde with creamy freckled skin. "And lady." Reese flashed that grin like Ryan's. Instantly, I was jealous. "Thank you for the game, but I'm being summoned." She stood, tipped the dealer, and slid her arm through mine. I straightened, assuming the role of escort, and led her back to Ryan.

"Whoa." Ryan looked up from the carpet he was studying. "You guys look like a couple."

Reese and I looked at each other. Her wide legged, dark gray pants looked good next to my slim charcoal slacks. Our shirts were different, mine was plain white, but the tie I was wearing was pale pink and gray. We looked like we'd dressed together. Like fuckin' high school prom.

"Shit, it's the tie isn't it?"

"I didn't even notice." Reese was as thrown as I was.

"Ryan, trade ties with me." I started loosening mine, until I looked at his. "Sailboats? That is so lame."

"Yeah, keep yours," Reese said after studying Ryan's tie.

"What's wrong with sailboats?" He lifted it closer to his face. "Your dad gave me this tie."

"And he's so fashionable." I loved my father, really, but there was no way I'd wear his clothes.

"Anyway, I like this one." Reese drew her fingers down my tie.

"Why are you guys agreeing?" Ryan looked shocked. "Don't be nice to each other. I don't like it."

"You always wanted us to get along. Why are you complaining now?" I teased him.

"Well, you can get along. Just don't team up on me."

"How drunk is he?" Reese leaned closer to look at his eyes. "I think it's time to slow down, bro."

"I think it's time to go clubbin'." He started making music and dancing by himself.

Reese glanced at me and I nodded. "Okay, we'll go clubbin'. I want to get something out of the room first though." She took him by the arm and steered him out of the casino. In the elevator, he fell asleep on my shoulder. We got him to the room and dumped him on the couch.

"All right, you ready to go?" I asked before he even hit the cushions.

"Go where?"

"The club downstairs. It's supposed to be cool." Reese looked pointedly at Ryan. "Just turn him on his side." I'd lost her.

"His side?"

"So if he pukes he won't choke." She grimaced at my explanation. I went to the bar, grabbed a bottle of water, and set it on the table next to Ryan. Then I turned him on his side. "There, he'll be fine."

"Really?"

"Yes. Now, come on." Reluctantly, she followed me to the door.

❖

The club was dark, as they should be, and seething with the sort of sexuality that only youth and misunderstood immaturity can inspire. We passed through a lounge of sorts, down a subtly lavish hallway, and descended into Tryst. There was a waterfall, we were told, but that didn't interest me.

"Let's dance." My grip on Reese tightened as she walked with me and I dragged her to the floor, the booze in my system making me stupid and bold.

Reese didn't pull away like I expected. She moved closer and, upon reflection, put her arms around my shoulders. The song was heavy, thick, like sweat, and desperate. When Reese's leg pressed between mine, I didn't even consider it. I just pulled her against me tighter. We moved like that, pushed closer by the crowds, not caring about our precarious embrace. Her warm breath on my neck was indistinguishable from the hot air in the club, except I knew it was hers. My heartbeat was probably visible under my no longer crisp shirt. Her hand slid down and rested just above my breast, over my heart, and I knew she could feel it. Those dark eyes looked up at mine, shot through with gray, like Ryan's had been. Reese wasn't drunk though and she wasn't mad either. She was something else.

I was going to make an ass of myself. There was no way I could play off a botched kiss or grope as a drunken mistake. I'd need a lot more booze to pull that off. Resigned to the insatiable hunger I was feeling, I just kept dancing. It bordered on pain considering my increasingly swollen clit and how my nipples rubbed against my unforgiving shirt. As if Reese knew, she pressed closer so her lips hovered above my neck. I needed something to distract myself, anything.

Ryan. The twins were practically indistinguishable from each other. I just had to tell myself it was him. I was dancing with Ryan. That was harmless. That curtain of silky hair was his. The hands roaming my body, Ryan's. That flash of opulent eyes, my best friend. Thinking about Ryan was like a cold shower. Painful and only slightly effective. I couldn't do it.

"I need a drink." I dropped back a step.

Her eyes narrowed slightly. "Me too."

I nodded and took her hand to drag her behind me to the bar. "Two single malts," I shouted to the bartender. When they were placed before me, I downed mine in one gulp and asked for another. It went in one smooth swallow as well. I'd barely picked up the third when Reese dragged me away and put me at a table.

"You okay there?" There was almost some concern in her voice.

"Fine. Just warm." That was sort of truthful.

"That probably won't help." She tried pulling on my hand. "Come on. Let's dance some more."

"I'm good for now, thanks." If I went back out there with her, there was a good chance I'd embarrass myself. The third drink was even easier.

"Come on."

"Really, thank you. I'm good." I was begging her to let me alone. She didn't see it that way.

"Fine. Have fun."

I saluted her with the glass she left behind then emptied it.

Her hands were buried in my hair. There's something about styling your hair that just makes chicks want to mess it up. I pushed my tongue into her mouth and out again, a teasing promise for later. She had great lips. I slid my hands up the outside of her thighs inching her skirt higher. I was considering taking her to the bathroom to finish the job when someone grabbed the back of my shirt and jerked me away. Not again.

"I want to go," Reese said. Her eyes shot back and forth between me and the girl I was making out with.

"So go," I said. I didn't need to hold her hand.

"You need to take me up to the room." Demanding.

"Sorry." The girl removed my hand from her skirt. "I didn't mean to get in the middle of anything."

"You didn't," I assured her.

"Cooper." Reese looked like she could kill.

"Damn it, Reese. What?"

"Take me back to the room."

"Fine." I turned to the girl. "I'm sorry."

She didn't look too upset.

"Can we go now?" Reese started to drag me out of the club.

I managed to restrain myself until we were in the elevator. "What the fuck is your problem?"

"My problem?" She managed to look innocent.

"Yes. Your fuckin' problem," I shouted. "Why'd you drag me out of there?"

"You needed help."

"Help?" Reese nodded. "Help with what?"

"That trashy chick was all over you." She turned away. "You're welcome."

"I'm welcome?" I grabbed her by the shoulders and spun her to face me. "Did it occur to you that my hand was up her skirt?" Reese glared at the hand gripping her shoulder. "And the fact that I was kissing her might have been an indication that I was having fun?" The elevator door opened.

"Oh, please. She was nasty. I did you a favor." Reese lowered her already calm voice as we walked through the hallway.

"A favor?" I had no intention of lowering my voice to indulge her. "Right. You just wanted me out of there. I've got no fucking idea why."

"It is a little rude to ditch someone you go to a club with to make out with some disgusting girl." Reese's etiquette for the insane.

"Yeah, if we were on a date." I opened the door to our room. "But we weren't on a fucking date."

"It's still rude."

"You know what? Just lay off, okay?" She turned her back on me. "And, Reese." She stopped walking. "You can't manipulate me like you do everyone else. Remember that."

She spun to face me. "You can't control yourself. What makes you think you have any control over me?"

"You've got issues, buttercup."

"You have issues."

With that, we went into our rooms and slammed the doors.

CHAPTER TWELVE

The next afternoon when I woke up, Ryan was gone. In his place was a note. *Went for stuff. Back tomorrow morning.* Great.

I had no intention of being there when Reese's door opened. Since it was almost three in the afternoon, that would probably be soon. I changed and was about to leave for the pool. My hand was on the door when I turned back. The guilt was killing me and I didn't even know what I was guilty about. I picked up the phone and ordered some room service for Reese's breakfast. Just some fruit and other stuff Reese liked. When it arrived, I wrote a note explaining where I was, but with no overt remorse. Then I went down to the pool feeling slightly less terrible.

I'd only been there twenty minutes when one of the ever-present waitresses brought me a mimosa.

"I, uh, didn't ask for that." A mimosa sounded damn good, but I wasn't sure where it came from.

"It was sent from a Ms. DiGiovanni," was her explanation before floating away.

I guess that meant we'd forgiven each other. For another twenty minutes, I procrastinated in the sun sipping my drink. It was boring by the pool. And hot. I decided to suck it up and go back to the room.

"Hey," I called when I opened the door.

"Hey," Reese responded. The suite smelled like her shampoo and she was only wearing a towel. That was trouble. "Thanks for breakfast."

"Uhh, yeah. No problem." I tried not to stare at the towel knotted above her breasts. No, fuck that. I tried not to stare at her breasts. "I'm gonna jump in." I indicated the shower. She nodded.

When I emerged from the bathroom with wet hair, Reese was dressed in tight, cuffed Bermuda shorts and a loose V-neck T-shirt with nothing underneath it. The outline of her fantastic nipples was just barely visible.

"You want to walk the Strip?" Reese asked without looking at me. I pretended to deliberate. She turned to look at me. "If we stay here we're just going to drive each other crazy. So we may as well blow a couple hundred bucks." It was a convincing argument. "If we go, you can play on the opposite side of the casino. You won't even have to see me." She was joking. I was almost sure of it.

"Just don't let me drink any booze." Because I might do something stupid.

"Me either. I'm already going to be hung over for a week."

"I'll be right back. I need clothes." At her nod, I went into my room. If we were walking the Strip, I needed to blend. Cargo shorts, my favorite western shirt, and flip-flops.

"You look like a tool," Reese said when I came out.

"What? You don't like the shirt?" I finished closing the little pearly snaps. What was wrong with western shirts?

"It's so been done."

"Not like this, buttercup." I looked good. Fuck her. "And you're the one who looks like a tool." Mature.

"Witty, that's why I like you."

"You're a bitch, you know that?"

"I've been told." Reese slid a folded stack of crisp hundred dollar bills into my pocket. Her fingertips dragged over my thigh through the cotton. My head went light. "Let's go." Dutifully, I followed her downstairs and onto the street.

"Do you think I should learn how to count cards?" I asked as we started walking.

"Assuming you could, which you can't, definitely not."

"It might be fun."

"Until a guy named Vinny with a thick neck wants to discuss it. This is Vegas, sweetheart." She had a point.

"Why are you always so condescending?" I slid an arm around her shoulders, presumably so we wouldn't be separated by the crowds. Really, I just wanted to annoy her.

"Because you're inferior," came the simple answer.

"Thank God I make up for it in looks." That got my arm removed real quick.

"So do you want to walk all the way down and then work our way back up? We can grab some food on the way if we get hungry."

It sounded like a good plan so that was what we did. In every casino, Reese lost me right away, and when I got bored, I could always find her at the poker tables. Maybe she was addicted and didn't know it. When I had to start carrying her chips for her because her pockets were too full, I realized the real reason. She was damn good at it.

"Why aren't you cashing these in again?" My pockets were getting full, making my shorts weighty. I should have worn a belt.

"Because the chips are easier than a stack of cash." Both seemed cumbersome. "What's wrong with them? I like the chips. They have a feel to them." Descriptive.

"I didn't know you were so good."

"Surprised me too. Want to get some food?" If she thought I wasn't going to notice the subject change, she was so wrong. I'd save it for an opportune moment.

"Sure." I followed her into one of the million themed restaurants on the Strip. The food wasn't great, but it was no worse than the decor. We both ordered soda.

Two casinos later, I started to actually win at blackjack. The night had been terrible for me so far, so I was totally pleased with myself. I was debating quitting while I was ahead when my phone vibrated. It was a text from Reese with one word. *GO.*

"Shit, what time is it?" I asked the guy sitting next to me.

He looked at his watch. "Almost midnight."

"Man, my girlfriend is going to kill me." The excuse was automatic. I tipped the dealer and made a show of worrying about the girlfriend. That worked well because my hands were so sweaty I dropped my handful of chips twice before I got them in my pocket.

Thirty seconds later, I was out the door. I texted Reese. *Where r u?* *Walk to Bellagio. Im behind you.* I turned toward the Bellagio. Ten seconds later, there was another text. *Buy hat.* In front of me was one of the many stands with everything from lighters shaped like women to beer T-shirts. I dug out a crumpled twenty and bought a Corona baseball hat. As I walked, I stuffed it into one of my cargo pockets. My hands were shaking. Maybe Reese was fucking with me.

When I got to the fountains in front of the Bellagio, I stopped in the middle of the sidewalk like every other person. It was a guaranteed crowd. I pretended to watch the water show. Where the fuck was she?

"Act normal." Next to me, that's where. Crouched down in the middle of the swarm of people. Reese wrestled the hat out of my pocket. She twisted her hair up and put the hat on. She was trying to disguise herself. So I unsnapped my shirt, slid it down my shoulders, and handed it to her. The girl caught on quick. She threw the shirt on and straightened.

"What's going on?" My heart rate was through the roof. I'd probably hyperventilate.

"Someone recognized me."

Yep, I was going to have a heart attack. "Who?"

"Just keep my face covered," Reese said.

I slung my arm around her shoulders as if we were a normal couple. The move also obscured her face. "Can you see them?"

"To your left. Big guy. Unbuttoned white shirt." Casually, I turned away from her. There he was. Except Reese didn't mention the bulge under his left arm.

"He's packing."

Reese glanced around me. Her eyes filled with panic. I tried to look calm for her sake.

"Fuck. He's coming over here." She was right. The guy was walking directly toward us, but he was watching the street. Slowly, he turned his head in our direction. "He can't see my face," Reese whispered desperately.

I did the only thing I could think of. I kissed her.

It worked in the movies.

Reese just went with it, which was good because I was worried she might have chosen getting shot over kissing me. Apparently not. She twisted so we were facing each other and I put my arms around her shoulders. When she moaned into my mouth, I knew it wasn't just for show. Her hips rocked into mine sending heat through my body. I swear, I knew fucking divinity in that moment.

Holding back was too much. I pressed past her lips with my tongue, searching her mouth. The hand gripping my shirt tightened. She pushed my tongue back, bit my lip, and sucked on it. Fuck. This time I moaned. Reese took that as an invitation to go further. She kissed me even harder, bruising my lips, cutting off my air. I was pretty sure I could survive without air as long as she didn't stop. That was when she pulled away. We were both breathing hard and staring at each other. She was still close enough for my biceps to cover her face.

"Do you think he's still here?" Reese whispered. I drew her into me so her face was tucked into my neck. The mass of people had dispersed. The water show was over. The guy who'd been following her was gone.

"He's gone." I released her.

"Are you sure?" We started walking back to the hotel. Neither of us saw him. For good measure, we ducked into a casino and left through a side entrance. After that, Reese pulled me across the street. We walked through two more casinos, a restaurant, and a hotel lobby before Reese seemed satisfied that we weren't being followed. Vegas was great for losing a tail.

"So who the hell was that?" It took only a little nerve to ask.

"My uncle Vito." Dude sounded like something out of *The Godfather*. "He's not actually my uncle. Just kind of."

"He in the mob or something?" I joked.

"Not really." What the hell did that mean? She didn't look like she was kidding. The silence that followed lasted us all the way to the room.

When we got there, I crossed to the windows. With my hands planted on the glass wall, I surveyed the Strip.

"We have a problem," Reese said quietly. She leaned her shoulder against the window next to me.

"A problem?" A rough laugh pushed out of my constricted throat. "Just one?" Reese closed her eyes and hung her head. "Are you talking about Uncle Vito," I spit out the name, "seeing you? Or how about the fact that you even have an Uncle Vito." She flinched. "Or," the jagged laugh escaped me again. "Or maybe." I turned and locked eyes with her. "That I've never, in my life, been kissed like that."

Reese's delicate hand moved to my trembling arm, still propped against the glass. She rubbed it, only for a second. "The last one." Then she pulled my arm down and spun me so my back was against the window. There was a pounding in my veins that made my hypersensitive clit ache.

I tried to push up to take control of the situation. Reese held me back with one palm against my chest. She opened the button fly of my shorts and they fell to my ankles with a shower of colorful clay chips. Those slate brown eyes never left mine. My tank top was forced up and over my head. Deft fingers slid under the elastic of my boxer briefs and dropped those too. I was naked, fucking wet, swollen, and so ready I thought I was going to die. This was not how it was supposed to happen. I was supposed to be in charge. I always was.

"Reese." She wasn't even touching me. Just staring. "Take off your clothes." Even with my forceful tone, it was a pathetic attempt to regain control.

"Don't talk. Don't move. Don't fucking breathe unless I tell you to." She planted one hand next to my head and slid the other between my legs. Holy fuck, that felt good. I started to double over from either pleasure or pain. I couldn't tell which. Reese grabbed a handful of my hair and held me in place. "Watch me." So I did.

I watched her tits sway as she circled my clit. I watched her bite her lip and I could tell holding back was killing her. When I begged her to fuck me harder, I watched the grin twitch at the corner of her mouth as she slowed down. Her eyes went liquid when she fucking finally pushed inside me. The muscles in her arm tensed with each thrust into me. Something resembling words flowed from my mouth as I cried, screamed, begged for release.

I didn't think. I didn't think about Ryan. I didn't think about the fourteen years of hell I'd put Reese through. I didn't think about the cruelty in her eyes, 'cause right then it was gone. No anger. Just this.

Reese didn't kiss me until that last second, the moment when I contracted around her fingers deep inside and stiffened. That was when her lips descended and let me know, this wasn't fucking; it was way beyond that.

I slid to the floor, all strength gone. She followed still kissing me, still inside me, but unable to hold me up. I looked at her and couldn't see a trace of her twin in the look on her face. Slowly, carefully, Reese extracted her hand. Just to make me crazy, she licked her fingers.

Roughly, I wrenched her shirts over her head, pushed her to the ground, and dragged off her shorts. "Now I'm in charge."

"Whatever you want to think, sweetheart." The last word came out a taunting drawl.

I gripped behind her knees and yanked her closer. Reese reached back and linked her hands behind her head like she was about to take a nap. I dipped my head between her thighs and blew lightly across her engorged clit. Her hips jumped so hard I laughed. When I looked at her, she had her hands over her eyes and her jaw was clenched.

"Watch me," I demanded. Reese dropped her hands and propped herself up on her elbows. She was looking at me with unadulterated need. When I licked the length of her clit, she didn't drop her gaze. It wasn't until I drove my tongue inside her that she moaned and dropped her head back. I stopped.

Her head snapped up. "Fuck, Coop. Please."

Fast enough to make her gasp, I moved up the length of her body, hovering, aching to press against the naked flesh under me. "I told you to watch me."

"Okay," she whimpered. My mouth dropped to her fantastic nipples. I alternated sucking on them until she was writhing and pleading, until I couldn't hang on any longer. That was when I pressed inside her cunt, pushing hard until she screamed my name. With each thrust, we slid across the floor. And then we were up against the glass again. Reese reached back and braced her hands. Her hips were in the air fucking my fingers. I couldn't even feel my arm anymore, just a mass of overworked muscle that ended inside of Reese DiGiovanni.

One of her hands left the window and curled around my head. She pulled me against her as she came. Our foreheads pressed together, slick with sweat, as we stared into each other's eyes.

At six a.m., we should have been sleeping. My back was propped against the flamboyant, padded headboard and Reese was in my lap gyrating against my hand. Moisture dripped between my fingers and landed with surprising accuracy on my already wet clit. Every time she rocked forward, our matching necklaces tapped against each other with a metallic ring.

"Fucking kiss me," Reese said.

With my free hand, I cupped behind her neck and drew her mouth to mine. I sucked her lip into my mouth savoring the taste of her flesh. Her slim fingers worked my nipples. They were going to hurt like a bitch later. Fuck it. I didn't care.

Reese's phone rang.

"Ignore it," I said.

"Just don't stop." The rhythm of her hips picked up. I curled my fingers forward urging Reese to come. The phone rang again. "Fuck, fucking, fuck." Reese grabbed the phone and opened it. She stopped thrusting into my hand, except for an involuntary twitch when I put my thumb to her clit. She grabbed my wrist as if that would stop me.

"Don't do it." I punctuated my second warning with a slow thrust into her.

"What?" she answered the phone. I could hear Ryan's voice. I was so screwed. "What the fuck do you think I'm doing?" Just to mess with her, I started to work my hand faster again. Her jaw clenched. "That's fine just—" I thrust into her pussy hard. Reese slammed the phone into the headboard and screamed as she came. Then she slumped forward against me breathing raggedly. She slowly brought the phone back to her ear. "Sorry, Ryan, what was that?" I grinned at her. "Yeah, guess I dozed off. No, that's fine. Okay, see you then." She closed the phone and tossed it behind her.

"Who was that?" I asked innocently.

"Bitch, I'm going to make you pay." The threat made my stomach drop with wanting.

"I told you to ignore it."

"Ignore this." Reese moved back, pushed my legs apart, and sucked my clit into her mouth. Bitch.

Reese and I slept until the afternoon. When I woke up, she was on top of me, one bare thigh between mine, her hand resting on my hip, with her hair spread across my chest.

"Babe." I rubbed up and down her naked back. "Hey, peanut butter."

She opened her eyes then closed them. "Morning." She yawned.

"It's afternoon."

"Good afternoon, then." Her eyes were still closed.

"When's Ryan coming back?" I was getting a little worried. Partially for his sake, but mostly for mine. If he came in and found us like this, I would be dead.

"Tomorrow."

"He's gonna kill me." I played with her velvety hair. It was never a good idea to sleep with your friend's sister.

"Me too," she murmured into my chest.

"Why's he gonna kill you?"

"Because of you." Reese opened her eyes again and raised her head to look at me. "I slept with his best friend." She smirked. "Of course, he'll probably kill you first."

"Great. I feel much better now."

"Let's get some food."

Food sounded way better than my imminent death so I agreed. We settled into coffee and croissants, almost wearing clothes, and looking everywhere except at each other. I was chillin' in my boxer briefs and a ribbed tank top. Reese was wearing my western shirt with not a thing under it, and I knew I'd never be able to wear it again.

"Are we going to talk about it?" Reese set her coffee cup down.

My pulse jumped. "Shit, I don't know." I was already sweating. I'd never done the morning after what-did-it-mean talk, and I told her as much.

"So we just ignore it? Pretend it never happened because Cooper doesn't like talking?"

"That's not what I said. I'm just no good at talking." There was never a girl I wanted to talk to either. Not like Reese.

"Learn fast." That tone was all bad.

"What do you want me to say?" At a loss, I shrugged dramatically. "I don't know what we should do. Do you?"

"No, that's why we're supposed to talk. You know, figure it out together," she said in that condescending voice of hers. Why was she so infuriating? In sixty seconds, I'd gone from the euphoria only inspired by a night of screwing to absolute revulsion.

"You seem to know everything," I said. "You talk."

"Okay, fine." The pouty lips were kind of sexy. "This will devastate my brother."

"Yep." That I agreed with.

"We both love my brother."

"More than anyone in the world." It was true. "Except my parents, maybe."

"Same here."

"So?" We already knew all of this. I didn't know why she was reviewing. "You want to act like nothing happened to spare him or something?" What a stupid idea. Ryan would understand. He would be pissed, but he would understand.

"Is that what you want?"

"What do you think?" It would have been a good idea to say what I actually felt. Those words just weren't popping into my head at the moment.

"I think that you don't give a fuck. And if I'm right then we should just pretend it never happened. I'm not willing to sacrifice my brother for you." Damned if she wasn't ice through that little speech. The girl didn't break a sweat, shed a tear, or look anywhere except at me.

"Then fucking don't, buttercup." I stood.

"So that's settled then?" I shrugged, clueless about what just happened. "We just ignore it? It never happened? It won't happen again?"

It felt like getting punched. Repeatedly. In the face. "You make the rules. I just live by them." With that, I left her sitting on the couch. I needed a shower. If I had to walk around all day smelling like Reese's sex, I would kill myself.

"We probably shouldn't leave the room either," Reese called before I shut the door.

"Why not?" I was never going to get out alive.

"Uncle Vito." She didn't need to explain.

"Uncle Vito." I slammed the door laughing in a scared, heartless way.

Chapter Thirteen

By the early evening, I was bored and tired of the silence that felt like fighting so I decided to make a stab at conversation. It couldn't be any worse than what we were already doing.

"So why is Ryan staying in the city another night?" I was at the bar pouring a scotch for myself so my back was to her. Reese was on the couch reading. The girl was still wearing only my western shirt, which I found infuriating and totally sexy. It was those muscled thighs, perfect for wrapping her legs around my hips.

She put her finger in her book and closed it. "He's looking for a place to sell some of the bars." What the hell was she talking about? Oh yeah. Ryan. "When we go back for the passports, he wants to sell a couple of them."

"That's a good idea, actually." I turned and propped my back against the bar feigning indifference. "We should've thought of it before."

Reese nodded. "If we don't get rid of some of them, we'll be in trouble. They're too hard to move."

"We should probably do the same, you know? Try and find a place to sell them." Gambling, drinking, and screwing were fun so it made it easy to forget what we were supposed to be doing. That was the plan. Sell some gold in the States; take the rest to Mexico. And then... something.

"Ideas?"

"Do you think the phone book has a section titled Selling Gold Bars?" That sure would make it easier. Reese smiled at my joke, a definite improvement.

"Why don't you check on that?"

"We could look online. The hotel has wireless, right?" I set my drink down and went to grab my laptop. When I got back, Reese was staring at a very blank spot on the wall. "Reese?"

"You know what I was thinking?"

"Not yet."

"We could ask around downstairs. They probably know everything."

"You want to go ask the concierge where to sell your gold bar?" I asked sarcastically.

"Yep." She looked serious.

"Knock yourself out, buttercup." It sounded like a bad idea to me.

"I wasn't asking for permission." Reese sounded all irritated. She got up and went into the bathroom. A couple minutes later, the shower turned on.

At least I could be alone. By the time Reese got out of the shower I'd made a list of places that bought scrap gold and jewelry.

"You solve all of our problems, yet?" she asked.

"All my problems," I said without looking away from the computer. "Can't help with yours. That'll cost you." I looked up and flashed a charming grin, which instantly died. Reese was naked. Damn, she was gorgeous, smooth skin with those full breasts, slightly more than a handful. Fucking amazing.

"I knew you were a whore." Could she tell I was thinking about sex? "Thanks, but I don't need your services."

"That's not what you said last night." It wasn't nearly as fun to say that when I meant it. What I got for my trouble was the view of her naked ass. Not a bad trade. She came back out a few minutes later when I was pouring another drink. I had the phone propped against my ear and was about to dial the first number from my list.

Reese reached over and hung up the phone. "Don't use the hotel phone."

"Why?" I attempted to convey as much of my displeasure as possible.

"Because it will be easy to trace." That sounded logical.

"Right, whatever." No way was I going to tell her it made sense.

"I'll be back." She waltzed out of the room. I wished I could hate her.

With Reese gone, I picked up my cell and started to dial. Damn. It was almost out of minutes. I couldn't exactly use a credit card to load more time onto it. Quickly, I wrote a note to let Reese know where I was and headed out the door. There had to be some place in Vegas that sold pre-paid cell phones. I'd just take Reese's car. That also had the advantage of irritating her.

Besides, Reese was being all weirdly paranoid about this Vito guy. So what, her uncle might call Christopher. We would be gone before he could catch up. It was better if I just went out and let her yell about the vague, theoretical risk later.

As I navigated the maze of the hotel's bottom floor, I caught a glimpse of Reese ahead of me. She looked like she was heading the same way I was. I'd almost caught up to her by the time she was at the valet pickup in front.

"Ms. DiGiovanni, so good to have you back," the valet greeted her warmly.

"Hey, Ricky. It's been a while." How did Reese know the valet?

"Yes, ma'am. We've missed you."

I wasn't proud, but I turned and pressed my back against one of the big pillars in the lobby. Nonchalantly, I leaned against it and took out my dead cell phone like I had some purpose.

"I need some help. Discreet help," Reese clarified.

"Of course," he said in a lower tone. After that, I couldn't hear any voices. They either walked away or were talking very quietly.

I turned away and went back the way I'd come.

The floor was going to have track marks from me pacing in front of the windows. Maybe when Reese came the year before she had stayed at the same hotel. Maybe the valet was just really good at remembering the names of beautiful women. Women who had stayed in the hotel once over a year ago. Maybe. It was probably a totally innocent conversation and I was making it into a sordid affair.

I couldn't ask her though. Not without telling her I'd been eavesdropping, and that would get me in a shitload of trouble. Ryan wouldn't be back until the next morning so I would just have to wait for him. I needed a drink.

Ten minutes of pacing and one forgotten drink later, Reese walked in. I opted to stare at nothing on my computer rather than confront her. What a loser.

"Get any hits with your calls?" Reese asked politely.

"Nope. No minutes on the phone." That about summed it up.

Ten minutes later, the room phone rang. I jumped and almost fell over. Smooth.

"Hello?" Reese quirked an eyebrow at me then turned away. "No way. No, that's perfect. Thanks. Where is that?" She started laughing at whatever it was the person on the phone said. I was immediately envious of them. "Yeah, I got you. All right, bye."

"Girlfriend?"

The look Reese gave me made my insides quiver. Not in a good way either. "There's a place near Highway Fifteen," she said. "The guy who runs it buys gold by weight and is good at keeping quiet."

"No shit."

"Let's go."

"What? No." That was a good thing that she found the place. Really, it was. It just seemed off, a little too easy. "Right now?"

"Why not?"

I didn't have a good reason. "Okay, fine. I need to put on shoes." Reluctantly, I shuffled into my room to pull on my shoes.

"Hurry up," Reese yelled.

She'd changed into a T-shirt and thrown on a navy blue, cropped blazer. The sleeves almost reached her wrists and it was a little tight. Totally hot. All I had on was a hoodie and shorts. Whatever. I looked like a heathen and she didn't. Nothing new there.

"Should I bring something to put the cash in? Will the guy give us cash? Are you sure this is a good idea?" Nervous? Me? No, not at all.

"Here." Reese tossed a heavy backpack to me. She'd already put the bar in it.

"You're prepared."

"I just think ahead," she said in a way that implied that I didn't.

We went back down to the valet pickup in silence. It wasn't until we were in Reese's car that she said, "Oww, fuck, I can't drive with this," and reached behind her to pull out a small, stainless steel handgun. "Hold it, okay?"

"Fuck no." There was no way I was going to take it. "Why the hell did you bring that?"

"Because I like it better than that massive Glock my brother swears by." Reese leaned over and settled the small, elegant Walther into my lap. The way she did it would have turned me on if it hadn't been a gun. Okay, it kind of did anyway.

"But why did you bring a damn gun in the first place?"

Reese gave me that you dumbass look.

"Don't you have a holster or something?"

"I'm wearing it." Reese pulled open her blazer to reveal a dark brown shoulder holster and another Walther. "Can't fit two in there."

"Why do you need two?" I yelled.

"You might need one." For such a smart girl she could be so stupid.

"What for?" She didn't have an answer for that.

Reese drove like she knew where she was going. Soon we were away from the chaos and decadence of the Strip driving through streets that looked increasingly shady. Without the pervasive flashing lights, the darkness seemed even more oppressive.

"Where the hell are we going?" I asked after we passed the fourth very obvious dealer.

"See that cement building? The one with no sign." She had to be kidding.

"Yeah?" We drove past it. I didn't get a good look inside.

"That's it." Reese found a spot on the side of the road and parallel parked. We were a block and a half away.

"You're out of your mind." She expected me to walk? "Drive closer."

"There aren't any spaces. Do you see any?" No. "You scared?"

"No. It's just a long way."

"Want one of my guns?" Reese started laughing at her own joke.

"I'll be fine, thanks." I yanked up the hood of my sweatshirt and got out of the car.

The sidewalk was empty. Recesses in the buildings to my left looked like the perfect place for someone to hide. I'd never see them coming. My instinct was to grip the backpack with both hands, but I knew that would be too obvious.

The building Reese had pointed out looked like it could survive Armageddon. Bars covered the scratched window, and I had to ring a buzzer to get in. A camera mounted above the door adjusted to get a good view of my face. Apparently, I was cool enough because the lock clicked open. I took a deep breath and stepped into the cubicle. Once the door closed behind me, the one in front of me clicked open as well. This place was covered just a little too well for the hood we were in.

"How may I help you?" the tall, stooped man behind the counter asked when I walked in. His heavy accent made it difficult to understand him. My best guess was Hungarian, but I'd only known one guy with a Hungarian accent so I wasn't sure.

"I was told you buy gold."

"Ricky sent you over," he said. I nodded. "Well, let us see the bar." His spindly hand waved me forward.

My hands were so shaky I almost dropped the bar when I tried to give it to him. For a second, I wondered if it was a fake and Christopher was laughing his ass off at us right now. No, Christopher was probably ready to kill us right now.

The man was carefully inspecting the bar, doing whatever it was he did to verify its authenticity. I glanced around while he did his thing. Glass cases formed a U along three walls and were filled with various jewelry, heavy gold cuffs, tennis bracelets, diamond encrusted Rolexes. The walls were covered in photographs of celebrities shaking hands with the guy. In some of the photos he was barely a man, maybe twenty-five, all the way up to his current sixty years. Everyone was up there, from Wayne Newton to Harrison Ford. What the hell were they doing in a dive like this? Or maybe this shop wasn't always located here.

When he made a noise of approval, I returned my attention to him. He ran his fingers over the numbers engraved on the top of the bar. Then he typed something into the ancient computer on the counter and told me the amount. Holy shit.

"So you'll buy it then?" I was playing cool.

"Yes, of course. It is quite beautiful," he mused. "Is it not?" We both gazed at the gleaming surface that seemed to emit light rather than reflect it.

"Very."

He nodded, satisfied that I appreciated the bar. "I will get your money."

"Thank you."

Ten minutes later, I was back on the sidewalk. The backpack was much fuller and much lighter. Up ahead, I could see the side of Reese's car. As I started going toward it, a guy turned the corner and started walking in my direction. He looked older than me, maybe forty, so I ignored him. He wasn't exactly young thug material. When he didn't move to one side for me to walk by, I got worried. I knew I was just paranoid though so I kept going. When I started to pass him, he grabbed my arm and dragged me into one of the alcoves.

"What the fuck?" I shrugged his hand off my arm. "Get the hell off me." I pushed him aside and walked into a wall of flesh. Shit.

"What's in the bag?" the guy behind me asked.

"Nothing. Let me go." The backpack was jerked down my arms and the wall of flesh laughed. He grabbed the front of my sweatshirt and pulled me up close to his face. The stench of old cigars and peppermint invaded my nostrils. The guy behind me unzipped the backpack.

"That's a lot of cash, kid," he said. "Take a look at that, Vic."

The grip on my sweatshirt was eased enough for Vic to lean forward and look in the bag.

"Where'd you get the money, kiddo?"

"Your mom." Why did I say that?

"What?" Vic yanked up so I was inches from his fat face.

"Your mom." Might as well roll with it. "She likes the way I lick her pu—"

I was thrown into the wall next to me. I tried to put my hands up in time to catch myself. It didn't work. Vic came up behind me and pushed my face into the rough cement. Then he pulled my head back by my hair, scraping my face against the wall.

"He thinks he's funny, Gino."

"I'm a girl, douche bag." It came out before I could stop it.

Vic let go of me. I stepped away from the wall. There was nowhere to go. Where the fuck was Reese with her PPKs now?

"You get that, Gino?" Vic grinned, an unnatural twist of flesh and too white teeth. "It's a girl." My stomach turned. I was an idiot.

"Are you done with the obvious? I gotta go." I tried to grab the backpack and push past them. The shorter one backhanded me. I stumbled back, tasting blood.

"Here's how this is going to work. We ask questions, you answer them. Got it?" I didn't answer fast enough. He slapped me again. "You got it?"

"Whatever." I wasn't telling them shit. My mouth started to slowly fill with blood.

"Where'd you get the cash?" Vic asked.

I hawked some blood and spit onto his loafers. "I told you. Your mom." This time he just punched me in the stomach. I doubled over and yelled obscenities at the pavement. He grabbed my sweatshirt again and made me stand up straight.

"New question. Where are those bastard kids?"

Shit. "I don't have any kids." I played dumb. Vic didn't buy it. He did punch me in the stomach again though.

"Where are the goddamn twins?" He tossed me back into the wall. My head smacked into the cement making it throb.

"Where's Ryan?" Gino stepped up to the plate when I didn't answer. Vic must have been tired. Beating up girls is hard.

"I don't know anyone named Ryan." Gino punched me in the ribs this time. I spit some more blood at him. He grabbed me by the hair and pushed my face back into the wall. His body pressed into mine, pinning me. I tried not to hyperventilate.

"How about pretty little Reese?" he murmured in my ear. The rasp of his voice when he said her name made me want to kill him.

"Bitch, I'm gonna drop you like a bad habit." I struggled to push him off. I was going to knock him out. I could do it.

They laughed. "Come on, kid. You're driving her car. We know she's with you," Vic said.

"I'm right here, you stupid fuck," came Reese's voice from behind us. I couldn't see anything, but Gino moved away from me. "That's right. Get the fuck off of her."

Finally free, I turned and looked at Reese. She had a handgun trained on each of them.

"Get over here, babe."

I didn't need to be told twice.

"We've been looking for you, Reese." Vic stepped toward her and started reaching into his jacket.

"Get up against the wall. Hands where I can see them." Gino laughed at her instructions. "Do I look like I'm fucking around?"

Neither answered, but they both turned and put their hands on the wall.

"Search them," she instructed me. "I want guns, cell phones, and car keys."

"I'm not touching them." Fighting some nineteen-year-old punk with my friends to back me up was way different from those fuckers kicking the crap out of me.

"Do it." One look into those cool gray eyes and I jumped to feel up Gino and Vic. They let me, but it was more like bored indulgence than fear.

"Come on, honey. Drop the act," Vic said. I patted him down. He was packing a massive handgun. I put that on the pavement. Lucky for me, their car keys were in his jacket pocket. I really didn't want to reach into his pants pocket. That would just be disgusting. When I dropped his cell phone next to his gun, Reese demolished it with a quick stomp and twist of her heel.

I moved on to Gino. The piece he was carrying joined Vic's, along with a knife, a scary serrated number.

"Stop this shit," Gino advised after Reese killed his cell phone too. "Just come with us. You won't be in any trouble." He sounded like he was consoling an unruly toddler.

"Sure, why not?" She was being sarcastic. Vic believed her though.

"Good girl." He spun to face her.

Reese pistol-whipped him. His head flung to the side. "Did I say you could turn around?" He cupped his face in response. A trickle of blood seeped between his fingers. "No, you dumb fuck. Now, face the wall."

"All right, kiddo, you made your point." Vic did as he was told. Warily, he glanced over his shoulder at her.

Reese handed me one of the guns and pointed at Gino. I directed it at his head. She picked up the knife and stepped closer to Vic.

"I haven't come close to making my point." Her tone was scarier than the gun cradled in her hand. She flicked the knife open. The gun went to the back of Vic's neck, forcing him to press his face into the wall. The knife went between his legs much higher than he wanted it. "Do you understand me?"

"Yes." His voice was strained.

"Where's your car?"

"On the street." Reese inched the knife higher. "Behind you. The blue Cadillac," he rushed to clarify.

"Good. Now walk over there," Reese said. "And move carefully. Wouldn't want to lose anything." Vic did as he was told. Each footstep was stilted.

"You too," I said to Gino. He didn't move. "Move your ass." He shuffled with his head down. Probably just happy there wasn't a knife to his balls.

"Open the trunk, babe." Reese had her hands rather full.

I squinted in the dim light at the piece of plastic until I figured out which button did what I wanted. The trunk popped open.

"Get in," Reese said. I laughed.

"We'll never fit in there." Vic's attempt to sway her was useless.

"Sure you will. You'll just have to spoon," I said.

Vic almost looked relieved when the knife was removed from his genitals so he could get in. Almost.

"Not you." Reese stopped Gino before he climbed in. "How did you find us?"

"It wasn't hard." He shrugged. Not smart.

"How did you find us?" she asked again.

"We looked."

Reese was livid, but in a cool, deadly sort of way. She traced the tip of the knife down Gino's cheek. He sucked in a mouthful of air and held it. The knife caressed his throat to his collarbone. Reese smiled. She twisted her wrist so the blade was at the neck of his shirt. Slowly, very slowly, she slit his shirt open.

"You want to talk?"

He didn't move, didn't breathe. I think he finally got that she was serious.

Reese started tracing down his chest again. This time pressing hard enough that the blade made a scraping noise on his skin. Every few inches she dug a little deeper so a bead of blood would emerge from his chest. It was freaky. I would have thought her cruel except for the eyes. This was killing her. She wasn't going to last long. As she approached the waistband of his slacks, he started to grind his teeth.

"You want to tell us now?" I asked Gino. Reese seemed relieved to have me take over.

Gino glanced up from the knife on his beer belly. His entire face had gone slack.

"How did you find us?" Reese asked.

"We got a tip," Gino gasped. "A pit boss at one of the casinos on the Strip. Don't know who. This guy told one of our contacts. I don't know anything else."

"Thank you. Now get in the trunk."

Reluctantly, Gino climbed in with his buddy. Reese slammed the trunk shut on their surprised faces. Methodically, she picked up the guns, wiped off any fingerprints with the bottom on her T-shirt, and tossed them into the front seat. She repeated the process with the knife. She took the keys from me and tossed them in a nearby trashcan.

"Are you okay?" Her hand trembled when I brushed my fingertips over it.

Reese nodded curtly. "Are you?"

"Yeah. Just a little beat up."

"All right. Good." She was fighting to keep her composure. I could tell.

Chapter Fourteen

At the hotel, I shed my clothes, grabbed clean ones, and went into the bathroom. I checked out my face in the mirror. One side was covered in scratches from the small peaks of cement. I was glad Reese held a knife to that dude's junk.

My shirt was a bitch to get off because my shoulders and ribs were hurting pretty bad. Other than that, I was fine. It was Reese I was worried about. She hadn't looked at me or talked to me the whole way back.

The steam and hot water felt damn good. As soon as I was under the spray, the tension in my back eased up a bit. My face stung a little, but if that was the worst of my problems then I was doing pretty well.

As I walked out of the bathroom in my boxer briefs and T-shirt, I looked around for Reese. She wasn't there. Not in her room either.

"Reese?" I tried not to panic.

"I'm right here," came her voice from the couch.

"Hey." I crossed the room in a few long strides to kneel in front of her.

She slowly sat up. Dark hair fell forward covering her face. I reached up and carefully brushed it back. There were tear tracks on her cheeks.

"Are you okay?" I asked softly.

She didn't seem to hear me. "I wanted to hurt them." Another tear fell. "When I saw that guy pushing you into the wall, I wanted to kill him."

"I wanted to kill Christopher when this happened." I brushed my thumb over the fading mark beneath her eye.

"Why?"

"I don't like seeing you hurt." I'd thought that was obvious.

"But you hate me," Reese said. Seemingly unaware, she slid her hands over mine. Her fingers drew patterns on my palms and wrists. My hands started to tremble.

"I've tried that, but I'm no good at follow through." My attempt at humor was lost when my voice shook.

"I don't hate you either." She wouldn't look at me.

"Good, I was real worried." I tilted her chin up so I could see her eyes.

"Shut up," she said when she saw that I was teasing her. We grinned at each other like idiots. "Does it hurt?" Her warm fingers traced over the scratches on my face. My spine started to tingle, the sensation rolling languidly down my back and into my limbs.

"Not really." I couldn't even feel the pain anymore. The more she touched me, the less I felt anything except really good.

"Take off your shirt so I can see."

I let go of her hands. "I don't think I should." Normally, taking off my shirt wouldn't have been a problem. Reese had bandaged me up a million times.

"Why not?"

"Because I can't be objective anymore." Either one of us naked equated to one thing for me now.

"So?" Her eyes went from brown to gray. The change was instantaneous.

I prayed that I was reading the invitation correctly and kissed her. Reese groaned and pulled me into her. We were in serious trouble.

"I was starting to think you were dead," Ryan said the second I came out of my room the next afternoon. I was glad I'd left Reese's bed in the small hours of the morning.

"Not yet. When did you get back?"

"Couple hours ago." He finally looked at me. "Shit. What happened to your face?"

"Long story." I didn't elaborate.

"Well?"

"Where's Reese?"

"She's sleeping. Your face?"

"Seriously, it's a long story. I'm going to get Reese and we'll tell you the whole thing." I started for Reese's closed door. "You want to order some coffee?"

"Anything else, princess?" Ryan poured himself a scotch. How late was it?

"Breakfast. Eggs and potatoes and sausage. Chicken sausage." As if he didn't know. "Double order of the potatoes and sausage. Oh, and see if I can eat the biscuits and gravy." I'd exerted myself a lot recently. There was a lot to make up for.

"Damn." He raised his eyebrows. "That all?"

"Maybe order something for Reese," I said before going into Reese's room. I accidentally on purpose let the door close behind me.

Reese was asleep wrapped up in an ill placed sheet. The curve of her naked ass was visible under the cover and a very sexy foot hung off the bed. I started with the foot. Gradually, I kissed my way up her calf to that spot at the back of her knee, up to her very sexy thigh. Reese moaned softly. Her back was exposed so I kissed that too. She tasted sweet like Reese and skin and sleep. She didn't wake up until I kissed the curve of her neck, up behind her ear.

She smiled first then whispered, "Hi."

"Hi." I rubbed my palm down her back to rest under the sheet on her ass. She lifted her hips slightly. I couldn't stop myself. I moved my hand the rest of the way until it was cupped between her thighs. I slid a finger on either side of her clit.

"We were at it until four this morning and you already want more?" She gasped.

"You're so wet." As if that explained my behavior.

"You're insatiable," Reese murmured appreciatively.

"I know." I pulled my hand away playing with the silky strands of wetness covering my fingers. "Your brother's here. We can't do anything."

"I hate you." She grinned and turned to kiss me. "What does he think you're doing in here?"

"Waking you up so we can explain my face."

"How about we lock the door and..." She kissed me again. Her tongue pushed inside my mouth and made me forget almost everything.

I stopped kissing her long enough to say, "I would if I didn't think he would come in here and shoot me when he heard you screaming."

"Hey." Reese pushed me away. "I'm not the screamer. You are."

"Right, babe." I grinned. "Whatever you want to think."

"You are so annoying." Her criticism was sort of lacking because she couldn't stop touching me.

"Let's go eat breakfast while I can still walk, okay?"

"You ordered breakfast?"

"Ryan did. I had to give him something to do to distract him."

"Got it." Reese started pushing me away again. "All right, go. Let me get dressed. I'll be right out."

"I'm okay with you being naked."

"Go," she ordered. I decided to do the intelligent thing and leave.

Over breakfast, Reese and I took turns updating Ryan on everything that had happened while he was gone. We forgot to mention the whole hooking up thing.

"So is anyone going to tell me who the hell Vito is?" I pushed Reese's fork away from my plate for the second time. She kept trying to eat my food when hers was perfectly good. "Stop it. Eat yours."

"I want biscuits and gravy." She stole another bite.

"Hey, guys, pay attention," Ryan demanded.

"Oh, yeah. Uncle Vito?" I asked again.

"I think he worked for Mom. And he was like her distant cousin or something," Ryan mumbled.

"You're related to that guy?"

"Not really." Reese wouldn't look at me. "Kind of. But it's like through marriage or something."

"Well, maybe he'll help us." If this guy was their uncle or whatever, he would probably be happy to help.

"Not likely. I think he works with Christopher now," Ryan said.

"What about those guys from last night?" I asked Reese. "Do you know them?" Yes, I was pissed.

"No." She scooted away from me a little. "Okay. I recognized them, but I don't know them. I don't even know their names." I was pretty sure she was lying.

"Vic and Gino," I supplied.

"What?" Ryan's eyes got real big. "Vic, big guy? Smokes a lot of cigars? And Gino? Fat little fucker with squinty eyes?"

"That's them." I was going to kick some ass. Reese never mentioned that she knew them. Not that I gave her a chance.

"Shit," muttered Ryan.

"I really didn't know." Reese sounded a little pissed too. "There wasn't time to ask if they were working for my asshole stepfather. Sorry." The apology was totally insincere.

"How about after we left? You couldn't have mentioned it then?"

"Guys," Ryan yelled. "I can't take it. No fighting today." When in doubt, he just shouted louder than us.

"Sorry," Reese said.

"Yeah, sorry," I said to my plate.

"Now. Did anything fun happen while I was gone? You win big or anything?" As usual, Ryan tried to distract us with a new subject as if it were a shiny toy.

"I didn't. Reese did pretty well."

"How much did you win?" Ryan asked her.

"No idea. Haven't counted it." Reese dug into her breakfast with renewed fervor.

"Where is it? Let's count it." He was totally excited. Reese nodded in the direction of the bar. There was a heavy glass bowl filled to the brim. The clouded glass distorted the outline of the chips, but the color shone through.

"Knock yourself out. I'm going to shower." Reese abandoned her seat.

"You want to help me count it, Coop? It looks like a couple thousand bucks." Only Ryan could get excited about a couple thousand dollars when he was sitting on thirty-four million. It was the clay chips. Color excited him.

"Sure. Why not?" I snagged the last piece of sausage and followed him to the bar.

"Damn." Ryan was already dipping his hands into the bowl. "There are some five hundred dollar chips in here."

"No way." I peered inside. Damn. "Dude, like half of these are five hundred dollar chips. I told you Reese was good."

We proceeded to stack the chips, first according to denomination, then according to casino. Reese was pushing twenty grand. Not bad for a couple hours.

"That's a lot for one night, right?" Ryan asked me.

"I'd say so."

"She's been before though," he attempted for an explanation.

"Once." Beginner's luck didn't go that far.

"What?" Ryan looked at me like I was crazy. "You're thinking something weird. I know it."

I had to tell him. "I kind of accidentally overheard Reese talking to the valet downstairs. They knew each other."

"I don't follow."

"I think Reese has been here more than once. A lot more." There. I'd finally said it. I didn't have the balls to say it to Reese, and besides, we'd been busy, but at least I'd said it.

"What do you mean?" Ryan rubbed his face and covered his eyes. A sure sign he knew what I was talking about.

"I think she comes here to play poker." Duh, Ryan. Get the picture.

"You think she's some kind of high roller?" The water shut off and we both looked at the closed door.

"Not exactly. She doesn't have the capital." Reese wasn't the type to flaunt it anyway. She would intentionally be discreet.

"You want to ask her?" He appeared a bit nauseous at the prospect.

"No, I want you to." The door opened before he could answer.

"Hey, Reese." Ryan sounded all guilty.

"Hi." So did I.

"You guys are weird." She disappeared into her room and took long enough to get dressed for us to excitedly gesture at each other. I won.

"So, Reese," Ryan began nonchalantly when she came back out. "You've got almost twenty thousand dollars."

"Damn. Good for me." She went over and gazed out the window.

"That's a lot for one night."

"I guess it is."

"Have you played poker before?" He sounded idiotic. I should have just asked her.

"Yes, Ryan."

"I knew it," he shouted. What a liar.

"You did not." I smacked him and looked back at Reese. "I knew it." Great, we sounded like a bad movie. "You come here all the time, don't you? That's why everyone at this fuckin' hotel knows you. The waitress on my birthday, the valet." Jumping to conclusions was my forte.

Reese turned from the window, her face totally blank. "What do you mean they know me?"

"When you went to ask about selling gold bars I thought you were crazy, but the valet knew you by name and ten fuckin' minutes later, he called up here with everything all arranged." I walked closer until I was standing directly in front of her.

"You followed me downstairs."

"And it was a damn good thing. What else are you not telling us?" Okay, I was acting a little irrational.

"You fucking followed me?" Now Reese was yelling. "Are you my keeper now? You have no right. What the hell were you thinking?"

"Don't make this about me. You're the one who's been lying."

"Hey, hey. Everyone just shut the fuck up." Ryan moved between us. "Reese, you should have told us. Cooper, you shouldn't have followed her. Let's just talk like adults. For once, please?"

"What should I have told you?" Reese wanted to know.

"That you've come here before like a billion times and you're a liar," I suggested.

"Coop." Ryan put up a hand to silence me. "Let her explain."

"All right. During school, I come about once a month," she confessed.

"Once a month?" Ryan stared at her like she'd gone crazy. "Why didn't you tell me?"

"I don't know." Reese slumped back against the glass. "I just like it I guess."

"Vegas?" he asked.

"Poker. And I can't stand Atlantic City so I guess I like Vegas too."

"The whole time we've been here. You never said a thing." The fight had gone out of my tone even though I was still pissed. I was feeling a little defeated. And deceived. "Why didn't you tell me?" I couldn't even see Ryan anymore, just her gorgeous, slightly apologetic face.

"Why didn't you ask?" Reese was quieter too and looking straight at me. Something passed between us, a sort of pain. Like we both knew she was lying. But she didn't trust me enough to give me the whole story. And I didn't trust her enough to ask.

"Maybe this is a good thing," Ryan said. He was always trying to be positive. He also had no idea what was going on. We didn't respond, so he continued. "Those guys might not know I'm here."

"Good for you, but where does that leave me and Reese?"

"Apparently, it's normal for her to be here. So she can start dropping hints that her asshole brother took off for Canada with a shitload of cash."

"What about you guys?" Reese wanted to know.

"You can just call us Justin"—Ryan pointed at me—"and Heather." He pointed at himself.

"Only if I get credit for the idea," I said.

"Which was totally Coop's idea."

"Thank you."

"So we're in the clear," Ryan said.

"We also might want to change hotels," I said. They'd already followed us once.

"Oh, yeah. Good call. Classic move." Ryan threw up his hand for a high five. I ignored it.

"Or not," Reese said.

"Why?" I asked.

"I think we should make it look like we changed hotels, you know, pack our bags, load the car, whatever. And then put you two in drag and come back here. They'll think we changed hotels, but we will just get another room here. Maybe ditch our cars and get rentals."

"Oh, yeah. Double back. Classic-er." Ryan attempted another high five. Reese ignored it.

"You in?" she asked me.

"Totally."

❖

Reese and I left the hotel first. We piled our bags in the small backseat just high enough to be visible out the window. A dark sedan started following us after half a block. We let them. Reese made a couple half-assed attempts to lose the tail. The dark sedan dropped away and was replaced by a slightly different sedan.

These dudes needed to broaden their taste in cars. Fucking boring.

Ryan texted twenty minutes later. He'd left the hotel in his own car. No one seemed to be following him.

Reese got on a freeway. Merged onto another freeway. Went south, then south again. The dark sedan was back.

"These guys must think we are really fucking stupid," I said. Reese glared at me. "Okay, we are sort of stupid. But you never told me that some *Goodfellas* reject might be following us. Where does Christopher get these tools from?"

Reese shrugged. I guess we weren't talking about it.

Ryan texted again. He was on Fifteen going south. Still no tail that he could see.

"Ryan's in the clear," I said.

"Good. We're not. They switched cars again."

"Awesome. Our exit is coming up." I pointed. Reese followed my directions to the hotel I'd picked out.

"Where the hell are we?"

"We're visiting the Hoover Dam, honey. I know you always wanted to go." I used my douche bag, suburban husband voice.

Reese waited a beat, then said, "Always making my dreams come true."

We pulled into the parking lot. Our plan was sketchy at best. The first part went fine. Reese and I checked into the hotel. I talked. Reese smiled. I carried our mostly empty bags. Once we got into our room, I got cold feet. Sort of.

Reese unpacked the one filled bag. I pulled a chair into the bathroom and waited.

"You ready for this?" Reese perched on the counter.

I pulled my chair closer and sat down. "I guess." Not at all. "It'll grow back, right?"

"Totally. You might even like it." She threaded her fingers through my hair as she talked. I was facing a wall so I didn't know if she was lying.

"Let's do it." I gave the go-ahead.

Methodically, Reese started trimming my hair close to my scalp. It actually felt good. Mostly because I knew it was Reese playing with my hair and I knew the legs pressed on either side of me were hers and I knew it was her breath skittering across my neck to get rid of the fallen hair. The electric razor switched on and Reese dragged it from my neck to my forehead. The amount of fuzzy blond hair in my lap increased with each stroke.

"There." The razor was switched off. "Turn around. Let me make sure I got all of it."

I stood and moved the chair against the far wall. I didn't bother looking at myself right away. Instead, I watched her face. That was the only way I'd know if she liked it.

She smiled. "Hi."

"You like?"

"Yeah, it's a bit weird, you know? Kind of sexy though." The smile grew until it reached her eyes.

I glanced up at the mirror. It was weird. With my hair cropped so close, I did look like a guy, a sort of pretty one, but a guy. My jaw was way more pronounced and so were my cheekbones. It also made my over bright eyes stand out.

"You really like it?" Experimentally, I ran my hand over my buzzed head.

"Uh-huh." She replaced my hand with hers. I stepped closer for her to touch it. Reese's eyes had gone to slate. Her legs automatically wrapped around my hips as she pulled me down to kiss her. My exposed scalp was really sensitive so her fingers drawing patterns was just turning me on.

"That feels good."

"How long till we have to meet Ryan?"

"Long enough." I pushed my hands inside her skirt, shoving the material high on her hips. Reese pulled my tank top up to suck my nipple into her mouth. Damn, she was good at that. She yanked the shirt over my head and tossed it to the floor. Then she wrapped her legs around me.

Her underwear were soaked through already. I moved them aside so I could push two fingers inside her.

"Oh, fuck." Reese released my nipple long enough to whimper. Then she moved to the other one. Hot muscles sucked on my fingers, pulling me in. "Harder," she said. So I used my body to thrust into her. I braced my other hand to keep up the motion.

She let up on my nipples so she could kiss me. She kept her mouth closed. Made me work to get her to open up. I licked her lip, just a little. Kissed her soft and slow to balance the way I was fucking her.

Reese's fingernails dug into the bare skin of my back, urging me on, bordering on pain. When she neared climax those nails dragged down, drawing blood, I was sure of it. She grabbed my ass, fumbled with my jeans to get them open. I used my free hand to shove my pants and underwear down. She was gonna come soon. Hell, I was gonna come soon. And she wasn't even touching me. Yet.

Reese kept one hand on my ass, kneading, squeezing. Her other went between my legs. She was moaning into my mouth. Or was I? Her fingers slid around my clit. Every time I thrust into her, her fingers massaged me.

"Inside," I whispered. "Please, Reese."

"More, I want more," was all she said.

I added a third finger. She groaned and lifted her hips. I leaned into her, kissing her hard now. I was halfway on top of the counter with her. My clit was twitching. I was so fucking wet, but still she wasn't inside me. I needed to come so bad. I was shaking now. So was she.

"Please, Reese," I asked again. She still ignored me. Just grabbed my ass harder. I pulled out of her, thrust back in. And again. And again.

"I'm gonna come," she screamed, but it was too late. She was already coming. Deep spasms wracked her body, making her curl up into me. I drove into her one last time, milking it until the last second.

That was when she went inside me.

"Oh, fuck." I wasn't even sure I said it out loud.

She didn't respond. Just edged my legs apart and started fucking me fast and deep. I might have said something. I might have just groaned. Reese kissed my neck, sucked on it. I sobbed.

"You can come now," she said. My stomach got tight and I spent into her hand. She slid forward on the counter. Tightened her legs around me. Moved her hand from my ass to my back to keep me from falling. I leaned into her, trying to breathe.

"You're so beautiful," I whispered into her hair. She laughed softly. "We should probably go."

"Yeah, but you need to shower." Reese was already taking off her shirt the rest of the way.

"So?"

"You might need help in there." She pushed me back and slid off the counter.

"What if Ryan calls?" I don't know why I bothered to ask. I was already kicking away my jeans.

She shrugged and turned on the water. "We better be fast." I could manage that.

❖

The Ace bandage was itchy as hell. How did people wear these all the time? Without realizing it, I reached to adjust it. Reese grabbed my hand.

"Don't you dare."

"It's itchy," I said.

"So is my wig, but I'm not complaining. So deal."

Reese had gone a honey brown. It was boring. And she was wearing unobtrusive glasses. Jeans that were a little too tight. She had a whole Middle America thing going on. I still wanted to fuck her though.

"Yes, honey." I linked my fingers through hers.

We walked to the front desk. There was a different kid working. That was a plus. Reese asked for the rental car we had reserved. It was already in the lot waiting for us. Reese smiled. Did he know which tours of the dam were the best? Yes, he had a few recommendations. And brochures. Great, we loved brochures. Her boyfriend—I smiled— just couldn't wait to see it.

During their entire exchange, a thick-necked dude was chillin' in the lobby and watching us. But he was also watching everyone else. He looked a little worried. We left. He didn't follow us.

The lighter sedan was parked two spaces down from Reese's Mercedes. When we pulled out in our very own boring rental sedan, they didn't seem to care.

And then we were on the road. I drove. We took different freeways this time. It took us about two hours to get to the obscene casino near the Nevada border that Ryan had picked.

Reese spent the entire time studying our mirrors, but there was no sign of Christopher's little bitches.

I left Reese in the car to go pick up Ryan. Literally. When I walked into the bar, it took me a second to realize the trashy blonde sitting by herself was my boy. I got a beer so I'd blend. We made eye contact. He smiled coyly.

Fuck, we were bad at this.

I waited a long five minutes before going over to sit at his table. Up close, he was a train wreck. The eye makeup was perfect, but his foundation was too thick and his lipstick was smeared.

"You're cute in like a lacking self-confidence sort of way," I said quietly.

He grinned as if it were a compliment. "Blow me."

"How long do you think it would take me to pick you up?"

"My self-confidence doesn't think it will take too long."

"Yeah, the makeup really says 'my daddy never loved me.' And the outfit. Dude, Walmart much?"

He'd been going for the same look as Reese. But his jeans were a little too loose. And his top was too tight. Off the rack had never looked worse.

"It's good my face makes up for it."

It did. There was a pretty face under all that disguise. But I wasn't going to tell him that.

"This bar is depressing. Wanna get out of here?" I asked.

"Oh yeah. You're so hot I can barely contain myself."

"You know it, girl."

"Hey, I'm a lady." He pretended to be offended. It didn't work.

I didn't think I could pull off offering my arm to him so I put my arm around his waist instead. The walk to the door and into the evening air was the longest of my life. We were pretending to flirt and look like we wanted to jump each other. But animal attraction had never entered our relationship and we were bad actors. Also, he was four inches taller than me. It was awkward.

Reese was stretched out in the backseat reading a book. I opened Ryan's door and helped him in. Reese started laughing.

"Fuck you. I'm pretty," Ryan said.

"Sure you are." She laughed some more.

I shut his door and went around to my own. When I got in, they were full-on arguing about how pretty he was. I was leaning toward Reese's side, but I wasn't going to tell them that.

It was a long ride back to Vegas.

CHAPTER FIFTEEN

There was some begging and a lot of complaining. Ryan even bordered on crying for a second. Reese finally relented though. "Okay, fine. Just shut up."

"Yes." Ryan gave me a high five.

"But I'm setting it up, you aren't buying it, and we are not taking it with us when we leave." Reese was mean.

"But we can get some weed?" Ryan wanted to make sure.

"Yeah, we'll get you some weed." Reese turned away, only slightly disgusted. The door of her room shut behind her.

"She's kind of touchy." Ryan flopped down onto the couch. "I think she just gave up so she could get out of this damn room."

"Probably." I took the other end of the couch and put my bare feet on his chest.

"Gross." He dragged his finger down the arch of my foot. It tickled like hell so I brought my heel down hard into his ribs. "Bitch." He grabbed my ankle and yanked me closer. It only took him a second to jump up and restrain my hands above my head. It actually hurt because my arms and shoulders were still tender.

"Let me go." I struggled against the weight of his body. The boy was surprisingly ripped.

"Hell no." Ryan started tickling me.

"Stop it," I screamed, but I was laughing pretty hard. With a good jerk of my hips, I rolled him onto the floor. He pulled me after him. We wrestled for a couple minutes, each trying to pin the other.

Reese came out of her room and stared. Ryan had me on my stomach and he was half lying on top of me. I had my arm twisted back at an uncomfortable angle around his neck. Our legs were twined together as I tried to kick him off. We were both breathing hard.

"Hey." I grinned at Reese. She didn't look amused.

Ryan used my moment of weakness to duck his head out from under my arm. He shifted until I was trapped under him.

"I win," Ryan said. Then he rolled off of me.

"Douche," I said.

"What is wrong with you guys?"

"We're bored, buttercup," I said.

"It's been five days. In this room. Five days." Ryan was a little fixated.

"We all agreed to lay low." She said it all slow as if we were dumb.

"Wrestling is cheap entertainment," I tried to explain.

"If you're a seven-year-old." So mean.

"I stopped maturing at seven." Ryan giggled. "Ask all my ex-girlfriends."

"Same here," I agreed with Ryan. Reese gave me a look that was pure disdain. It made me horny. "I love when you look at me like that."

"Get up," she said. "You need to get dressed."

"Whatever you say, babe." More disdain.

"I wanna go." Ryan started whimpering.

"No."

"Why not?" Maybe Ryan really did stop maturing at seven.

"I don't trust you." Reese could be brutal. "If you meet the dealer, you'll blow all our cash."

"Nuh-uh. Pot's not that expensive." He smiled at her some more.

"And we agreed not to leave the room. Coop's going alone. She's the least recognizable."

"Heather's a babe."

Reese rolled her eyes. "Let's go, Justin." She made a point of drawing the name out. I guess that meant I was going in drag. "I'll help you if you need it."

A chance to be alone with Reese? In a room with a bed? Fuck yeah. "I think I'll need it." With a last slap against Ryan's stomach, I got up from the floor. Reese grabbed an Ace off the table and followed me into my room.

"Take off your shirt," she said the second the door was shut.

I pushed her back against the door and kissed her hard. "You take off your shirt." I grinned and started lifting away her clothing.

"Come on." Annoyed, she brushed my hands away.

"I know." I tried not to take it personally. "I just missed you."

"We can't do this with him out there."

"Why not?" I backed away and started taking off my shirt, careful to turn away from her. If she didn't want me, that was fine.

"Don't do that. I'm sorry." Reese slid her hands up my back.

"It's fine." I shrugged her hands away. Okay, I was pouting like a child.

"Coop. Turn around." Reluctantly, I complied. "I'm sorry, that wasn't cool."

"Maybe I should be sorry. I just assumed..." I turned away again and pulled out some clothes to change into.

"Don't pout. It's unbecoming." She was so fuckin' high and mighty.

That was all I needed to snap. "I'll do whatever I damn well please."

"You always have."

"What is your problem?" The girl had issues.

"You want to know?" I nodded in response. I wouldn't have asked if I didn't want to know. "I'm jealous, okay?"

"Of what?" I returned my attention to her, shocked into forgetting my anger.

Reese was studying her feet. "Ryan." It had to take a lot for her to admit that.

"Why?"

"I don't know." A fact that seemed to frustrate her. "You guys are just different together. That's a part of you he'll always have."

My eyebrows must have been floating above my head like a cartoon. "You want to wrestle with me and make stupid jokes about getting stoned?"

"Not really."

"How about wild, crazy sex?"

"Are we still talking about things you do with my brother?" She knew we weren't, but the glare was still convincing.

"Nope, that's all you." It only took me a second to walk back to her and press her against the wall with the length of my body. "Now," I said in between licking and biting her neck, "will you help me get dressed?"

She started taking off my shirt for real this time, though I wasn't sure that putting clothes on me was one of her priorities. Not that I was doing so well with holding back. For the last five days, I'd been watching her, wanting her, and unable to do more than yell at her. So I didn't care when her hands tightened on my ribs where they were sore. I didn't even care when she brushed her hands over the raw nail marks she'd left. It wasn't until her forearms tightened around my shoulders that I winced.

"Babe?"

"Sorry. I'm just a little sore. It's fine though." I went to kiss her again, but she stopped me.

"I want to see." Reese forced me to spin around. When she saw my back, she gasped.

"It looks gross, but it's not bad." I'd been checking it when I got dressed and showered. The original bruises from getting tackled in Christopher's office had faded to a really sexy, faint yellow. Those she had seen. The new bruises from Vic and Gino ranged from an awesome puke green to a purple that usually only existed in Crayola boxes.

"Babe," she sort of moaned. "These have to be killing you."

A fist pounded on the door. "Whatcha guys doing?"

"Screwing like rabbits," I answered immediately. Reese smacked my arm leaving a little red mark.

"Put this on." Reese handed me a ribbed tank top. "Come in."

"It's locked. I tried."

"That's why we lock it," I whispered to Reese as I pulled on the tank top.

Reese let Ryan in. "Go check out her back."

"What's wrong with it?" He bounded in. "Oh, shit. Cooper's got leprosy."

"It's from you, Ryan." I mustered my most pathetic voice. "I told you we shouldn't roughhouse."

"Doesn't it look bad?" Reese pushed my tank top up so it was stretched above my shoulders.

"I kind of like it. It's like *Fight Club* Chic."

"You guys are impossible." Reese let the shirt drop.

"What do you want me to say?" he asked her. "It's a bruise. If I push it, then it'll hurt." Ryan poked his finger into my back.

"Oww." Jerk.

"So we won't do that." His hand dropped. "It'll heal."

"You're no help."

Ryan looked at me all confused. I shrugged. Neither of us knew how to heal a bruise faster.

"Get out so Coop can get dressed." Reese directed him toward the door. He dragged his feet. "The faster you move, the faster your weed arrives." That got him going. Reese closed and locked the door behind him.

"I told you not to worry."

"No, you didn't." So literal.

"Well, it was implied."

The heat from before had left the room sometime between her seeing my back and her brother joining us. Getting dressed wasn't nearly as fun as it could have been.

❖

Twists of metal rail of New York-New York's roller coaster loomed behind the gaudy flame-covered façade of the bar Reese had sent me to. The fading sunlight in the background was hardly a match for the wattage emanating from the overdone sports bar. Vegas sure as hell had the whole excess thing down.

There was a game playing on the screens covering every wall in the place. I made my way through the masses of people, mostly male. Half walls of glass separated the various rooms into semblances of bars and restaurants. It was all the same though.

I chose a stool at one of the bars facing a glass wall. From there I could see in front of me and behind because of the reflections in the glass. A few minutes later, a guy with a cropped Mohawk sat next to me. His dark, unkempt goatee stood out against the pale tone of his skin.

"You Justin?"

I nodded. "Chad?" We proceeded to act like we knew each other. In a bar this packed, it didn't really matter, but it was still a good idea to be cool.

"How much you want?" There was a trace of a Southern twang in his voice.

"Half a zip." I was trying to make my voice sound a bit deeper. I was also trying to say as little as possible. It wouldn't be good to let him know I was a chick.

"Cool. Two thirty." Damn, markup in Vegas was high.

I pulled out a wad of cash and counted it in my lap where he could see, but no one else could. "You got the shit?" There was no way I'd hand it over without making sure he had something to give me.

"Right here." Chad reached into his jacket pocket and flashed me a bag of weed.

"Awesome." With the bills rolled into my palm, I smacked his hand, twisted my palm up, and pulled close so our shoulders touched. Traditional bro hug. In the process, he took the cash and handed me the bag of green with his free hand. I shoved it into the pocket of my baggy jeans.

"Give me a call if you need anything else," Chad said.

"For sure." It was doubtful that we would need more. We only had another week or so left until the passports came in. Chad and I went our separate ways. He walked back into the casino and I went out the front entrance. I was about to open the door and leave when I turned and saw someone who made my hands shake and breathing pick up considerably. Gino. He made eye contact, looked me up and down, and, just as easily, looked away.

It wasn't possible. The fucker didn't recognize me. The second I was outside, I started walking toward the Wynn. It required all my effort not to run. Instead, I called Reese.

"You get it?" she asked.

"Yeah. But Gino was in the bar."

"What? Get your ass back here. We're leaving."

"No, no. It's cool. He didn't recognize me. We made eye contact and he kind of checked me out, but he totally didn't recognize me."

"Shut up. What a dumbass." She sounded as incredulous as I felt.

"Weird that he was in there." I wouldn't have chosen a cheesy sports bar for a meal if I lived in Vegas. If you lived there, you'd know the actual cool places. "You know what that probably means?"

"What?"

"He's probably here just to find you guys. That's a total vacation place."

"I think you're right."

By the time I got back to the room, I was completely full of myself for avoiding Gino. The room smelled like pizza.

"I hear you're pretty happy with yourself." Ryan looked away from the window to tell me. Then he twisted back and pressed his face against the window again.

"I saw Gino," I said. "He didn't recognize me."

"Reese told me. But, like, did he even see you?" Ryan sounded a little dubious.

"Yes, he saw me." I joined him at the window. "He looked me up and down."

"We ordered a couple pizzas." Ryan wasn't as excited about Gino as I had been. "And beer. You guys wanna watch a movie?"

"Sure." I dug into my pocket and handed him the snack size Ziploc filled with pot. "Got this for you."

"I love you." He grinned and took the bag to the couch where he proceeded to crack it open and smell inside. Judging by his faraway smile, it was acceptable. He rolled ten slim joints and filled his case with them. Reese and I joined him on the couch.

With Reese's blessing, I chose the most horrific movie the hotel offered and we settled in with our pizza, beer, and pot. Not a bad way to spend a night really. The first scene made Reese jump. She moved closer to hold my hand. I ate my pizza and drank my beer one-handed. Half an hour later, Ryan jumped too. After that, I didn't have any free hands.

About halfway through, I reclined across the couch with my head in Reese's lap and my feet in Ryan's. They passed a joint back and forth between them. Whenever Reese had it, she would hold it to my lips. She had a way of doing it. Her fingers would trace over my mouth, let me inhale some pot, and I would blow it out. Through the haze I would sometimes suck her thumb into my mouth. Just enough to make her rock her hips forward. Reese's breathing slowly increased.

Ryan didn't notice anything.

The movie was a dark one. Literally. At one point, the screen went black for over a minute. I quietly lifted Reese's shirt and kissed the warm skin of her stomach. My tongue traced around her bellybutton.

Just as silently, I dropped the material back in place. When light from the screen filled the room again, Reese wasn't watching it. She was looking down at me with murky eyes somewhere between horny and angry. A desperate smile twitched at the corner of her lips.

The movie ended soon after. Ryan went to change out of his jeans. Reese and I stayed on the couch. The second his door closed, she leaned over and kissed me. We couldn't get enough of each other. Her hands moved under my T-shirt, pushing it up to scratch down my ribs. I twisted my hands into her hair, pulling her closer.

"I want you so bad right now," Reese whispered against my mouth.

"I know. It's killing me. We have to find a way to get rid of him for a couple hours tomorrow." I bit her lip and sucked on it lightly.

Ryan's door opened and we broke apart looking guilty. I got up off the couch and stretched. Damn, I was a little fucked up. The room spun and Ryan laughed.

"Good shit," he said.

"Yeah, I guess we're not going out tonight."

"We're not going out any night," Reese said.

"Whatever. You know what I mean."

"Not really. What do you mean?" Reese asked. It hadn't really hit her yet. She was probably just dreamy and happy.

"Stand up. You'll feel it." I told her.

She did and swayed a little like I had. I reached out to steady her.

"I'm going to bed," she said.

"Why?" I still had my hand cupped under her elbow holding her close to me.

"Because I don't like being high as much as you guys do." Reese moved past me brushing her body against the length of mine. That smile was back on her lips.

"So boring." Ryan was totally oblivious. I felt sort of bad for lying to him. Not bad enough to tell him though.

"I know." Reese disappeared into her room.

"So whatcha wanna do?" Ryan fell less than gracefully onto the couch.

"I dunno." I flopped down next to him.

We spent the next hour playing video games. I couldn't pay attention though. All I could think about was Reese.

Finally, Ryan tossed down his controller and shrugged. "I'm gonna crash."

"That's not a bad idea." I followed his lead and stumbled to my room. It wasn't very late, but it was better than sitting alone and lusting over Reese.

My bed was just as oppressive as the couch. What was Reese doing? Was she already asleep? I tossed and turned for half an hour. Maybe I'd go see if Reese was awake to, uh, talk.

I climbed out of bed and opened my door. The suite was illuminated by the garish lights from the strip, which cast bizarre neon shapes onto the walls and left most of the room in shadow. Both of their doors were shut. I quietly closed my door and started padding over to Reese's until I heard a noise. It sounded like someone breathing, and it wasn't coming from either of their rooms. Someone was in the suite.

CHAPTER SIXTEEN

Fuck. Automatically, I flattened myself against the wall as if that would help. The shadow did nothing to hide me. Probably due to my white shirt and pale skin.

"Cooper?" Reese's voice floated across the room.

"Shit. You fuckin' scared me." I stepped away from the wall feeling like a total loser.

"Right." Her form appeared next to the bar. "You scared me. I thought you were Ryan."

"I thought you were a bad guy." It came out before I could stop it. Not my fault. Her pajamas consisted of my western shirt. It made it hard to concentrate. I'd been wondering where my shirt was.

"A bad guy?" A huge grin spread across her face. "A bad guy?"

"Shut up. What are you doing out here?" The closer she got, the harder I tried to come up with a way to look under her shirt.

"The same as you." Reese stopped in front of me.

"Oh." And then she was on me. One hand fisted in my shirt, a rogue foot curling up my leg, her other hand guiding mine under her still-buttoned shirt. "I love the way you think."

She laughed in response and pulled me into my room. We collapsed onto the bed in a tangle of skin and partially removed clothing.

"We have to be quiet," I mumbled into her mouth.

"He's asleep." She arched enough for me to push the shirt off her shoulders.

I moved my lips to the soft skin of her breasts, erratically going between them, trying to decide which one to suck. Reese grabbed my hand and pushed it between her legs again. When I slid a finger around her clit, she moaned.

"I missed you," she said. So quiet I could barely hear her. But I did hear her. And I missed her too. I was going to tell her. Except there was no way to admit it. Blind agreement would sound insincere. And sincerity would sound like a lie. So I said nothing. Just decided on a nipple and started sucking.

Reese put her hand at the back of my head. When there was no hair to grab, she cupped my chin instead and forced me to look at her.

"I mean it."

I went still. The only movement was the erratic rise and fall of her chest. Reese searched my eyes. I let her.

"I know," I said. Maybe I didn't say it. Maybe we both just felt it. That was enough. "Now be quiet." But we both knew she would never keep quiet. I put my free hand over her mouth. She smiled against it and bit my fingertips.

I slid into her. Real slow. Even though she wanted it fast. Reese lifted her hips, let me take my time, let me fuck her the way I wanted to.

My thumb was on her bottom lip. She licked it, bit it, sucked on it. Then she pulled my face down and kissed me through the fingers still against her mouth.

Her hands skittered down my sides. She grabbed my ass and pulled me into her firmly, bracing a thigh between my legs. It was fucking distracting, the shock that traveled up my spine and spread through my shoulders. I just wanted to pump hard against her muscle until I came. I forced my concentration back to her. Not that it was hard to concentrate on the wet rush beneath my fingertips; the smell of Reese and sex permeating my everything; the small, incoherent moans in her throat; the way she curled her leg around me, giving me more. So it was a surprise as she came beneath me that I succumbed too. We went over the edge in a swirl of slick skin and ultimate submission. Together.

I'd missed her.

I woke to the stench of pot seeping under my door. I wasn't entirely awake yet, just that floating, grasping sensation where the clock and the sunlight don't seem nearly as important as the warm body next to you. It was involuntary, my shift closer to rest my face on her smooth stomach. She moved in her sleep, I think, to place her hand on my neck. Those long fingers brushed over my buzzed head and I just felt good.

I closed my eyes and breathed her in. Her skin was so soft. And I liked the hint of muscle beneath that. She smelled good. So did the pot. Warm skin and weed. Good way to wake up. 'Cause there's nothing like a joint in the morning, and the smell was making me crave it. Great way to start the day out mellow. Have some coffee to counter the effect. All good. Where was the smell of pot coming from? Oh yeah, under the door.

Shit. From Ryan. And Reese was still in my room, in my bed. All the good morning thoughts of naked girl and my drug of choice soured.

"Reese," I whispered. "Wake up."

She opened her eyes slowly. Her long lashes fluttered against her cheek and she smiled. Damn, I loved that smile.

"Babe, Ryan's up."

"Huh?" Her eyes shot open. "What?" At least she had the good sense to keep her voice down.

"He's out there. I can smell weed."

"Shit. What are we going to do?"

"We could just tell him." Not one of my better ideas. From the look she gave me, she thought it was a terrible idea as well. "Or I could go distract him and you could sneak back to your room."

She liked that better. "How will you distract him?"

"Tell him to change into his bathing suit so we can hit up the pool?"

"Yeah, good." Reese nodded. "Just let me know when he's in his room."

"All right." I got out of bed and put on some clothes. As I headed for the door, she stopped me.

"Wait." Reese got up, all naked and sexy. She kissed me long and hard. "I don't know when I'll get you alone again." More kissing. "Now you can go."

"You're such a tease." I was turned on. Again. Damn her.

"Go." She pushed me toward the door.

I went out into the suite and shut the door behind me. Ryan was at the window smoking.

"Hey, give me some of that." I joined him.

"Morning." He handed the joint over.

"Reese up yet?" I played dumb.

"Nope. Just me." Ryan took the joint back. His eyes were totally red.

"Know what we should do?" I asked. He raised his eyebrows in question. "Hit up the pool before it gets too hot."

"Chill." Ryan was the master of one-word non-responses. He held the joint out to me. I took it from him. "I'm gonna change." He ambled away. High Ryan was a little out of it. Sleepy Ryan was the same. Any combination of the two made you wonder if his heart was still beating.

The second his door shut. I rushed over and opened my door. Reese had the shirt back on as well as a pair of my boxer briefs. She ran her hand over my chest when she went past me. I shut the door and watched that cute ass twitch as she walked. Reese was just opening her door when Ryan came back out.

"Hey. You finally up?" Ryan took the joint back from me.

"Yep." Reese acted like she was coming out instead of going in. "I'm ordering coffee. You guys want?"

"Uh-huh." Ryan nodded. "I'm tired."

Reese plucked the joint from between his lips. "Can't imagine why." She inhaled a mouthful of smoke and held it in.

"You guys heard them too?" He made a grab for the joint, but she stepped back out of his reach.

"Heard who?" My heart rate picked up a little.

"The people in the suite next to ours." Ryan made another grab for the joint, and again Reese danced away. She so wasn't listening to him. "They were going at it half the night."

I decided not to make a big deal out of it. It would only tip him off. "Weird."

"Reeeeessssee." Ryan didn't care about the noisy neighbors. He just wanted the weed.

Reese handed it to me instead of him. I sucked on it and blew the smoke into Ryan's face. That slowed him down. He smiled and breathed it in.

"I think you got a problem," I told him when I gave the joint back.

"I got two. You and her." Ryan pouted.

"Right." I left them to squabble over the weed so I could change into my suit. Swimming actually sounded like a good idea.

By the time coffee got there, Reese had put on her suit too. Fuck swimming. Fuck coffee. I just wanted to get busy with that bikini. Instead, I stared out the window so I wouldn't give myself away.

"I was thinking." Reese handed me a cup of coffee. "We're taking the gold to Mexico, right?"

"Yeah," Ryan said like she was dumb.

"How?"

"What do you mean?" I asked. Maybe she was dumb. "We put it in the car and drive. The same way we got down here." Reese raised her eyebrow. "Oh, shit. I get it." We couldn't fit all the gold in one car. Damn.

"Get what?" Ryan was slower to catch on.

"Remember how we took two cars down here?" I asked him.

"Fuck." There it was. "Guys, we can't put it all in one car," he said like he just thought of it.

"No shit." Reese was less patient than me.

"What are we going to do?" If I knew Reese, she'd already thought about it.

"I think we should leave half of it."

"Like buried?" Ryan was drinking his coffee. It was helping, sort of.

"Yeah, but I think we should re-bury it. Deeper down and maybe in a different location." She really had thought about it.

"Why a different location?" I asked.

"It'll be more hidden if we bury it farther away from Vegas. Like middle of fuckin' nowhere."

"Works for me." We both looked at Ryan. His forehead was against the glass and his eyes were shut. "What do you think Ryan?"

"Does this mean we have to dig another hole?" He seemed pained by the idea.

❖

"Reese, I need help too," I yelled at my closed door.

"Hold on. I'm helping Ryan."

Some genius decided that if we were going out, we should sell another bar. That might have been my fault. A different sort of genius decided that if we were going to be seen, then Ryan and I had to be disguised. Damn Reese.

"Reese," I called again.

"Damn it. I'll be there in a second." It was closer to ten minutes.

"Finally," I complained the second she was through the door.

"You're like a child." Reese snatched the Ace off the bed and approached me. "Arms up." I did as I was told. She started wrapping the bandage under.

"You want me to push my tits down?"

"It would be helpful." So I did. "Not like that. That's just cleavage. Like you did before." Reese tossed the bandage on the bed. An annoyed grin tugged at the corner of her mouth as she flattened her palms over my chest. My nipples got hard.

"I like it when you do it." I placed my hands over hers.

"Too bad." Reese slid her hands out from under mine. Great, now I was just feeling myself up. "Don't move."

After that, it didn't take long for her to wrap my chest so it looked like I had awesome pecs instead of tits. Reese checked to make sure it was secure then handed me a T-shirt. I pulled it on and faced her.

"What do you think?"

"If I were into boys, I'd be so into you." Reese tweaked the bottom of my shirt like she was going to pull it off again.

"How about girls dressed like boys?" I put my arms around her.

"I could be into that." She finally let me kiss her. That girl could kiss. She was all warm, smooth lips and teasing tongue.

Ryan pounded at the door. "Reese, I need help again."

"I'm coming," Reese shouted back.

"Stay. Help me." I grinned and tightened my grip on her.

Reese removed my arms and stepped away. "Put your pants on." She grabbed the pair of Ryan's jeans that were on my bed and held them out at arm's length.

"I don't know how." I took the jeans and tried to look helpless.

"You can handle it. I'm sure." She headed for the door. "It shouldn't take much longer to get him ready," she said before she went out.

With the door shut, I resumed getting dressed. We'd already decided against me wearing tight jeans and packing. I wanted to blend in, and most guys wore baggy jeans that didn't outline their junk. A few minutes later, I went out into the suite. The twins were in Ryan's room with the door shut. I poured myself a drink and waited. I had a feeling that Reese helping Ryan get into drag might have better results so I was a little curious. But it was still probably going to be a disaster. I sure as hell wasn't expecting what came out of his room.

"Holy shit. You're smokin'." He was fucking gorgeous. In a hot slut kind of way. Reese had obviously done the hair and makeup. His face was just made for it. Even the body, which totally surprised me, was sexy. He had just enough ass, standing there in a skimpy dress with a short skirt and stripper heels. "And you've totally got a streetwalker thing going on, by the way."

"It's Vegas," was his explanation. "I was going to go classier, but I figured I should go all-out."

"It works." It did. "I'd totally hit on you."

"Thanks." His sensuous lips curled into a smile.

"Want to make out?" I was only half kidding. He was that pretty.

"Okay."

He attempted sexy when he walked toward me, but he couldn't pull it off. We were moments away from a disgusting, sloppy, fake kiss when Reese had the good sense to stop us.

"You really want to kiss him with that bulge between his legs?" She snagged the scotch out of my hand and took a sip.

I glanced down and there it was. Gross. "Ewww, you gotta tuck your junk."

"I did." He stepped back all indignant.

Reese and I pointedly looked at the very noticeable tent in his dress.

"I tucked my junk, okay?" To our horror, he reached under his skirt and pulled out one of Reese's Walthers. He was right though, no visible dick after that.

"Ryan," Reese screamed. "Now I'll never be able to use that again."

"Calm down. It wasn't touching anything." He tried to hand it back to her. She backed away fearful of the possible STDs.

"Bro," was all I could think of to say.

"Where else was I supposed to put it?" Ryan asked. Neither of us had an answer. The dress was skintight.

"Just don't carry it," I finally told him.

"Fine." Ryan tried to give the gun to Reese again, but she still wouldn't touch it.

"Can we just go?" Reese seemed pretty unhappy.

❖

This time, Reese parked in front of the scary cinderblock building instead of miles away. We learned quick.

"For real?" Ryan stared at it with his mouth open. "It's shady."

"Just go to the door and hit the buzzer and he'll let you in." I acted like it was no big deal. Just casually selling a piece of metal that could have paid for my entire education. Like ten times.

"You guys aren't going to leave me here, right? Because that would be really mean." He actually seemed to think it was a possibility.

"We'll be right here." Reese patted his knee awkwardly.

"All right." Ryan took his purse that was way heavier than it should have been and got out of the car. "If you abandon me, I'll never forgive you."

"We won't leave you. Promise," Reese said.

The second he slammed the door shut, I asked, "Should we take off?"

"It would be amusing." Reese considered for a second. "Probably not a great idea though."

"Oh, well." I leaned forward into the front seat. "Want to make out?"

"Not so much." Reese waved to Ryan. He was watching us from the vestibule inside the first door. He smiled back at her.

"Why did I have to be in drag again?" The bandage on my chest was itchy.

"Because all of us decided that if either of you left the room, you had to be disguised." Stupid idea. "Move over." Reese pushed me to the side and climbed into the backseat with me. At least our rental car had a bigger backseat than the Mercedes.

"How long do you think he'll take?" We turned toward each other. Reese put her legs around my waist. The movement pulled her shorts tight against her thighs.

"Not sure. You think he can see us?" I glanced behind me. With the tinted windows, I was pretty sure he couldn't.

"Probably not. As long as we don't make out, we'll be fine." In the dim light I couldn't really see her eyes, but I could see that smile. Mischievous.

I tucked my hand under the bottom edge of her shorts. Reese scooted closer. I moved my hand higher and scratched my nails down her thigh.

"That's making me wet." Reese groaned softly.

"That was kind of my intention."

"You're crazy." Reese curled her fingers around my forearm and pushed my hand farther up her shorts. The backs of my fingers brushed her soaked underwear.

"I'm not the crazy one." I edged the last barrier aside with my thumb so I could press the tips of my fingers into her pussy. Reese rocked forward until my first knuckle was buried. I pulled out.

"Damn it." Her breathing had picked up. "We don't have time for that. Just fuck me."

"I never said I was going to fuck you." I tapped her clit lightly, repeatedly. The muscles in her thighs tightened, inching us closer together.

"Either you do it or I will." Was that supposed to be a threat?

"Works for me." I stopped touching her.

"Come on." She gripped my arm again and tried to force my hand back to where it had been. "Please."

She did say please. "All right." I pushed back into her fast and hard. The grip on my arm tightened. I kept up the rhythm and added pressure to her clit with my thumb.

"Babe," Reese groaned. She braced her hands on the seat behind her so she could raise her hips. I picked up speed. It wasn't easy the way we were sitting, but I couldn't stop. Every time I pushed into her, she whimpered until she was constantly moaning, begging. It was addicting.

"Reese." Her head snapped up. "Do it. Come," I told her.

She was already going to. I could feel it in the tightening of her cunt. With my permission, she did. Moisture flooded my hand one last time. As I evoked that last spasm from her, she collapsed back on the seat.

"Fuck," Reese breathed. "You are so damn good at that." Couldn't hear that enough.

"It's you." I carefully pulled out of her. "You make me good."

"Kiss me."

I leaned down to steal a kiss. She sucked my lip into her mouth, made me feel inside of her again, then let me go.

When Ryan returned to the car, we were sitting in the front seat acting nonchalant with the windows down. It had seriously smelled like sex, but I was pretty sure the scent was dissipating.

"That wasn't so bad." Ryan got in the backseat. "You guys were right."

"Told you so." I had told him.

"You ready for some strenuous labor?" Reese started up the car.

"Shit, guys." We both turned back to look at him. "I'm wearing a dress."

Chapter Seventeen

"Pull off here." I pointed to the side of the freeway.

"You're not even looking at the GPS." Reese pulled over anyway.

"Yes, I am." I was. "And it doesn't matter anyway. I recognize it." There was a weird light pole.

"You can't remember it. You only drove here once." Reese checked the GPS. The girl never believed a word I said.

"I have no idea where we are," Ryan announced. I glanced back and saw him holding out the neckline of his dress to stare at his fake boobs.

"Probably because you're checking out your tits."

Reese spun to look so fast I was afraid she was going to lose control of the car. The second she saw him, she started laughing her ass off. "I told you they were nothing like the real thing."

"You think I can't tell that?" Ryan cupped his chest. "If I'm going to dress like a chick I should at least get the benefits."

"Chicks don't feel themselves up." Even though we'd had this conversation, I figured I'd remind him. He opened his mouth to protest so I cut him off. "Not even lesbians."

"You guys are so boring." He gave up on touching himself.

"Where am I supposed to stop?" Reese glanced at the GPS unit again.

"Now you want my help?" I said and was rewarded with a serious glare. "Calm down." More glaring. "Go more to the left. We only have another mile or so."

After Reese stopped the car, Ryan and I got out and found the spot where we needed to dig. Reese opened the trunk of the car and pulled out a shovel.

"Is there any chance I can convince you guys to do all the digging?" She attempted to shove the shovel in the ground. It bounced, hit her, and dropped. Ryan and I really tried not to laugh. It didn't go so well. Reese pouted and attempted to cry. Which just made us laugh more.

"Suck it up, babe." I picked up the offending tool and handed it back.

"I hate both of you." But she did take the shovel.

Ryan went through his little routine of putting on his shoulder holster and gun. Then he took off his heels and tossed them in the backseat. He looked like an idiot. Okay, the whorish dress and the holster were kind of a hot combination, but whatever. He was still dumb.

"You're such a tool." I had to make sure he knew. The holster tightened his stretchy dress across his chest. The black leather contrasted against the shimmering material, but not in a good way.

"You just wish you had this." Ryan did a little shimmy and ran his hands over his body. The sexy chick from earlier was officially gone. In her place was a dumb boy in a dress.

"I think I might hurl." I reached out like I was feeling weak and caught myself by grabbing his boob. "I'm feeling a little better."

"Guys." Reese looked pissed. "Focus."

"Fine, I'm almost ready." Ryan removed my hand and opened the backpack his gun had been in. He pulled out a fresh bottle of scotch. Reese and I just stared. He cracked it open, took a swig, and held it out to us.

"Really, Ryan? Really?" Reese was about ready to smack him.

"What? It'll make digging more fun." He acted like that was rational.

"Bro, you brought a gun, a holster, and a bottle of scotch?" He nodded as I listed things off. "And it never occurred to you to bring pants?"

"No." He set the bottle down. "I didn't think of that."

"Way to go." I picked up the bottle and drank some. Might as well partake. "Let's get started."

In between shoveling dirt out of the hole, Ryan and I passed the bottle back and forth. We built a cadence. He'd dig and I'd drink, then we'd switch. By the time we hit the bricks, we were tipsy. Not drunk yet, but that didn't matter to Reese. She was straight up pissed. I didn't see why. She barely did any work, just protested the entire time. Ryan got in the hole and started handing us bars. Reese and I went back and forth between the hole and the car carrying the bricks and stacking them.

"Can you guys move faster?" He perched on the edge of the hole and crossed his arms.

"You just worry about getting the bars out, okay, Heather?" Reese responded with a sneer.

"I'm waiting on you, princess." Ryan pointed to the pile on the ground. He picked up the scotch and drank some more.

"The faster you get those out, the sooner you can start filling the hole back in." Yes, I was annoyed.

"I'm tired of shoveling dirt," he complained.

"Okay, just get the gold out and I'll fill in the hole." I had to do everything. Between the two of them, there was constant whining. Reese didn't want to dig. Ryan didn't want to dig in a dress. I just wanted to finish. "Give me that." I held out my hand for the booze. Ryan handed it over. I took a last swig and put it back in the car.

Thankfully, Ryan started stacking gold again. Once he was done, I started filling in the hole. It didn't take them much longer to finish putting the bricks back in the car and count them to make sure we had them all. Instead of helping me, they passed the scotch back and forth and watched. Assholes. Hell, maybe it would help Reese loosen up a little.

I really tried to stay mad at them. It was difficult though. I liked pretty things and they were damn pretty. With the headlights shining right at me, I couldn't even see the twins that well because they were behind the light. I could see enough though. Reese leaned against the side of the car with that fuckin' bottle dangling from those gorgeous slender fingers. Ryan had his head on her shoulder and his arms around her waist. For some reason, that totally turned me on, the sight of their slender silhouettes wrapped around each other.

"Thanks for helping, guys." I decided to go for annoyed when I was done. That way they wouldn't know what I was really thinking about. Irritated, I tossed my shovel on top of the gold. Then I threw the two they'd been using in as well.

"You looked like you had rhythm." Reese acted all naïve.

"Yeah." I looked her straight in the eye. "Wouldn't want to throw off my rhythm." She got what I was saying. Her eyes went straight to gray, though I wasn't sure if it was from anger or memories from earlier.

"Sorry," she said it kind of quiet. Almost as if she meant it.

We piled back in the car and went back to the highway. Forty minutes later, we found a good spot to pull off the road and drove out for another twenty minutes. This time when we got out the shovels, they both actually helped. We were digging deeper this time, maybe five feet. It was wider too, so we could actually stand in it. A couple feet down, only one of us fit anyway so I stepped up. They started unloading and stacking our loot so it would be ready.

"What do you think?" I grabbed the bottle sitting on the edge of the hole I was in and had some more. It was almost gone. We were all definitely drunk. It was good it wasn't a huge bottle. "Is it deep enough?"

They peered down and nodded.

"Looks good to me," Reese confirmed.

"Hand me the flashlight." Unlike the night when we originally buried the gold, the moon was non-existent. We had the sedan facing us with the headlights on again, but that didn't do much good in the hole. The light went right over.

"Here." Reese handed me the light.

I flashed the beam into the corners and around the sides. Square enough for me.

"You want us to hand the bars down?" Ryan crouched next to Reese.

"Sure." I gave the flashlight back. The first brick Ryan handed me went fine. The second he lost his balance and tipped forward. Reese grabbed his shoulder to steady him.

"Maybe I should hand them to her." Reese was slightly more sober.

"Why don't you hold the flashlight?" I tried to make it sound like an important job.

Ryan bought it. "I can do that." He grabbed the light and held it over my head. It was sort of wobbly because he kept moving, but it helped a little.

Reese didn't do much better than Ryan. About every fifth bar, she would drop it too quickly so it smacked into my hand.

"Fuck, Reese. Pay attention," I demanded after it happened one too many times. "These weigh like thirty pounds."

"Sorry. I am sorry." She handed me the next one. "Was that an improvement?" It wasn't exactly clear which she was struggling with more, speaking in that drunken, perfect way of hers or handing me bars.

"Yes, that was fine." Sometimes, I felt as if I was babysitting them.

Five minutes later, she missed my hand entirely. I tried to catch it before it hit my foot and succeeded in slowing the descent at the expense of a couple fingers.

"Shit. Fuck." The bar dropped loudly to the ground. "Damn it, Reese. I told you to pay attention." I inspected my fingers in the feeble light. They looked fine; hurt like a bitch though.

"Oh, fuck. Sorry. I am sorry," she said. "Did I get you?"

"Yes, you fuckin' got me."

"Are you all right?" Reese grabbed my hand and looked at it. "Does it hurt?"

"What do you think?" I snapped.

"What happened?" Ryan caught on that something was wrong.

"Reese dropped a bar on my hand."

"Shit." Ryan started to lean closer then stopped when he realized that doing so would make him fall.

"I said sorry." Reese felt bad. I could tell that much. "Maybe you and Ryan should switch. What do you think?" She asked him.

He just stared, presumably trying to understand the question.

"Maybe not," I said. Babysitting, I swear. "Hey, Ryan, do you want to go sit in the car?" I made it sound fun.

"Okay." He turned off the flashlight and wandered away.

"Is he stoned too?" I asked Reese once he was out of earshot.

"It is possible. Let me see your fingers." Reese dropped into the hole next to me less than gracefully. I held up my hand for her to inspect. "I am sorry, Cooper." She kissed my hand. I wasn't sure when she went from contrite to sexy, but suddenly there was tongue involved and my spine started to melt.

"We're never going to finish." The gravity of my statement was sort of lost because I just let her do her thing.

"Hey, guys?"

Reese and I stepped away from each other real fast.

"Guys?" he said again.

"What's up?" I looked up at him.

"It's late. We gotta finish." So bright. "Maybe I should get in the hole and take over."

"What a new and great idea," Reese exclaimed. "You are so smart."

"Is that a yes?" He was confused. "I guess I'll go get the flashlight." And he was gone again.

"You are so mean to him," I scolded Reese.

"Right. And you're not?" Reese braced her hands on the ground and jumped up. I grabbed her ass. It was a great target. "Stop it," she said.

"Oh, sorry. I thought you wanted help."

"I can handle it." Reese pivoted and sat with her feet dangling in front of me.

I planted my hands and jumped out of the hole as well. As I turned to sit next to her, she slapped my ass.

"Reese." I used my best serious voice.

"Oh, sorry. I thought you wanted me to do that," Reese mimicked me.

"Did you just smack Coop's ass?" Ryan came back.

"She asked for it." Reese smiled her little drunk grin.

Great, Ryan was going to shoot me. "I did not."

"Never mind. I don't want to know." Ryan held out the flashlight. "Who's holding the light?"

"I will." Reese took it from him.

Handing the bars to Ryan was a bit smoother than what we'd been doing before. Still, it took forever to pile the rest of the bricks in the hole. We were getting sleepy.

"Last one," I told Ryan as I handed it to him.

"Finally. I'm dying." Ryan placed the bar and climbed out. I gave him a hand to keep him steady. "I can't believe we still have to fill this in."

"For real." Reese turned off the light. "I'll go get the shovels. With three of us, it shouldn't take long."

"Yeah." I followed to help her. When we were far enough away, I whispered, "All I want is to take a hot shower with you and climb in bed."

"That sounds amazing." Reese closed her eyes and leaned closer to me. "Maybe we should tell him just so we can sleep together."

"I'd pretty much give my life at this point to have you and a bed." I was so serious. Naked Reese was worth dying for.

"Well, don't. If you're dead, I'll be bored out of my mind."

"Glad to know you care." I smiled at her so she'd know I was playing, kind of.

"You know it." Reese dragged the shovels out and handed me one. We turned back to the hole, but there was no Ryan.

"Where is he?" I asked. Didn't twins always know where their other halves were?

"I have no idea." She looked around then shouted, "Ryan?" No answer. "All right, Ryan. Good one. Where are you?"

Nothing.

"Let's just get started," I suggested. "He'll get bored of hiding."

"Yeah. Good point." She swayed a little.

I started putting dirt back in the hole. After the second shovelful, I heard a weird moaning sound.

"Was that you?"

"No." Reese tossed another scoop of dirt in. "He just doesn't want to help." Reese came to the same conclusion as me.

We threw in some more dirt.

"You guys," Ryan called out. "Stop. It's in my eyes."

"Where are you, Ryan?" Reese called again. He moaned in response. I was about to shovel more dirt in when there was a bright flash and sharp crack in the hole. A gunshot. Reese screamed and dropped her shovel. I jumped back too.

"Fuck, Ryan." I tossed my spade to the ground. "Are you in the fucking hole?"

"Duh, I'm stuck."

"You idiot," Reese screamed at him. "You could have shot one of us."

"Don't shoot. I'm coming in," I said in as calm a voice as I could manage. I dropped down into the hole that now had a half a foot of dirt in it. One of my feet hit something squishy.

"Oww. You bitch, that hurt."

"Sorry." I couldn't see shit, just the glimmer of Ryan's dress.

A couple seconds later, Reese shone the flashlight down. Ryan was propped on his elbows and had dirt covering most of his body.

"I fell," he said.

"I can see that, you idiot. Why didn't you say something?"

"Is he okay?" Reese asked.

"He's fine." I cupped under his armpits and helped him stand up.

"You guys tried to bury me," Ryan said.

"We wouldn't have if you told us." I pinned him against the wall of dirt with one hand. "Reese, I'm going to help him out. Steady him, all right?"

"I can get out on my own," Ryan told me.

"Then why didn't you?" He didn't have an answer for that.

Ryan placed his hands on the ground and jumped up. It wasn't that high. With the gold in the hole, it was only four feet or so. I grabbed him around the waist and pushed him up. Reese helped him stand. I followed him up a moment later. Ryan was covered in dirt. The dress was a little torn. His once perfect makeup was marred by the pale streaks of dirt on his gorgeous face. And he was pouting. I struggled not to laugh.

"Go sit in the car. We will be done soon." Reese pointed him in the direction of the headlights.

"Okay." He stumbled toward the car. The second the door shut, Reese and I started laughing. She almost fell over she was laughing so hard.

"He is so dumb." I gasped. "Who falls in a hole?"

"My brother," Reese responded.

We were terrible at this shit.

I have no idea how we got back. Ryan and I were drunk. Reese drove. Ryan slept. At the hotel, the valet didn't even blink when he saw three dirt-covered twenty-year-olds, one of whom was a boy in a dress, get out of the car. Maybe that was normal for dawn in Vegas.

CHAPTER EIGHTEEN

Paulie called and said the passports would be ready within twenty-four hours so we got another rental car for Ryan to go up and get them. While he waited for them to arrive, he was going to sell two bars. He left the final brick for us to get rid of. I was a bit worried about selling the bar. We'd sold one two days before, and I didn't think our buyer would have enough cash on hand for another. Reese insisted he would though. Logistics are so fucking boring.

"I'm going in again, right?" We stopped in front of the cinderblock building. It looked different in the daylight, less sinister, but more decrepit.

"Yeah. Have fun." Reese handed me a backpack with the bar inside.

"Don't miss me too much." I got out of her car.

"I'm sure I'll be fine." She grinned, just a little.

There was a different guy working this time. A younger version, probably his son. I hesitated once I was in the vestibule waiting to be buzzed into the store itself, but after a moment, the elder shopkeeper emerged from the back.

"Hello," he said. "You are back to sell another?"

"Yep." I took out the bar and handed it to him. "Do you have enough cash on hand?"

"Do not worry," he chided me. His son disappeared into the backroom. "It is interesting," he mused. "I tend to know the movements of gold like this." After a small hesitation, he continued, "but I have not heard of any missing amounts." The speech was delivered carefully. It could have been his seemingly limited English. It wasn't.

"You're wondering if I stole it?" I chuckled a little.

He looked up sharply. "I would not imply such a thing. It is idle curiosity."

"I inherited it." I was telling a partial truth. The twins were supposed to inherit it.

"I see." His gaze returned to the brick in his hands. "There was a…" Another hesitation. "A woman in here a few days ago. She sold me a bar whose serial number was very close to this one and the other that you sold me." His thin forefinger traced the number.

"Heather? Yeah, she's my friend." I chose not to elaborate any further.

"I see," he said. I didn't care whether he believed me or not. Besides, I was pretty sure he was just curious. "My assistant will have counted your money by now. I will get it for you." He disappeared into the back. Both of them reappeared moments later carrying stacks of cash. I didn't bother to count it. Like before, I flipped through and did some math in my head. It looked to be the correct amount, and this guy didn't seem the type to short someone. He didn't have all of those photos on the wall from being dishonest.

When I got back to the car, Reese took the bag from me and put it at her feet. She couldn't help gloating a little.

"I told you he would have enough."

"Yep," I indulged her. "You were right. You're super smart."

"Shut up."

"Where to next?" I asked as I drove back to the hotel.

"We need to cash out. As soon as Ryan's back, I want to get out of here."

"How many casinos do we need to cash out at?" By my count, there were two, not including the one we were staying at.

"Four, I think. The place we're staying, that one near that Eiffel tower thing, the one with those neon drinks, and the one Vito saw me in. What's it called? By Circus Circus?" So damn descriptive.

"I don't know. You can't go back there though."

"No shit."

"So I should do that," I said. Reese agreed so I went back to the hotel to pick up her chips.

❖

The chips weren't too bulky in my pocket, but they weren't comfortable either. I had about eight thousand worth, mostly in five hundred dollar chips. Before, when Reese made me carry her little loot, it didn't bother me. Now that I knew how much it actually was, it made me a little nervous.

The cashier at the casino didn't even blink when I stacked the chips and pushed them toward her. She coolly counted out the cash in hundreds and thanked me. I separated the bills into two smaller stacks and shoved one in each of my front pockets.

As I sauntered out of the casino, I started to pull out my phone to call Reese. Maybe she wanted to grab dinner.

"Don't move, Vivian," someone said quietly. His hand grabbed my arm to keep me still. "Get in the car." A dark blue sedan was waiting at the curb.

"Fuck you." I tried to shrug him off.

"Don't be stupid," he told me. The sidewalk was flooded with people talking, laughing, calling to each other. Still, I heard the distinctive click of a gun cocking. Maybe I felt it.

"You're not going to shoot me on a crowded sidewalk." I couldn't believe I was having that conversation.

"I have no problem doing so. But right now, I just want to talk. Would you rather I sent my men after Reese? I won't be kind to her. She has made me very angry."

"And I haven't?"

"Not yet. Get in the car and we talk. You live. Or I can kill you and torture Reese. Your call."

There was a chance I could run, but there was an even better chance he'd shoot me, so I let him lead me to the car. I got into the backseat and he immediately followed. The driver started the car and pulled into traffic.

Later, much later, I thought of a thousand things I could have done or said to get away. But I didn't do any of those things.

"See? That wasn't hard." He closed the door.

"What do you want, Vito?"

If he was surprised I knew him, he didn't show it. "I just want to talk."

"Knock yourself out." I gave him the go-ahead. "You guys can just drop me at my hotel. It's up there." I pointed in the opposite direction.

"You must be turned around." Vito smiled softly. "Your hotel is that way." He indicated the correct direction. "The Wynn? In the Tower Suites, right?"

"What do you want?" Shit, fuck, and double shit.

"I told you. I just want to ask you a couple questions."

"Get on with it then." I was going for annoyed and bored to cover what I was really feeling, fucking terrified.

"All right." He smiled again. It made my skin crawl. "Where's Ryan?"

"You know, Vic and Gino asked me the same question," I said.

"Vic and Gino are idiots." The two guys in the front seat started laughing. "They shouldn't have been sent to do man's work. Now." He brought it back to the point. Not too easily distracted, this guy. "Where's Ryan?"

"Which one?" I asked. He raised his eyebrows, probably amazed that I was going to play dumb. Well, buckle down, Vito. "I know a lot of Ryans. There are three or four guys I went to high school with. One of them went to UCSD. Another's in Texas, I think. Not sure about the others. There's a couple at Sac State. I work with a Ryan. So I'm guessing he's still in EDH." Vito's eyebrows climbed continually higher and his creepy grin got even bigger. Glad to know I amused him. "Oh, and I dated a chick named Ryan last semester. But I don't know where she is. After she dumped me, we didn't really talk. That bitch was crazy."

"That's cute," Vito said like he didn't find it so cute. "But I'd rather you just answer the questions."

"I don't get it." I slouched down in my seat like a teenager.

"You're going to make this difficult aren't you?"

"Maybe your questions should be more concise." I shrugged. "It's hard to answer when I don't know what you're asking."

Vito leaned back in his seat like he had all night to make me understand his questions. "How about you just sit tight? We'll be at our destination soon." After that, he didn't say another word.

We left the Strip and after that the city. I recognized that we were on Highway 15, but it all pretty much looked the same. The sun was dropping low so the shadows of the scrub and small boulders elongated to three times their size. My stomach was twisting in fear and desperation by the time the guy driving turned off the road and drove out into the desert. A second car followed us. I was dead. There was no other reason to drive out to the middle of the fucking desert. I was just so fucking dead.

The car stopped and Vito hauled me out of the backseat. The second car stopped and there was a chorus of slamming doors as a bunch of mini-Vitos got out. Vic and Gino were among them. Despite the heat waves rising off every available surface and the spine melting, brain-killing hot air, all of them were in suits. Vito was the only one smart enough to wear linen. The others were such tools trying to be tough.

"What's the deal, Vito?" I threw up my hands, waiting.

"Where's Ryan?" he asked. The other guys formed a loose circle around us. Awesome. I was back in ninth grade and about to get beat up. Not a great feeling.

"Which one?" I asked again. Instead of the cheap grin, I was rewarded with a punch in the face. Awesome. "Fuck you." I moved my jaw around. It was going to be bruised tomorrow. If I made it to tomorrow.

"Where's Ryan?"

"Which one?" I ducked the punch, but one of the guys shoved me forward. Vito swung again and connected. I could already taste blood.

"Where is Ryan?" He was a fucking broken record.

"Oh, are you talking about Ryan DiGiovanni?" I asked, all innocence.

"Good kid," Vito congratulated me. "Where is he?"

"I don't know." He slugged me on the other side of my face. Good, mix it up a little. A couple more and I'd be crying like a little girl.

"How about the money? Where's that?" Not much variety with Christopher's bitches.

"I've got a couple hundred. I'll give it to you for a ride back to Vegas." I feigned like I was going to reach into my pocket. Vito fucking punched me again. Fuck that. I hauled off and hit him back in his meaty face. Don't know why I didn't do it earlier.

Vito laughed. "Spunky. I like that." Three of his minions dragged me backward.

"What's with the bodyguards, Vito? Can't beat up a kid without help?" I struggled to break free. They tightened their hold on me.

"I just bring them for show." Vito worked his face into that smile thing again. Did he have any other expressions? Or was it just serious no feeling man and smiling no feeling man? "Let her go." He waved a hand at the guys holding me. They complied. "Where's the money, sweetheart?"

"I don't have any fuckin' money." Yes, I was pissed off. No, I wasn't thinking about the future.

Vito hit my nose straight on. There was a nauseating crunch as my nose broke.

"You broke my fuckin' nose, douche bag." I cupped my hands to my face. That was a bad idea. No touching the broken nose. Warm blood started to pour down my face, into my mouth, off my chin. Not a slow trickle, a nice healthy faucet of sticky, metallic blood. For good measure, I spit a stream of it onto his pretty cream suit.

"Do you really want me to hit you again?" he asked like I was really trying his patience.

"I'd rather you didn't." I decided to just let the blood pour. Not much I could do about it.

"Then tell me where the money is."

"I don't know."

Vito did it again. Blood sprayed in an arc on the sand. It was sort of merciful though. He hit right below my eye instead of on my broken nose. If I lived, my face was going to be all kinds of purple. I shook my head to clear it, which only made me want to heave. Then I punched him again. After that, the underlings didn't let me go. It was kind of good after a while because Vito kept asking where Ryan and the money were and I kept telling him I didn't know and he kept hitting me, so if it weren't for them holding me up, I would have fallen. Not just fallen, but curled up and cried. I didn't tell him shit though.

The pain became a sluggish pound through my head. I wasn't thinking so clear. The thugs holding me up got lazy and I dropped to my knees. They still held my arms, and one was kind enough to grip under my chin so Vito could hit my face directly. None of this pansy shit. Vito's ring opened a gash on my cheek so fresh blood ran from my face to the dirt.

The sun had fallen to just below the horizon by the time they dropped me to the ground on my back. Blood dripped down my throat and from my face into my ears. Vito delivered one swift kick to my ribs that sent a different, sharper sting through my chest and stomach. I curled up on my side and covered my head. The heated dirt grated against my face, infiltrating the cut in my cheek. It made me know I was still alive. He just kept fucking kicking. I wasn't even answering him anymore. There were no more creative ways to say I don't know.

"Pick her up again," Vito said.

His men roughly grabbed my arms and heaved until I wasn't quite standing, just hanging there with my feet dragging on the ground. Vito stepped closer and my forehead pressed into the soft coolness of his jacket. His fingers brushed over the back of my head and made me want to sleep.

"Boss?" one of the guys asked. Vito silenced him with a raised hand.

"Vivian, sweetheart." Vito knelt in front of me. He lifted my chin so I was looking in his eyes. "You think you're hurting right now?" I nodded pathetically. "You don't even know what pain is yet."

"Fuck you." Droplets of blood spewed from my mouth onto his cheek.

"Listen to me, kid. This is Tommy."

One of the underlings stepped away from his buddies into my sightline. Tommy was a boy, a child. He could have been fifteen or he could have been thirty with a face like that, like it was sculpted from creamy wax. Every feature was too perfect and unnatural for reality. The fading sunset cast him in shadow, so the only true details I could see were the slice of his cheekbones and his slender, pretty fingers.

"Tommy has a way with women," Vito continued.

Tommy began to stroke something in his hands. It looked like a knife, but that wasn't right. Was it?

"Do you understand me? Tommy can redefine pain for you."

A shuddering started between my shoulder blades and spread through my arms, chest, legs. It was a burning ice, the sudden knowledge that no matter how much my friends, girlfriends, parents treated me like one of the guys, I wasn't. I was a girl, and they could inflict things upon me I'd never even fathomed. The beating Vito had given me would heal; I knew that much. But what he was saying about Tommy, I wasn't sure I'd survive that.

"I like you, Cooper." He used my real name. That made me listen. "When Tommy's done with you, I will consider being merciful. Maybe

I'll put a bullet between those pretty eyes of yours. You'd like that, wouldn't you? We'll bury you here. Understand?" I could only nod my head. "But we need the information." Vito got to his feet. The throbbing in my head increased tenfold when I lifted my head to see his face, so I just stared at the ground. "If you don't give it to us, we'll go for Reese." Hot tears began to course down my cheeks melting the congealed blood and pooling in the dirt. "And what we did to you, what we'll do still? Oh, Cooper. It will be so much worse for her." I forced myself to look at him. "I won't touch her," Vito promised. "I'll just let Tommy take care of her."

I never actually wanted to kill someone. Literally, just rip out their fucking heart with my hands, but right then? Man, give me a gun and I'd blow Vito's head off. Tommy's too, just to do the world a favor.

The thought of rotting in a shallow grave outside of Vegas after Tommy's brand of punishment was impossible to swallow. Maybe that was why my throat was so thick and dry. And never seeing the twins again? Fuck that. I couldn't stomach it either. I was going to break. Vito knew it. I knew it. Threatening Reese was just his twisted form of whipped cream. And I fell for it hook, line, and motherfuckin' sinker.

"San Francisco." I wouldn't sell Ryan out. Not all the way. Just enough for them to back off because if thirty-four million didn't sate my hunger, then revenge did, and the twins and I were going to get the fuck out if only to show them that we could.

"Ryan or the money?" Vito was fucking gleeful.

"Both, I think." I took a moment to hawk up some bloody mucus. "He's going to Canada, but I think he put whatever it was he stole in a storage unit in San Francisco." I took my time committing to the lie, convincing myself it was real. If it were true, how would I feel?

"Where in Canada?"

"Don't hit me," I begged. "I don't know."

"But you have an idea," Vito said.

I started to nod, but the pressure in my skull ratcheted up a couple notches. "He once told me that if he was going to disappear it would be where no one could find him, where no one would think to look." I tried to remember the name of a city in Canada, any city. Hell, a province would do. What was in Canada? Damn, it was hard to focus. "Best guess, Nova Scotia." That was a province or something, I was sure of it.

"And the money?" Vito was probably envisioning a fat bonus from Christopher.

"He gave Reese two gold bars, gave me one. Told us to get the fuck out of EDH, and the next morning, he was gone. I don't know anything else." The ache that was my body had mellowed so I could pinpoint the various centers of pain. My head hurt, of course, the whole thing was just a mass of blood and pressure and nausea. My back and ribs all along my sides and spine felt broken and splintered. I got visions of my shredded bones floating through me. Even my arms, where I had a set of meaty hands gripping my biceps on either side, burned from holding up my body. At least I'd stopped crying.

"How do you know he went to San Francisco?"

"I got a call." I tried to lie, but the truth bled out a little. "From a friend, a guy I knew at Sac State. He saw Ryan in a bar. Said he didn't look too good. So the guy called me. By the time I got the message, Ryan was gone."

"Good kid." Vito praised me again. "That wasn't so hard was it?"

I didn't answer because all I knew was pain and it showed no signs of abating.

CHAPTER NINETEEN

I tried, I really tried to stay conscious, but it so wasn't happening. At that point, why bother? So I could relive the past few hours? Fuck that. I'm not sure if I passed out or fell asleep, but I woke up to car doors slamming and a sudden rush of noise. It was wind and voices and competing strains of music. Then there were hands grabbing me and yanking me onto a floor that was really hard. There were people and buildings and enough chaos that nobody noticed when I hit the curb and the car squealed away. I sat there trying to orient myself, but it was hard because the world kept moving and I couldn't tell if the lights and colors were real.

"Sugar, are you all right?" A woman crouched in front of me, her knees to one side because of her skintight dress. The wind blew her teased blond hair across her cheek and she brushed it away with long blue nails.

"I think…I don't know," I said. "My head hurts."

"You look pretty beat up." That wasn't a woman. Her voice, it was slow and melodic and just a little too deep. I liked the sound of it. "Can you stand?"

"Maybe." My mouth was all metallic. The blood caked on my lips made them tight and dry. Experimentally, I opened my mouth and moved my jaw around a little. At least it was working. I attempted unsuccessfully to get up.

"Careful, sugar. Take it slow." Her wide hand gripped my elbow and guided me to my feet. As we stood, she slid an arm around my waist. Fuck, that hurt. It was like shards of glass were in my stomach and just fucking stabbing everything. "There. Better?" She started to let go and I swayed.

"Uh-oh."

She tightened her grip again and I gritted my teeth against the onslaught of pain, which just made my head hurt more.

"Let's get you inside." She guided me toward a doorway facing the street. I tried to read the sign, but the lights were so damn bright. Inside it was darker and somehow pinker. There were half naked women dancing, gyrating together, with poles, and walls of glass. My savior guided me to an even darker corner where I fell into a padded chair.

"I need to call my girlfriend." I dug into my pocket for my cell phone. A fan of hundreds came out with it and floated to the chair and floor. The woman was kind enough to gather them and stuff them back into my pocket. I pushed the green button on my phone until I heard it ringing.

"Where the hell have you been? I've been fucking worried." Reese's voice was easily the best thing I'd ever heard in my life.

"Babe. Vito got me."

"Vito? What do you mean he got you?" She sounded scared now.

"I…he…" I couldn't really remember how to talk. My face hurt; talking hurt. "I'm hurt." I just told her what I was thinking.

"Where are you?"

"It's, like, a bar, I guess. There are lots of women here." Eloquent. "They're dancing." Helpful. Man, I was tired.

"Can you walk?"

"I'm sleepy."

"Just stay there. Can you talk to me?"

"Yep," I promised and promptly fell asleep.

I loved the smell of Reese. She smelled like…Reese. And Reese smelled good.

"Cooper. Sweetheart. Wake up." Warm hands held my face.

I opened my eyes and it was Reese. "You smell good," I told her.

"Good to know. I need you to wake up though. Can you do that?"

I wanted to do what she wanted, really I did. The problem was that everything hurt. Just fucking everything. Even my eyelashes and toenails. I raised a hand to touch my eyes. I wanted to know how they could hurt so much. My hand brushed my nose and then I really hurt. It came away with fresh blood.

"Coop, look at me." I did. Reese was so pretty. "We need to get you out of here, okay?"

"Okay. Be careful." She probably already knew we had to be careful.

"I know, babe." She slid an arm around me and someone on my other side did the same. We navigated through a dark, sultry room and were suddenly on the street. My head was kind of hanging and I saw that I was leaving a trail of blood. It was dripping off my face every couple steps.

"I'm bleeding."

"Don't worry about that," came a melodic voice from the side that wasn't Reese.

I turned to look into some of the most serious eyes I'd seen on a woman. Or was that a woman? "Who are you?"

"Don't worry about it." She smiled. It was a real smile. It went all the way to her eyes, not like Vito.

"Shit. Reese. Vito. They got me." The past few hours started coming back to me and I remembered. "We gotta get out. They're coming." We reached the rental car. Reese opened the door and the woman half lifted me into the seat.

"Thank you," Reese told the woman. "You're very kind."

"Just trying to help, sugar." There was that smile again. "You kids try to be safe, all right?"

"We will, thank you." Reese went around and got in the driver's seat.

"Reese." I had to tell her. "Vito knows Ryan's in San Francisco. We've got to tell him."

"What do you mean?" She wasn't even listening, just watching the road. She thought I was crazy.

"I had to tell him something. They already had me, but Tommy was going to get you and so I told them Ryan was in San Francisco." It made sense in my head. Not as much when I said it out loud.

We drove another block and Reese pulled to the side of the road again. "I'll call him, okay?" Reese traced a finger over my cheek. Her hand was shaking. "Tell me what happened."

"I told you. Tommy—"

"No. Start at the beginning."

"Vito told me to get in the car. I shouldn't have gotten in the car." What a dumbass. "He hit me. In the head. A lot." I tried to remember. It was all messed up though, a jumble of sound and feeling. "He kicked me. It hurts. Right here." I waved my hand from pelvis to shoulders.

"Did anything else happen?" For once, Reese's eyes were unreadable. They looked a lot like when Ryan was about to lose a video game, but more. Way more.

"There was a guy—Tommy." I wanted to explain what kind of guy Tommy was so Reese would know. If she thought I just sold Ryan out, she'd never forgive me. I was protecting her though. "He has, like, a specialty." Very carefully, I wiped my upper lip with the back of my hand. Half-congealed blood left a streak on my skin.

"I know Tommy." Her jaw started working back and forth. "What happened, Coop?"

"Vito threatened me with Tommy and I was like fuck that. But, Reese," I was begging her to understand. "Reese, he was going to come after you. I had to do it."

"Do what, babe?" She seemed frustrated and I didn't know why. Maybe she was mad about Ryan.

"Tell them where Ryan was. I swear I lied about most of it, but I told them he was in San Francisco."

"But what about Tommy?"

I turned to stare out the windshield. "He's a creepy motherfucker." A shudder went through my shoulders.

"But he didn't..." Reese swallowed hard and tears started to gather in her brown-gray eyes. "He didn't get out his knife, right?"

"No. He had it out." Her tears started to fall. "Thank God he didn't fucking use it. I mean, what a douche bag."

"Oh. My. Fucking. God." She gasped through her tears. "Cooper, you asshole."

"What?" I hated when girls cried. I always thought it was my fault.

"I thought he raped you." More gasping and sobbing. She wasn't listening.

"That's what I'm trying to tell you."

"What?" she screamed.

"He threatened me and he said they were going to come after you. I had to tell them where Ryan was," I explained for the millionth time.

Reese collapsed back in her seat breathing hard and staring at nothing.

"Reese?" It finally clicked. "Are you crying because you thought he raped me?"

"I can't believe we dragged you into this," she whispered. "Money isn't worth it. Nothing is."

"But he didn't. They just beat me up."

"What?" Screaming again. "You fucking asshole."

"Stop yelling. It hurts my head."

"Sorry." Reese finally looked at me. "But you're okay? Fuck. I was so fucking scared."

"I still feel like shit." I don't know if that was supposed to make her feel better or worse.

"You look pretty fucked up."

"Thanks." I attempted to grin. It hurt so I stopped. "I wanna go to sleep."

"That's a bad idea." Reese started the car up.

"Why?" I leaned back and closed my eyes. My whole body was killing me. I just wanted to take some painkillers, curl up, and sleep. Except I was pretty sure curling up would hurt.

"You need to stay awake."

"Nuh-uh." I was already drifting.

"Don't fall asleep," Reese said.

"Whatever you say." I opened my eyes to look at her. She had her cell phone out and was dialing a number. "Who you calling?"

"Hey, it's me," Reese said to the person on the other end of the line. "Sorry to wake you up. I've got a problem."

"Who you talkin' to?"

"I'm with Cooper. She got beat up really bad." She paused. "Hit in the head repeatedly and kicked in the ribs." Another pause. "I'm not sure. She seems coherent, but a little out of it."

"You're out of it," I told her.

"I don't know, Kerry." What the fuck? "I'm kind of freaking out."

"Fucking Kerry?" That pissed me off. She called her ex to see what to do with me? Bitch. I snatched the phone away from her, clicked it shut, and tossed it in the backseat. "Why are you calling your fuckin' ex?"

"What the fuck?" Reese kept one hand on the wheel and reached into the backseat. It took her a second to find the phone.

"What are you doing?" I demanded.

"What are you doing? What is wrong with you?" Reese started dialing again. "She's an EMT. I want to know if I should take you to a hospital or not. If not, she can walk me through how to take care of you."

"Well, call someone else."

"You think I want to call her?" Yes. "I don't. I'm doing this for you."

"Yeah, right. Fuck that." I reached for the door handle and opened it. We weren't going that fast.

Reese grabbed my T-shirt and yanked me back as she tapped the breaks then sped up. The door slammed shut. "Sit down and shut the fuck up," she yelled at me. "Don't even think about moving." Her hand was still fisted in my shirt. "What the fuck is wrong with you?"

"Don't use me as an excuse to call her," I said. I wasn't going to be some pawn for her.

"You. Are. An. Idiot." Reese started dialing again. "Do you know any EMTs?"

"No."

"Anyone who's pre-med?"

"No."

"Any nurses? Doctors?"

"No." I made another grab for the phone.

"Then sit tight, sweetheart."

After that, I sat still.

Reese moved the phone to her other ear. "Hey, sorry she grabbed the phone and threw it." I could hear Kerry's voice. "No, she's not normally like that…So that's normal?" The more I heard her voice, the angrier I got. "I'll check." Reese pulled to the curb and engaged the locks. She turned toward me.

"What are you doing?"

"Look at my eyes," Reese said. I did as I was told. Reese picked up the phone again. "Yeah, her pupils are uneven."

"Your pupils are uneven," I responded like a genius.

"Yeah, she's acting belligerent."

"You're acting belligerent." I couldn't stop myself.

"So I should take her in?" In where? "Is she going to be okay?" I was fuckin' fantastic. Except the whole sitting thing was brutally painful because of my ribs and standing was brutally painful because of my head thing. "Thanks, Kerry. Yeah, okay. Bye."

"Did Kerry send her love?"

"She told me you were probably acting like this because you have a concussion." Reese could kill with that look.

"Fuck that. I'm fine."

"I'm taking you to a hospital." Reese got on the road again. "We'll just pay cash so we don't have to deal, all right? Do you have your fake ID?"

"Yeah, and I got cash." Somehow, that seemed helpful. I dug in my pocket and started pulling out hundreds. One by one, I crumpled and threw them at Reese while making explosion noises.

"Cooper, I fuckin' swear…" Apparently, she swore nothing except empty threats.

I didn't want to go to a hospital. Reese didn't seem to care though so we spent half the night getting my head looked at so they could tell us my ribs were broken and I was pissing blood. Like I didn't already know that.

❖

"Did you talk to Ryan?" was the first thing I asked when Reese woke me up late the next afternoon. We were in some random hotel. I remembered that much.

"Yeah. He's in San Jose hiding out in a motel." Reese rolled over to look at me. She very softly trailed her hand down my chest. "You want a pain pill?"

"Maybe." It only took one deep breath for me to say, "Yeah, that's probably a good idea."

"I'll go get it." Reese threw off the sheet and got out of bed. She was wearing nothing but a little tiny pair of boy briefs. Very nice.

"Did he say anything? Was he pissed?" I was a little groggy, but I could remember most of what happened.

"Not at you." Reese helped me sit up, which felt like hell, and handed me a pill and a glass of water. "He was ready to kill Vito and his guys though."

"You sure?" That water was fuckin' ambrosia.

"Yeah, he thought you should have told them sooner to avoid the beating. Actually, he said, and I quote, 'You're not in a bullshit movie and it's okay to break.'" Reese slid her cool hand to the back of my neck and rubbed lightly.

"That feels good." My chin dropped to my chest and I closed my eyes. Reese rubbed more. She was amazing. I opened my eyes again and saw my hands against the sheets. Rivers of rusty red filled the creases in my skin. Dried blood. It was on my arms too, matting the pale hair. "Does my face look as bad as my hands?"

"Pretty much." Reese stopped rubbing, but left her hand on my neck. "But I still think you're hot."

"Thanks." When I smiled, I could feel the pull of dried blood on my lips too. "Can I shower? Or is that not allowed?"

"You sure you don't want to sleep some more? I'll have to wake you up again in an hour anyway. Head checks."

"No, I'm done sleeping."

"All right. You want help?"

"Just with getting undressed." We started the slow progression to the bathroom. Once there, Reese worked the shirt I was wearing over my head and dropped my underwear to the floor. I wasn't really paying attention. I was just looking at my face in the mirror. It was like an Easter egg a kid would make, all blue and purple and green. Both my eyes were black. My now twice broken nose was slightly off where it had once been perfectly straight. A couple butterfly dressings were holding the cut on my cheek closed. I looked like absolute shit.

"Make sure you're careful in the shower. Don't touch your nose. Oh, and those butterfly things are waterproof." Reese avoided making eye contact as she left. Not that I blamed her.

The worst part of showering was getting the blood out of my ears. Gross. It was caked in the weirdest places, the hollow of my collarbones, my eyebrows, my fingernails, even some in my bellybutton. All the places the nurses didn't clean at the hospital. At least my head was buzzed. Otherwise, my hair would have been a bitch to get clean.

Reese was staring out the window when I got out, a glass of scotch in her hand. She heard me and twisted around. The towel hanging off my hips didn't do much for me though because she immediately turned back to the window.

"You okay?" I asked hesitantly. It wasn't my imagination that she couldn't look at me. What I didn't know was why.

"I'm fine." Reese sipped her drink then held the glass to her temple.

"Come here." I leaned against the couch with my arms hanging limply at my sides. Crossing them hurt too much.

"You want a drink?" She ignored me and crossed to the bar.

"No. Come here."

Reese set down her glass and kept her eyes on the floor as she walked toward me.

"Reese." I tipped her chin up. "Why won't you look at me?"

A hint of tears came into her eyes. "I can't." She studied the expanse of windows. When I turned her chin so she was looking at me again, she broke. "It hurts too much. I can't believe they did this to you." Her fingers traced my jaw. Very, very lightly, she kissed my lips.

That was all it took. The throbbing in my head stopped, the ache in my chest and ribs faded, and all I felt was Reese.

"Don't look at me then." I moved behind her, pushing her thighs against the back of the couch. My lips found that spot at the back of her neck that made her shiver and tense.

"Coop, you're hurt," came the mild protest.

"I need it." My voice sounded hoarse and desperate. "I need you."

"Then I'm yours." Damn right. Reese stripped off her shirt. Immediately, I cupped her tits, playing her nipples between my fingertips. She arched back, filling my hands. Damn, she felt good. Reese slid her little briefs down, catching my towel along the way. Her bare ass pushed back into me. That feeling of Reese skin and Cooper skin all pressed together, it was fuckin' perfect. Fuckin' world peace presented in skin. I gripped her hips, my fingertips dug into that depression where thigh met stomach, and pulled her tighter against me.

Reese leaned forward, her elbows on the couch, and linked her hands over her neck. She was waiting.

I allowed myself the luxury of tracing the contours of her ass. Her breathing picked up. She wanted me to fuck her. What else could I do? I wet my thumb and pushed into her ass as I slid two fingers into her cunt.

"Oh, fuck," Reese whispered.

"Okay?" I asked a little late.

"Fuck, yeah," she gasped and spread her legs further apart.

Slowly, I built it up, that rhythm that made her groan and twitch and beg. My hand closed over her shoulder so I could control her thrusting back. Sweat broke out between her shoulder blades making my hand slide on the perfect sheen. I couldn't take it, that image of her light chocolate skin and my pale hand, thumb buried in her ass, fingers thrusting into her cunt. Damn.

Vaguely, I was aware of pain in my own body. It was eclipsed by the low moans emanating from Reese, her pleas that I not stop. So I didn't, I went faster. I wanted to, no, had to kiss her. I leaned down. Kissed across her shoulders. Licked the sweat on her spine. Bit the base of her neck. She groaned. Reached one hand back and pulled my head tighter against her. Then, she stiffened, gasping my name, pushing back one last time so I could fill her all the way.

Then she was turned around, open mouth against my shoulder, face buried in my neck, whispering, chanting, "Need you. So much. Afraid, I was so afraid."

All I could do was hold and tell her, "I know, I know."

CHAPTER TWENTY

We were ready, cashed out, bags packed, showered, and dressed. I was wearing the H&K P2000 SK Reese got for me. She said she didn't want me going anywhere unless I was packing. I couldn't really disagree. The .40 cal seemed a little extreme, but Ryan told her she had to butch up my piece. As if a gun wasn't butch enough all on its own.

All I had to do was wait for the twins. They made the decision to pack the car and leave me in the room with the so-called important stuff, the cash. It was just an excuse to keep me safe for the ten minutes it took to come back to The Wynn and check out. How boring. I called Reese's cell phone for the second time.

"Are you guys done yet? I don't want to sit in the room anymore."

"Keep your pants on." I could hear the faint echo of the parking garage they were in. "We have a lot of shit to pack."

"Let me talk to Ryan." I unsnapped and re-snapped the holster against my ribs. May as well have put handcuffs on me.

"No, we'll be done soon. I'll call when we're on the way up."

"Fine. Hurry, okay?"

She hung up on me.

I paced around the room. I took off my jacket and checked out my holster in the mirror. It looked good on me. If you liked guns, which I didn't. I put my jacket back on. Couldn't walk around a casino with heat like that, had to keep it covered. I looked in the duffle bag holding the cash. Yep, it was still in there. How surprising. I slung the bag over my shoulder and looked in the mirror again. Yep, it looked like a duffle bag over my shoulder. Boring.

The phone rang. Finally. It was the room phone, not my cell phone. Weird.

"Hello."

"Ms. Cooper?" a slightly high, but decidedly masculine voice asked.

"Yes?"

"This is Ricky. I'm one of the valets downstairs." He spoke rapidly.

"Reese's friend," I said.

"Yes. I'm watching one of the monitors for the garage." It wasn't just rushed I decided, it sounded like fear in his voice. "Your friends are in trouble, I think."

"What do you mean?" Now I didn't sound much better than him.

"There is another car, a sedan, two men just got out. I think they have guns, but I can't tell. It looks like they're trying to force your friends into their car."

"Fuck. Can you stop them?"

"How?" Damn. Good question. "Do you want me to call the police?"

"No." I responded by instinct then thought about it. And then I thought about why my instinct was to say no to the cops. "I'm coming down. Have our rental car for me. If they leave the garage before I get there, then call the cops." I didn't wait for a response. I just slammed the phone down, grabbed the duffle bag, and ran.

Ricky was in the lobby near the valet pickup. Sweat glinted on his brow, though I wasn't sure if it was from the heat or nerves. He followed me to Ryan's rental while spouting directions to the garage and trying to keep up without sprinting. That would probably look bad.

I only had one question. "How many exits are there?"

"Two. Back and front. They are kind of in the middle of the garage."

"Where does the back come out?" Guess I had two questions.

"Service road behind the casino. Front is on the main road." He opened the car door for me.

I dug a couple of bills out of my pocket, hundreds, and pressed them into his hand. "Thanks, Ricky." Then I tossed the bag in ahead of me, jumped in, and gunned that motherfucker. With my free hand, I dug into the duffle bag and pulled out Ryan's Glock. Two men, I'd need two guns.

The tires screeched as I rounded the casino and rocketed into the parking garage. Once inside, I knew I could drive around for hours and never find them. That place was huge. I chose a spot near the back exit, about four rows away, and waited. It was a gamble. Hell, it was Vegas.

After thirty seconds, I was sweating. Gambling is great with money, not so much with your best friends' lives. One minute had me drumming my fingers on the gun pinned between my palm and the steering wheel. I must have chosen the wrong exit. Three minutes, I was ready to piss myself. Where the fuck were they? How long did it take to shove a couple scrawny kids into a car? At four minutes and change, I heard a car. I sort of ducked down, but that just made my ribs feel like shattered glass. I bit my lip and tried to ignore the sting.

Then it was there, a dark sedan with a thick-necked dude behind the wheel. Next to him, Vito was scanning the garage as they drove toward the exit. The first time he looked, his gaze slid right past me. The second time he looked it clicked. He smacked the guy driving and pointed. They sped up real fast. He probably thought I was going to follow them. Nope, I was way dumber than that.

I punched the gas and aimed right for him. It was hard to steer with the gun in my hand. First gear, second, third, and the engine screamed at me. Vito raised his hand and squeezed off a single shot that seemed unbelievably loud. When I slammed into their car, fuck. Bone-jarring? Hell, no. Try enough impact to make my sides feel like they were splitting open and shredding any remaining bone, flesh, muscle I had left. Try my headache reaching levels I'd only imagined before that fucker Vito.

All forward motion stopped as the driver's side of the sedan smashed into a cement pillar. The grill of the rental implanted into the opposite fender. They were trapped and they were fucking mine.

I got out of the car with my hand already wrapped around Ryan's gun and pointed it at the driver. I yanked my H&K out of its holster and aimed it at Vito's head. At that point, I had few qualms about pulling the trigger.

It didn't look like I'd have a problem. Vito was definitely alive, just sitting there staring at me, stunned. The driver was shaking his head, trying to figure out what happened. It gave me enough time to glance in the backseat at the twins. They had the same expression as Vito.

"Move," I screamed.

They did. Everyone. Ryan grabbed Reese and hauled her out of the backseat. His door opened fine. Vito started trying to muscle his door open, but that so wasn't happening. There was a car rammed into the side of it. Dumbass. Same with the guy behind the wheel. His door was glued to a cement post. They were lucky I hadn't been going faster.

"Holy shit," Ryan nearly whispered. Then he screamed, "Are you fuckin' crazy?" He was only a couple feet away so his voice was deafening.

"Yes," I told him without taking my eyes off their captor.

Vito realized his door wasn't going to magically open. He unloaded a couple rounds into the already cracked windshield then kicked it releasing a shower of glass on himself. Not too smart. He and his buddy started to climb out.

"Guys. Get in the fuckin' car." I yelled to the twins. It took a second for them to understand. Finally, Ryan started pushing Reese toward the car. Slowly. Vito and his buddy were scrambling over the hood of their car when I shouted for them to stop. They paused.

"Why?" Vito asked. "You won't shoot us."

"You sure about that?" Maybe it was my tone or the way I was grinning, but he actually stopped moving. Just stood there on the hood of his car. The twins had also stopped. They were watching me, studying me. I turned to tell them to get in the car. What I saw made me freeze, a bright red handprint across Reese's cheek. Immediately, I spun back to face Vito.

"Is there a problem?" Vito sort of chuckled.

"Which one of you was stupid enough to touch her?"

"That was Jimmy." Vito gave a nod to the guy next to him. Jimmy laughed. That really pissed me off.

I dropped the gun in my right hand a few inches and squeezed the trigger. I was close enough that I couldn't miss. The kick from the gun forced me to take a step back. Probably should have taken it to a range to get a feel for it.

Jimmy screamed and fell clutching his knee. Blood seeped through the cracks between his fingers. The shards of glass on the hood scraped and echoed as he twitched. I felt oddly satisfied and only a little nauseous.

At least I'd talked Reese out of the hollow points.

"Was that really necessary?" Vito asked like he was trying to be cool. Judging by the amount of sweat on his face, it wasn't working.

"I'm not in the mood to fuck around."

Vito took another step closer. "Let's talk. Work this out." His hands were in the air like a surrender. Screw that.

"You know?" I moved both guns so one was pointed at his head, the other at his body. "I'm not really feeling it. So just shut the fuck up and don't come any closer."

"Oh, Cooper." Vito sighed like I was a recalcitrant toddler. But I wasn't. I was a recalcitrant adult. Much worse. At least he wasn't walking forward anymore. Next to him, Jimmy screamed some more.

"What part of shut the fuck up did you not get?" More screaming. "And make him shut up too," I said as if Vito could make it happen.

"You just shot him in the knee. That's pretty painful," Vito said. Damn, he was annoying. Condescending too.

"Whatever." I couldn't take my eyes of Vito, but I could still talk to the twins. "Will you guys go get the car so we can get the hell out of here?"

"Sure. Whatever you say." Ryan backed away from me.

"I'll stay here." Reese finally spoke.

"Here." I handed her Ryan's gun, which she trained on Vito. Jimmy finally stopped screaming. He must have passed out.

"I'll be back in a sec." Ryan got in the rental. When he backed it out of the sedan, the shaking made Vito stumble and fall to the ground. Ryan screeched away leaving Reese and me with their uncle on all fours on the cement. Shit.

"Don't try anything," I said. "Just stand up real slow."

"Sure, kid," Vito assured me.

I didn't believe him for a second. As he stood, I stepped forward to cover Reese. Good thing too. Vito was clutching a handgun, which he pointed right at me. I froze.

"Now we're going to do things my way."

"No," I said.

"Drop the gun. Move away from Reese."

"I said no, dumbass." I pointed at the gun I was holding. "I've got a gun too." Was he fucking slow?

"What are you doing?" Reese tried to push me away.

"I got this, buttercup."

"Would you rather stand here and see who's a better shot?" Vito straightened his clothing with his free hand. "It won't turn out well for you."

"What can you do, kill me?" I asked. Actually, that seemed pretty shitty. I didn't go through all that just to get killed in a parking garage in Vegas. "I'm the only one who knows where your money is."

"I don't believe you, Vivian. You proved to be a pretty good liar before." Vito shrugged in a dignified way. "Besides, I was only asked to retrieve the twins. No one said you had to be alive."

"Would you two stop the pissing contest?" Reese grabbed the waistband of my jeans and hauled me backward so she could step in front of me.

"What the fuck?" was all I could manage.

"There's the Reese I know." Vito grinned. I could barely see him from behind Reese.

"Shut up, Vito." Reese still had the gun trained on him, but it was kind of pointless. He'd let his drop so it was pointing at the ground.

"That's my girl." He sounded like he meant it. "You really haven't changed have you?"

"Please shut up?"

"Just like when you were little," Vito continued, leaving no question about who was in charge of the situation, guns or not. "You know, once when you were just a tiny thing you pulled a stunt exactly like that. Your grandfather slapped Ryan and told him he was a bastard." Vito laughed at his own story. Their grandfather sounded like a douche bag to me. "You pulled Ryan away and stepped in front of him. Exactly like that," he repeated. "It was classic." As he spoke, Reese started to straighten. Her shoulders squared and her jaw started to clench. "You couldn't have been older than six. It was right before your mother ran away," he mused. "She wanted to keep you safe, kid. Carissa always was naive."

"Vito. Stop. Fucking. Talking." Reese raised the gun as if she suddenly meant it. "You don't know shit."

"Really, honey? I think I do." Vito smiled. I believed him. "She came back into the fold, you know? Couldn't keep away. You'll come back too." What the fuck was he talking about?

"No, she didn't," Reese screamed. It was like the petulant eight-year-old I once knew was standing in front of me and I was just a fly on the wall. "And I'm never going back." I half expected her to stomp her foot.

"What do you think you're doing right now? That gun feels good doesn't it?" His voice was low, taunting, like tainted honey.

"Shut up. Just shut up." Her gun trembled.

"You have a choice, kiddo. Come home now. We'll protect you. Give you everything you ever wanted." Stern tone now, very fatherly. "If you don't, you'll end up just like your mother."

Reese let go of the gun. The sound of it dropping echoed through the cement surrounding us. "It was an accident. He told us it was an accident."

"You believed Christopher?" Vito asked incredulously. "You're smarter than that."

Reese looked like she was going to cry. I was so totally lost. What the fuck was going on?

Ryan chose that moment to pull up in the second rental car. Reese was just standing there gasping for air and trying not to cry or hyperventilate. It wasn't working. Vito looked like he was waiting for her to rush back into his arms. I could have just walked away. No one would have stopped me.

Instead, I raised my gun again and pointed it at Vito's head. Ryan stepped out of the car. I put my other arm around Reese's waist and steered her toward Ryan. He put her in the backseat. I picked up the gun Reese had dropped and shoved it in my holster.

"We'll never stop looking, Reese," Vito said right before her door slammed shut.

"You'll stop right fucking now," I said as I backed toward the car.

"Do you even know what we're talking about?" Back to the pissing contest.

Nope. "I know as much as I need to." He was right though. I didn't know anything about them. Not like I thought I did. And not knowing was starting to worry me.

Behind me, Ryan started the car.

"They've already marked you as one of us," Vito said as if I knew what the hell he was talking about. "That necklace was Carissa's, wasn't it?"

"Jealous?" I guessed.

Vito laughed. "You should ask them where they came from. What it is that they are dragging you into."

I went around the front to get in the passenger side. My gaze never left Vito's face. "I already know more about them than you ever will."

"I doubt that."

I got in the car. Ryan gunned it out of there. Vito watched us drive away without moving.

"What just happened?" Ryan asked once we were on the main road.

Reese didn't answer. Neither did I.

"Guys, what happened?"

"Nothing. Vito's just a douche." Reese wiped her eyes and straightened her shoulders.

"I'd like to know what happened." I pivoted to look at Reese.

"Nothing. He was just trying to get to me. It worked." She lied.

"What was he saying about your mom?" I chose to ask the question I was sure would get an answer. Even though I knew I wouldn't like the answer.

"That she was murdered." Reese didn't break our eye contact as she said it.

"What?" Ryan yelled. He turned away from the road to study Reese. His grip on the wheel tightened.

"Drive, Ryan," Reese said.

"What the fuck?" He did what she told him, but his eyes flickered between the road and the mirror.

"Come on. We knew it. We just didn't want to." She sounded surprisingly calm.

"Fuck." He took a deep breath, drummed his fingers on the steering wheel, took another breath. "Yeah, but we didn't *know* know." He was kind of pleading. Hoping she would take it back. "Really?"

"Yeah." Reese nodded. She looked so sad and adorable, I just wanted to climb back there and hold her. Not really an option. Also I was pissed. And weirded out. Something was going on. Vito was right. I didn't know shit.

"Are you two fuckin' high?" They just found out their mom's death wasn't an accident and that was their reaction?

"No, why?" Ryan was either callous or stupid.

"Indulge me. Tell me you're stoned. I'll feel better."

"Coop. We knew," Reese told me. "We just never admitted it."

"You knew your mom was killed?" They had to be high.

"There are just things you know." Ryan twisted his grip on the wheel. The sound of creaking leather made me glance at him. There were tears in his eyes.

"Does anyone want to tell me what exactly is going on?" I asked even though I was pretty sure I wouldn't like that answer either.

"I don't know." Reese shrugged apologetically, dishonestly. "But he's right. They're never going to stop looking for us."

That much I knew. Christopher just didn't know that we weren't going to stop fighting him. I decided to let the twins keep their secrets a while longer.

CHAPTER TWENTY-ONE

There was sort of a sense of accomplishment when we were digging for the final time. Sure, we'd have to come back for the other half later, but for now, we were practically home free. We'd gotten rid of the rental and picked up the 4Runner. All we had to do was get across the border. Ryan even broke out another bottle of scotch. He must have bought it in bulk or something.

"It's easier to do this when we're practically sober." Ryan set two more bars on the ground. He was in the hole this time.

"Yeah, it's real easy," I said.

They both glared. I wasn't doing any work, just observing. With broken ribs, I couldn't do much. Payback was awesome.

"If you weren't already hurt, I'd kick your ass," Reese said.

"Anytime you like, babe." I grinned. Now that I could sort of move my face, I was much happier.

"Is it me or are you guys actually getting along?" Ryan straightened to study us. "Since we've been in Vegas, you guys have barely fought. Hell, if I'd known locking you in a room together for a couple weeks was all it took, I would have done it years ago."

That was the moment. The perfect opportunity to tell him. Reese and I both stared at each other, mouths open, trying to figure out if the other was cool with it. We took too long to decide. The moment passed. Ryan bent down for more bricks.

"These are the last two." He set the bars next to the others.

"Here." Reese handed me two bars and picked up the remaining ones. We walked toward the car in silence. When we were behind the

SUV, I glanced over at her. Both of us started laughing. Hysterically. It felt a little mean.

"He has no idea," I said. An unnecessary announcement.

"I know. We've got to tell him sometime." Like we hadn't already had this conversation a thousand times.

"Yeah. Soon or he'll be really pissed." I pulled the blanket spread in the back over the remaining gold bars. Then I dug around until I found a fresh bottle of scotch.

"He's already going to be pissed." Reese held out her hand for the bottle after I swigged some.

"So let's wait until he doesn't have a gun in easy reach." I took the bottle back.

"After we're done here? When we're driving?" Reese asked.

"I'll drive. That way we know he won't hit me or anything." Yes, I was afraid. No, I didn't think either of us was actually going to tell him.

"Pansy," she said.

"You like it."

"I like it a lot." Reese tucked her fingers into the front of my pants and yanked me closer.

It had been way too long since I kissed her. Her mouth was all soft and tasted of scotch. Even though my head was buzzed, she still tried to play with my hair, working her fingers over my scalp.

"Reese, babe." I broke away. "He's right there." My control was already slipping.

"I know." She kissed me again. I couldn't stop it after that. She felt too good.

"Come on." I grabbed her hand and dragged her away from the car, in the opposite direction from Ryan, into the darkness.

"You're crazy," she told me, but she followed anyway.

As we walked, I loosened her shoulder holster in order to push up her shirt and suck one of her nipples into my mouth. It was hard to walk, but who gave a fuck? Reese gripped the bottom of my T-shirt and tugged it over my head so it and my gun were hanging off one shoulder. Her hands worked at my belt so my pants only stayed at my hips because I was holding them there, which was hard since I was still carrying a nearly full bottle of booze. We were far from the circle of light created by the headlights when we finally stopped. I reached for her, but she smacked my hand away.

"You don't always get to be in charge."

"Right." I tried to grab at her again and was rewarded with another slap. "Stop hitting me. I'm injured."

"Shut up." Reese punctuated her demand by kissing me. More smooth tongue and hard liquor. Difficult to argue with that. She flattened her hand against my stomach and leisurely started the teasing glide over my scorched skin into my boxer briefs. We both dropped to our knees in the dirt. I didn't care. I couldn't feel anything except that so damn good feeling of Reese filling me, taking me, unlike any girl I'd ever known. The easy, hard, cadence of her fucking me was like being known. She knew when to stop, to tease, to go, to take me higher so I was poised, wanting.

Through the groans pushing past our lips, mingling in each other's breath I whispered, "Fuck, Reese. I'm gonna…You make me…." I couldn't speak.

She didn't stop. Not that it mattered. I was gone anyway, collapsing forward into her. Reese placed an arm around my waist, the other still in the depths between us. She let me feel strong when I had nothing else to offer.

"Coop, Cooper." Reese wanted my attention.

"Yeah." I raised my face to hers, afraid of what she would say.

Nothing. She just kissed me and dragged my hands to her body.

Her muscles twitched as I brushed her stomach, traced her bellybutton. I cupped those perfect breasts and gasped when her nipples hardened against my palms. Reese buried her face in my neck.

"Please touch me."

Without thinking, I cupped her sex in my hand, encouraged by the waiting moisture. When I pushed to fill her, she started working her fingers, still inside me, slowly, echoing my movements.

My thumb had just pressed against her clit when she froze.

"Come on. Don't stop."

"What the fuck?" She eased out of me and pulled her hand away letting my underwear slap back against my abdomen. Not exactly what I was hoping for.

"What?"

"That?" She pointed behind me, toward Ryan.

I didn't see anything. "I don't get it." What was her deal? Reluctantly, I removed my hand from between her thighs. This wasn't going well.

ASHLEY BARTLETT

"I think someone is driving toward Ryan." She pointed in the direction of the freeway. "Do you see a car driving without headlights?"

"No." I didn't see anything and now I was way less turned on. "Where?"

"Right there." She didn't seem to be joking.

I actually looked where she was pointing, and sure enough. "Shit. I think I see two cars. I thought you were fucking with me."

"Fuck. There are two." Reese grabbed my arm with both hands. "What are we going to do?" The first car stopped behind the 4Runner. The sound of car doors closing echoed out to us.

"Shit. Fuck. I don't know." The second car continued and parked on the far edge of the circle from Ryan's headlights, surrounding him.

"We have to go back. Help Ryan."

"No shit." I pulled my shirt back over my head and closed my pants with shaking hands. Next to me Reese, started fixing her clothes as well. We stood and started walking, not very well either. "How many guys do you count?" I kept my voice low. "I can't tell if it's five or six."

"I count six."

"Damn. Why can't they just leave us alone?"

"It's not what they do." That sounded ominous.

I put out a hand to stop Reese. "Is there any way I can convince you to stay here?" The thought of dragging her back to those assholes made me feel ill. Better that she stay out here in the relative safety of darkness.

"Any chance I could convince you to let me handle my family's bullshit? Because I'd rather you didn't get the shit kicked out of you again." Okay, I could see where she was coming from.

"We need a plan." I blew off her question. No way in hell were we going to run in, shoot the shit out of everyone, and hope for the best.

It took a couple minutes to work out what we were going to do. Soon I found myself dragging my body over the sand behind the sedan closest to the highway. I could hear shouting from Vito's goons and Ryan. Too bad I couldn't understand what they were saying.

Careful to stay far enough away from the circle of light, I propped myself up on my elbows, ignored the smoldering pain in my ribs, and waited. This sucked.

"Come on, you stupid punk." Vito was shouting at Ryan. "Where's the other half?"

"Half of what?" Ryan spat back. Like with me, Vito's guys were surrounding Ryan, keeping him without holding him. Vic and Gino flanked either side, Tommy and a guy I didn't recognize behind, and a fifth one was leaning against the car parked on the far side of the pool of light in case Ryan ran.

"You little shit. We'll get it one way or another." Vito bitch-slapped him.

"For once in my goddamn life, would you show me just a little"— Ryan held up his thumb and forefinger—"respect? Would that be so fucking hard?"

"If you acted like a man, I would treat you like one."

"What could I possibly have that you want so much?" Ryan was taunting Vito now, his default way of dealing with anger. "Balls?" He cupped his junk. "Because there's no way I can give you that."

Where the fuck was Reese? She needed to get this show started. I already had my H&K gripped tight enough to leave an imprint on my palm.

"You're useless." Vito shoved a fat finger in Ryan's face. "Just like your piece of shit father."

"You don't know a damn thing about my father."

"I know more than you do," Vito said. Mature.

"Fuck you." Genius response, Ryan.

"You know, boy, I think I'll put you out of your misery." Vito reached into his jacket and pulled out a gun. "We should have put you down at birth."

I was practically hyperventilating. If Reese didn't show in about one second, I'd have to step up.

"Thanks, by the way." Vito nodded at the hole and laughed. "I hate digging, but you've already done all the work." The men surrounding Ryan started laughing too. "That must really get you, huh, kiddo? Digging your own grave and not even knowing it."

"You're not going to shoot me." Ryan taunted Vito, despite the color draining from his face. "You'd never find the girls."

"We found you." That resonated. We were in the middle of the fucking desert, the middle of nowhere.

"I think we both know they're smarter than me. You'll never get them."

"True," Vito acknowledged. He raised the gun to Ryan's face.

"If you're going to do it then get on with it."

"Sorry, Ryan." Vito shrugged without a trace of remorse.

I was surprised he couldn't hear my heart beating. Someone was pointing a gun at the guy I loved. The only one I would ever truly love. I started to stand. Vito heard my foot scuff on the ground and lowered his gun as he pivoted to peer into the darkness.

Opposite me, a glass bottle spewing liquid flew into the light. It clipped the guy leaning against the sedan in the head then shattered against the car. He dropped to the ground. Damn, Reese could throw. Air suddenly rushed into my lungs. I didn't even know I had stopped breathing.

Instantly, every man standing drew a gun. They rushed at the darkness. Vic saw Reese's outline and aimed at her. I focused on his outstretched arm and fired. He dropped to his knees screaming. The goons were confused now. Vito was shouting instructions at them. Gino and the guy I didn't know ran toward me. Suddenly, Gino pitched forward. On the ground he shuddered, red blossoming from his shoulder blade. Thanks, Reese.

I felt more than saw the moment his buddy finally made me out of the darkness. He started to raise his gun. Without hesitation, I shot him in the chest. My body was numb. I didn't even feel the kickback. He jerked, stumbled a few steps, and went down.

I didn't want to kill anybody, and I was afraid. Afraid of that place deep inside where my soul went as I pulled the trigger. That place where I didn't care about pointing a machine made for killing at another human.

Christopher made me do it. They made me do it. When they threatened the two people who mattered most to me. They wanted one of them dead and the other they wanted something else from. I didn't know why they wanted her, but it seemed, somehow, worse than death.

I pushed myself to walk by the bodies on the ground, without looking, trying to maintain the cold that pumped through my veins. To my left, Vito and Ryan were fist fighting, their weapons thrown away. I passed them to where Vic was kneeling cradling his injured arm. With a kick to his chest, he landed on the ground. There was blood everywhere. It made me wonder if I'd hit something important. Then I remembered the way he talked to Reese. That gave me the anger to place my foot on the wound and press down with all of my weight. The pain on his face imprinted in my mind along with screams to give me nightmares. Then, finally, he blacked out.

Behind me, Ryan and Vito were still grappling like little boys in a schoolyard fight. Vito was stronger, but Ryan was faster. It only took three strides to reach them. I gripped the barrel of my gun and hit Vito's head with the butt of it. He collapsed. Five down. Where was Tommy?

"Thanks." Ryan straightened and wiped a streak of blood from his nose. "Where's Reese?" Shit.

I spun and surveyed the pool of light. Bodies, spilled scotch, blood, shell casings, no Reese. "Fuck. He's got her."

"Who?" Ryan located his gun in the dirt and put it in his holster.

"Tommy." I crossed the pool of light to where I'd last seen her. Nothing. I turned back to Ryan.

The gun was back in his hand. "Where the hell are they? If he touched my sister, I'll fuckin' kill him."

"But, Ryan," a smooth voice behind us intoned. "She's so pretty."

We both spun to face him. Reese was standing in front of Tommy, pressed back into him by a long knife held flat against her belly. He had a gun to her temple and a feral grin plastered on his face. Something wasn't right with that man.

"Let her go," I said. The gun gripped in my hand hung like dead weight at my side because that's what it was. Useless. Dead weight.

"Why?" Tommy used the barrel of his gun to pull her hair back. "I think she likes me." He kissed the exposed skin on her neck. Right behind her ear.

That was my fucking spot to kiss her. Hot, sick anger rolled through me. The look on her face made me stay still. She was ice. Not a muscle moving. Her eyes gave away all the pain and fear, but to someone who couldn't read her, nothing. Tommy couldn't read her.

"Just let her go, Tommy." Ryan was trembling. "Make this easier on everyone."

"Drop your guns," Tommy said.

"No." When faced with intelligence and anger, the anger won. I wasn't doing a damn thing he wanted.

"Okay, you can just watch if you want." Tommy lowered the knife from her stomach. "She wants me, you know?" He used the blade to lift her skirt and traced it along her thigh. "They say I have a way with women."

I was going to vomit.

"Funny." Ryan managed to stop shaking. "I've always heard you had a way with men." He shrugged. "Or they have a way with you."

"Shut up."

"They always said you were a faggot." What the hell was Ryan doing? "Only put up with you because they had to. Fuckin' pansy." Since when did Ryan spew shit like that?

"You want to see how much man I am?" Tommy raised the knife another inch. The tip dug into Reese's flesh. A small stream of blood trailed down her thigh. I wanted to kill him. I was going to kill him.

"Man enough to fuck a girl?" Ryan laughed. "Seriously, dude. Cooper can do that." I finally caught on to what he was doing.

So did Reese. "She's good at it too." She made it a benediction.

"Shut up, bitch." Tommy pressed the gun into her skull harder.

"You don't have the balls to kill someone though, do you, Tommy?" Ryan asked, taunting him. "That's why no one ever liked you. Said you could never finish the job. You always had Vito do it for you."

I kept my mouth shut and prayed Tommy would forget I was standing there.

"That's not true," he spat at Ryan.

"Really? I don't think you have it in you." Ryan let his gun fall. "You afraid of something?" He held up his hands, a silent offering.

Tommy took it. "I'm not afraid." He moved the gun from Reese's temple to point at Ryan.

It was instantaneous. Reese twisted Tommy's wrist away with both hands and dove for the ground. Ryan hit the dirt as Tommy aimed at him. I raised my gun and fired.

Three bodies hit the ground. Reese, Ryan, Tommy. I remained standing, my gun pointed at air.

Ryan picked himself up, his shirtsleeve turning crimson. Reese disentangled herself from Tommy's dead weight. I dropped my gun. Both twins hit me running. Reese threw her arms around my neck. I wasn't even thinking when I kissed her. I just needed her, real and alive, consuming me. She kissed me back, pulling me into her. Tears ran down her cheeks, wetting mine. Ryan, with his arms thrown around us, didn't notice. Right away.

"What the fuck?" Ryan said when he realized what was happening. He took a step back. "What the fuck are you doing?"

Reese and I broke apart.

"No, no, no."

"Ryan, it's okay." I held my hand out to him. The other was firmly around Reese.

"No, no, it's not. What the fuck?" he yelled. "You and…And you. No, no, no, no."

"Ryan. Listen to us," Reese tried.

"She's my sister," he screamed at me. "My sister."

"I know."

He turned to Reese. "And…and she's my best friend."

"We're sorry," Reese told him. "We wanted to tell you. We just…" She shrugged.

"Couldn't," I finished.

"Great. Now you finish each other's sentences? What the fuck?" Ryan gripped his arm. Blood started slowly dripping through his fingertips. Damn, he was really hurt.

"No," Reese and I shouted. That was unfortunate timing.

"Isn't that just fucking adorable?" Ryan retrieved his gun. Uh-oh.

"Put the gun away," Reese demanded.

He did. "You think I'm going to shoot either of you?" He laughed without a trace of humor. "I can't. You're my best friend and my sister."

"Let's just talk," I suggested.

"No," Ryan screamed. "How could you?" He waved his arms around dramatically. "And how could you not tell me?" He tapped his chest with the flat of his hand. It left a bloody print behind.

"We were afraid," Reese said.

"You should be." He pointed at us and took a step forward. "Throwing away everything we've got just so you could get fucking laid?"

"Ryan, stop." Reese held up a hand. "Please. You don't understand. We're not just fucking."

That made him stop. "You what?"

"We're not. And we're not trying to hurt you," I said. I couldn't bring myself to say I loved her. That would just be too pathetic.

"Then maybe you shouldn't have fucked my sister." Ryan nodded in her direction.

"I'm not fucking your sister." I let go of Reese to step closer to Ryan. "And show her some respect."

"You show her some respect." Ryan got close enough so our faces were almost touching. "Oh, wait, you don't respect women do you?" He shoved me back with a shot to my chest.

"Coming from you, that's real nice." I stepped closer then pushed him back a step.

"Hey." Reese stepped between us. "Enough."

"How you going to get out of this one, Coop?" Ryan peered around Reese to taunt me. "Cheat on her, stop answering her phone calls, or maybe you could just be an asshole until she dumps you. That seems effective."

"Ryan. Shut up. She's different, okay?" I stopped pressing against Reese to get to Ryan. "She makes me different."

"What?" Reese turned away from Ryan to gaze at me.

"What the hell does that mean?" Ryan wanted to know too.

"It means I don't feel…" I didn't know what I felt. "Trapped. She makes me want to be better. Not an asshole, you know?" I acted like I was telling Ryan, but right then I didn't give a shit what he thought.

"Babe." Reese's eyes turned to gray.

I did what I knew she wanted. I kissed her. Her pelvis tilted forward, shoulders back, teasing me. I circled my fingers at the base of her spine, willing her closer.

"Well, that's just fuckin' great," Ryan scoffed. "Stop. You're making me want to hurl."

Reese pulled away with a smirk on her lips. Tease.

"I really am sorry we didn't tell you." I finally met Ryan's eyes. They were gray too. But a different sort of gray. "But I'm not sorry it happened."

"I'm sorry too." Reese reached out and petted Ryan's hair, pushing it away from his face.

"Yeah, well." He studied the ground, then returned his gaze to my face. "You fuck up, I'll kill you." I didn't believe him for a second. "Same with you." He pointed at Reese.

"Sure you will." Reese pulled him in for a hug. "Now can I look at your arm? You're bleeding all over the place."

"It hurts really bad." There was the Ryan I knew. Reese released him so I yanked him closer to hug him. He let me.

"What happened to your arm?" I asked once Ryan let go of me.

"I think Tommy shot me." His face was a bit pale, eyes filled with pain.

"Fuck. Why didn't you tell us?" I pushed up his sleeve, and sure enough, there was a deep streak across his bicep. The bullet hadn't penetrated, just grazed him. Still, it couldn't feel good.

"Dunno." Ryan closed his eyes and turned away.

"Reese, go see if we have anything to tie on his arm." She thought I was crazy. "To slow down the bleeding," I explained.

"Just a sec." She went back to the 4Runner and came back with a shredded T-shirt.

"Thanks." I took a strip and tied it as tight as I could around his upper arm. "That'll have to work for now. Let's hurry though. I want to clean that." Ryan nodded, eyes still pressed shut. "So what are we going to do about these assholes?" I asked.

"Leave 'em," Reese suggested.

"Yeah, fuck 'em," Ryan said.

"Guys." They both looked at me. "If we leave them, they'll probably die." Both seemed uncomfortable with that. "Let's just, like, check them."

They nodded. I started to walk and they followed me. Apparently, they wanted me to do the checking because neither made a move to touch the bodies. In fact, they stayed in a single file line behind me. Vic was definitely alive, enough that I was afraid he'd come to when I touched him. I tied another strip of material around his arm like I'd done for Ryan. Good enough.

"Babe, check those two." I pointed at Vito and the guy by the car.

Reese sauntered off looking anything but happy. Ryan stayed still, watching us. Now that we were acknowledging that he was hurt, he was going to milk it.

I went to where Gino and the guy I'd shot in the chest were. Both alive. Not doing so good though. There was blood fucking everywhere. Not much I could do about it. Fuck.

Tommy was the last one, the only one I didn't give a shit about. I'd like to say I hit him right between the eyes, that would be beautiful, but I didn't. The hole in his forehead was slightly off-center, a trickle of blood ran down his forehead. No pulse.

"Check them for cell phones," I shouted to Reese.

"Why?"

"Just find me one."

"Fine." She glared.

A minute later, Reese gave me a phone.

"You guys ready? We'll need to drive fast."

"Sure." Reese grabbed Ryan's uninjured arm. "Let me put him in the car."

I waited until they were strapped in. Ryan was in back, Reese in the passenger seat. I dialed 911, listed off the body count and GPS coordinates, hung up, and tossed the phone. Then ran like hell for the car.

We hit the highway and pulled out. As I sped up and moved into the fast lane, a single police car with its lights on appeared in the distance. It pulled to the shoulder as we sped away.

None of us could stomach the idea of giving Ryan stitches. So Reese and I poured half a bottle of peroxide on his arm and made sure the wound looked clean. Then I filled the gash with superglue and slapped a piece of duct tape over it, it was stronger than Steri-Strips. He didn't seem to mind. Peroxide, superglue, and duct tape were almost as good as the emergency room. Right.

The three of us left our no-name motel room, clean and bandaged, or in the case of Ryan, duct taped, as the sun was coming up. We were crossing the Mexican border by mid morning, just college students looking for summer fun. Nothing out of the ordinary.

By then, we should have figured out how to tell if we were being followed. Too bad none of us thought to check.

About the Author

Ashley Bartlett was born and raised in California. She is from Sacramento, and her life consists of reading and writing. Most of the time, Ashley engages in these pursuits while sitting in front of a coffee shop with her girlfriend and smoking cigarettes.

It's a glamorous life.

She is an obnoxious, sarcastic, punk-ass, but her friends don't hold that against her. She currently lives in Long Beach, but you can find her at ashbartlett.com.

Books Available from Bold Strokes Books

Crossroads by Radclyffe. Dr. Hollis Monroe specializes in short-term relationships but when she meets pregnant mother-to-be Annie Colfax, fate brings them together at a crossroads that will change their lives forever. (978-1-60282-756-1)

Beyond Innocence by Carsen Taite. When a life is on the line, love has to wait. Doesn't it? (978-1-60282-757-8)

Heart Block by Melissa Brayden. Socialite Emory Owen and struggling single mom Sarah Matamoros are perfectly suited for each other but face a difficult time when trying to merge their contrasting worlds and the people in them. If love truly exists, can it find a way? (978-1-60282-758-5)

Pride and Joy by M.L. Rice. Perfect Bryce Montgomery is her parents' pride and joy, but when they discover that their daughter is a lesbian, her world changes forever. (978-1-60282-759-2)

Timothy by Greg Herren. Timothy is a romantic suspense thriller from award-winning mystery writer Greg Herren set in the fabulous Hamptons. (978-1-60282-760-8)

In Stone: A Grotesque Faerie Tale by Jeremy Jordan King. A young New Yorker is rescued from a hate crime by a mysterious someone who turns out to be more of a *something*. (978-1-60282-761-5)

The Jesus Injection by Eric Andrews-Katz. Murderous statues, demented drag queens, political bombings, ex-gay ministries, espionage, and romance are all in a day's work for a top-secret agent. But the gloves are off when Agent Buck 98 comes up against The Jesus Injection. (978-1-60282-762-2)

Combustion by Daniel W. Kelly. Bearish detective Deck Waxer comes to the city of Kremfort Cove to investigate why the hottest men in town are bursting into flames in broad daylight. (978-1-60282-763-9)

Silver Collar by Gill McKnight. Werewolf Luc Garoul is outlawed and out of control, but can her family track her down before a sinister predator gets there first? Fourth in the Garoul series. (978-1-60282-764-6)

The Dragon Tree Legacy by Ali Vali. For Aubrey Tarver time hasn't dulled the pain of losing her first love Wiley Gremillion, but she has to set that aside when her choices put her life and her family's lives in real danger. (978-1-60282-765-3)

The Midnight Room by Ronnie Black. After a chance encounter with the mysterious and brooding Lillian Gray in the "midnight room" of The Griffin, a local lesbian bar, confident and gorgeous Audrey McCarthy learns that her bad girl behavior isn't bulletproof. (978-1-60282-766-0)

Dirty Sex by Ashley Bartlett. Vivian Cooper and twins Reese and Ryan DiGiovanni stole a lot of money and the guy they took it from wants it back. Like now. (978-1-60282-767-7)

Raising Hell: Demonic Gay Erotica edited by Todd Gregory. *Raising Hell*: hot stories of gay erotica featuring demons. (978-1-60282-768-4)

Pursued by Joel Gomez-Dossi. Openly gay college student Jamie Bradford becomes romantically involved with two men at the same time, and his hell begins when one of his boyfriends becomes intent on killing him. (978-1-60282-769-1)

Young Bucks: Novellas of Twenty-Something Lust & Love edited by Richard Labonte. Four writers still in their twenties-or with their twenties a nearby memory-write about what it's like to be young, on the prowl for sex, or looking to fall in love. (978-1-60282-770-7)

The Storm by Shelley Thrasher. Rural East Texas. 1918. War-weary Jaq Bergeron and marriage-scarred musician Molly Russell try to salvage love from the devastation of the war abroad and natural disasters at home. (978-1-60282-780-6)

Ladyfish by Andrea Bramhall. Finn's escape to the Florida Keys leads her straight into the arms of scuba diving instructor Oz as she fights for her freedom, their blossoming love…and her life! (978-1-60282-747-9)

Spanish Heart by Rachel Spangler. While on a mission to find herself in Spain, Ren Molson runs the risk of losing her heart to her tour guide, Lina Montero. (978-1-60282-748-6)

Love Match by Ali Vali. When Parker "Kong" King, the number one tennis player in the world, meets commercial pilot Captain Sydney Parish, sparks fly—but not from attraction. They have the summer to see if they have a love match. (978-1-60282-749-3)

One Touch by L.T. Marie. A romance writer and a travel agent come together at their high school reunion, only to find out that the memory of that one touch never fades. (978-1-60282-750-9)

Night Shadows: Queer Horror edited by Greg Herren and J.M. Redmann. *Night Shadows* features delightfully wicked stories by some of the biggest names in queer publishing. (978-1-60282-751-6)

Secret Societies by William Holden. An outcast hustler, his unlikely "mother," his faithless lovers, and his religious persecutors—all in 1726. (978-1-60282-752-3)

The Raid by Lee Lynch. Before Stonewall, having a drink with friends or your girl could mean jail. Would these women and men still have family, a job, a place to live after…The Raid? (978-1-60282-753-0)

The You Know Who Girls: Freshman Year by Annameekee Hesik. As they begin freshman year, Abbey Brooks and her best friend, Kate, pinkie swear they'll keep away from the lesbians in Gila High, but Abbey already suspects she's one of those you-know-who girls herself and slowly learns who her true friends really are. (978-1-60282-754-7)

Wyatt: Doc Holliday's Account of an Intimate Friendship by Dale Chase. Erotica writer Dale Chase takes the remarkable friendship between Wyatt Earp, upright lawman, and Doc Holliday, Southern gentlemen turned gambler and killer, to an entirely new level: hot! (978-1-60282-755-4)

Month of Sundays by Yolanda Wallace. Love doesn't always happen overnight; sometimes it takes a month of Sundays. (978-1-60282-739-4)

Jacob's War by C.P. Rowlands. ATF Special Agent Allison Jacob's task force is in the middle of an all-out war, from the streets to the boardrooms of America. Small business owner Katie Blackburn is the latest victim who accidentally breaks it wide open, but she may break AJ's heart at the same time. (978-1-60282-740-0)

The Pyramid Waltz by Barbara Ann Wright. Princess Katya Nar Umbriel wants a perfect romance, but her Fiendish nature and duties to the crown mean she can never tell the truth—until she meets Starbride, a woman who gets to the heart of every secret, even if it will be the death of her. (978-1-60282-741-7)

The Secret of Othello by Sam Cameron. Florida teen detectives Steven and Denny risk their lives to search for a sunken NASA satellite—but under the waves, no one can hear you scream… (978-1-60282-742-4)

Finding Bluefield by Elan Barnehama. Set in the backdrop of Virginia and New York and spanning the years 1960–1982, *Finding Bluefield* chronicles the lives of Nicky Stewart, Barbara Philips, and their son, Paul, as they struggle to define themselves as a family. (978-1-60282-744-8)

The Jetsetters by David-Matthew Barnes. As rock band the Jetsetters skyrockets from obscurity to superstardom, Justin Holt, a lonely barista, and Diego Delgado, the band's guitarist, fight with everything they have to stay together, despite the chaos and fame. (978-1-60282-745-5)

Strange Bedfellows by Rob Byrnes. Partners in life and crime, Grant Lambert and Chase LaMarca are hired to make a politician's compromising photo disappear, but what should be an easy job quickly spins out of control. (978-1-60282-746-2)

Dreaming of Her by Maggie Morton. Isa has begun to dream of the most amazing woman—a woman named Lilith with a gorgeous face, an amazing body, and the ability to turn Isa on like no other. But Lilith is just a dream...isn't she? (978-1-60282-847-6)

Summoning Shadows: A Rosso Lussuria Vampire Novel by Winter Pennington. The Rosso Lussuria vampires face enemies both old and new, and to prevail they must call on even more strange alliances, unite as a clan, and draw on every weapon within their reach—but with a clan of vampires, that's easier said than done. (978-1-60282-679-3)

Sometime Yesterday by Yvonne Heidt. When Natalie Chambers learns her Victorian house is haunted by a pair of lovers and a Dark Man, can she and her lover Van Easton solve the mystery that will set the ghosts free and banish the evil presence in the house? Or will they have to run to survive as well? (978-1-60282-680-9)